The Road
—— *to* ——
REVELATION

THE ROAD
to
REVELATION
World at War

Clifford T. Wellman Jr.

The Road to Revelation - World at War
Copyright © 2018 by Clifford T. Wellman Jr. All rights reserved.

No part of this publication may be reproduced, stored in a retrieval system or transmitted in any way by any means, electronic, mechanical, photocopy, recording or otherwise without the prior permission of the author except as provided by USA copyright law.

Scripture quotations marked (NIV) are taken from the Holy Bible, New International Version®, niv®. Copyright © 1973, 1978, 1984 by Biblica, Inc.™ Used by permission of Zondervan. All rights reserved worldwide. www.zondervan.com

This novel is a work of fiction. Names, descriptions, entities, and incidents included in the story are products of the author's imagination. Any resemblance to actual persons, events, and entities is entirely coincidental.

Published by Clifford T. Wellman Jr.
www.theroadtorevelation.com
www.facebook.com/TheRoadToRev
www.twitter.com/RoadRevelation
RoadToRevelation13@gmail.com

Book design copyright © 2018 by Clifford T. Wellman Jr. All rights reserved.
Cover design by Clifford T. Wellman Jr.
Cover photo taken by unknown photographer.
Interior design by Clifford T. Wellman Jr.

Published in the United States of America

ISBN: 978-1-73089-575-3

1. Fiction / Christian / Suspense
2. Fiction / Thrillers / General

In memory of my father.

Your days in this world were too short for all of us that remain.

You made the most of the time that you spent here.

You were loved in life and still in death.

To my mother.

Dad was the head of the family, but you are the heart.

Your capacity for love shows us how we are supposed to live.

I cannot express enough how much you mean to our family.

We love you with all our hearts.

Other Books by Clifford T. Wellman Jr.

The Road to Revelation Series:

#1 - The Beginning

#2 - World at War

#3 - Darkness Falls

#4 - Life & Death (coming soon)

Real Estate and Investing:

- How I Retired By Age 45

ACKNOWLEDGEMENTS

I would like to thank Jesus Christ, my God and my savior. Without you, I would not have been able to share this story.
"I can do everything through him who gives me strength." (Philippians 4:13)

I would also like to thank my friends and family for the support and love that they have given me throughout this journey. For those of you who shared my excitement in writing this book, your excitement helped keep me going.

Thank you to my wife, who spent hours reading and editing. I had pages and pages of edits and changes. I could not have done it without you.

Prologue

Present Day

Somewhere over the Atlantic Ocean, the Turkish Ambassador to the United Nations was flying toward New York City. Over the intercom, the pilot of the Turkish Airlines 747 announced that they are flying at an elevation of 36,000 feet and that he had turned off the fasten seat belt sign.

Within minutes of this announcement, the first class flight attendant came over to the Ambassador and asked if he would like a drink.

"Yes, I would like the 50 year old Sovereign Scotch by Port Dundas, neat," the Ambassador said. "Make it a double."

The Ambassador knew that alcohol was forbidden within Islam, but during his tenure at the United Nations he became accustomed to some of the ways of the West.

"Yes, Sir, fine choice," the flight attendant replied.

A moment later, the Ambassador was sipping his forbidden scotch as he admired the ocean below. The man in the seat next to the Ambassador slowly turned toward him and shook his head.

"You are no better than the rest of those devils," the man said to the Ambassador.

The Ambassador turned to the man with an inquisitive look and his eyes widened when he saw the ceramic knife in the man's hand. In a split second, the Ambassador's consciousness ended as the knife was forced into his right eye socket. The quick motions of the man caught the attention of several of the first class passengers. The sight of the ceramic knife sticking out of the eye socket of the Ambassador and the blood pouring down his face raised many frightened screams.

As they watched in disbelief, the murderer stood and turned toward the front of the plane. He moved to the front and turned back to those who remained seated. With an evil grin, he pulled a small device from his jacket pocket and screamed "Allahu Akbar" right before pressing the red button on its face. Somewhere in the belly of the airplane there was an explosion that ripped the 747 into pieces.

Ali Basharat closed the door behind him and knelt on the rug that lay in front of him. He was familiar with room 66 on the 6th floor of the United Nations building, but for some reason it felt different.

"Come!" a voice commanded.

Ali stood quickly and walked toward the large desk at the end of the room. The man sitting behind the 900 year old desk had a solemn look on his face. In the past, he had greeted Ali in front of the desk, but this time he sat patiently waiting for Ali to speak.

Ali walked toward the man until he was a couple feet from the front of the desk and bowed his head. As he bowed, he could see the name plate of the man who sat behind the desk and thought to himself that his title would have to be changed from Deputy Ambassador to Ambassador, after the tragic explosion of the Turkish Airlines 747.

"Do you have news for me?" the man behind the desk asked.

"Yes, Mahdi, I do," Ali answered with a pause. "It is done."

When the Lamb opened the second seal, I heard the second living creature say, 'Come!' Then another horse came out, a fiery red one. Its rider was given power to take peace from the earth and to make men slay each other. To him was given a large sword.

— Revelation 6:3-4

Chapter 1

Abby

Traffic on the street was very light for a Thursday afternoon. Normally, even the small town that Abby called home was far busier than it was that day. Ford liked to drive, so as usual, he drove them into town. As they reached their destination, Ford slowly pulled the truck over and parked on the side of the street. He looked over to Abby who was in the passenger seat and smiled.

"I'm going to head to the bank for a minute while you go to the hardware store," Abby said. Ford leaned over and kissed her on the cheek.

"Okay, I'll see you back here in a few minutes," Ford replied.

Abby watched Ford walk the opposite way down the street for a few moments before turning to walk toward the bank. When she reached the front door of the bank, she turned to see if Ford was watching her. He always seemed to watch her from a distance when they went into town. She found his protectiveness very charming. Abby saw him standing in front of the hardware store looking at her. When he saw her look at him, he smiled and waved at her.

He has such a sweet smile, Abby thought to herself as the world erupted around her.

Chapter 2

Ford

After he left Abby and started walking toward the hardware store, he had a strange feeling. He remembered the shudder that he had felt last winter before the world had erupted into chaos. This feeling was very similar to what he felt back then. He reached the hardware store and turned toward Abby. She was still walking down the street almost twenty feet from the bank. He admired the way her hips swayed as she walked. That always put a smile on his face. A moment later she reached the bank and saw him looking at her. A slight grin raised on her face as he waved to his beloved and then an explosion tore through the bank. Glass and flame erupted outward toward the street and Ford witnessed in horror as Abby was tossed like a ragdoll halfway across the road.

Ford almost froze for a moment as time seemed to come to a halt, and then in a split second the clock rushed forward into the reality that consumed him. He moved slowly at first, but then built up speed as he raced toward Abby who lay in a pile on the street. As he ran, he noted how thankful he was that there hadn't been any passing cars that might have struck Abby as she was tossed into the street. When he reached her, he found that she was still breathing. He knew that he had to call for help or she was going to die. Before he knew it, he had pulled out his phone and dialed 911.

"911. What's your emergency?" the dispatcher asked.

"There has been an explosion at the corner of Main and 4th. My wife is hurt and I'm sure many inside the bank are as well," Ford said calmly.

"Ok, Sir, I've already dispatched police and fire onto the scene."

"Thank you, but my wife needs an ambulance immediately!" Ford exclaimed.

"One is on the way, Sir."

The dispatcher continued to talk to Ford, but later he wouldn't recall anything that she said. In that moment, he was focused solely on Abby. She had several cuts on her face and there was a large amount of blood on the right side of her head. He could only guess that it had been from hitting the pavement so hard. Her left leg was twisted beneath her body and he knew that it was broken. Ford knew some basic first aid, but this trauma was far beyond his skill level.

"Lord Jesus, please be with my wife, Abby, and please see her through this terrible..." Ford began praying, but trailed off as he heard sirens in the distance.

"Lord, I can't lose her. I just can't," Ford began to sob over his wife, as the first responders finally arrived at the scene.

Chapter 3

Nigel

He knew that he shouldn't be there, but something told him to wait. He had parked the van on the opposite side of the street from the bank, on the next block south. His orders were to set the bomb and get out of town, but a small voice inside had said *stay*.

From his driver's side mirror he could see the bank and most of the street. A couple minutes after he left the bank, a truck stopped near the bank and a middle aged couple got out. The man headed south toward the hardware store and the woman north toward the bank. He watched their interaction and thought to himself that they seemed like they were truly happy. He wondered how anyone could be happy in this world. The last several months had been very trying for him. Instead of love, he only brought destruction. His mentor, Ali Basharat, told him that he was doing the will of

Allah, but more and more, he just wasn't sure. He continued to watch the couple as she reached the bank and he the hardware store. They both turned to one another as if they just couldn't be apart. She waved to him and he to her.

A moment later, the explosion tore through the bank and the woman was thrown out into the street. His attention moved to the man in front of the hardware store and Nigel's heart wrenched at the look on the man's face. He didn't know these people, yet his heart broke for them. He watched the man race toward his wife. The pain on his face was complete.

What have I done? Nigel thought to himself.

A moment later, sirens sounded in the distance. Nigel knew that his time was up, so he put the van in gear and sped out of town.

Chapter 4

Ford

It had been over a month and Abby was still in the hospital. She had suffered a broken leg and hip, a broken collarbone, and a severe concussion. She also suffered many cuts and bruises all over her body. The doctors said that the bones would mend and the cuts and bruises would heal, but they were concerned about her head injury. They placed Abby in a coma for the first several days to give her body a chance to heal, but she hadn't improved. She had some bleeding on the brain and they were forced to relieve the pressure by drilling a hole in her skull. That first week, Ford spent every moment in the hospital at his wife's side, but soon the chores of everyday life at the lodge were catching up with him. He had chickens to feed and a garden to maintain. His youngest son, John, was home and would be going to college in the Fall. He was able to help with some of the work, but Ford still found himself getting further behind. His oldest son, Tom, had taken a job in Oklahoma City as a software developer and wasn't able to help out. Tom came home when he first heard about the explosion, but he could only take off so much time. Ford recalled arguing with Tom, telling him that he needed to go back to work.

"Dad! I need to be here with Mom!" Tom exclaimed.

"Tom, I understand that you are worried and I know that your mother appreciates you being here. I appreciate you being here, but there is nothing that you can do right now. Your mother's life is in God's hands now."

"My job can wait, Dad," Tom said, almost pleading to stay with his mother.

"I love you, kid," Ford started as he felt a tear roll down his cheek. He unconsciously wiped the tear away and continued. "But you need to get back to work. I will call you immediately when your mother's condition changes."

In the end, Tom relented and went back to Oklahoma City. Just two months ago, he was hired by Steel Oil as a Software Specialist. Ford and Abby were very proud of him and told him so many times. Tom told them about some of the cutting edge projects that he was working on. Tom explained to his father that Steel Oil was primarily into fracking technologies and the software that Tom was working on helped monitor the operations of each well.

After Tom left, Ford went to the hospital every evening to spend a couple of hours with his wife. He would sit beside her bed and read the Bible to her. He read a verse that struck a nerve in him. Philippians 2:14 said, "Do everything without complaining or arguing." Ford didn't complain a lot, but he realized as he read this verse that he had so much to be thankful for. God gave him a great wife and two amazing children. He also provided the land that Ford and Abby had always wanted.

"God is good!" Ford said out loud. He looked up and smiled. Somewhere in his heart he knew that God would bring Abby back to him soon.

Chapter 5

Abby

The clouds were a dark gray color and there was a hint of deep red throughout. It was as if the sunset was trying to force its way through a storm cloud. Lightning flashed down in the distance and was followed by the rumble of thunder. It seemed to Abby that there was a war in the heavens. No rain had fallen yet, but she was concerned that she might get caught in the coming downpour. Abby looked down at herself in astonishment. She wore a long white dress that flowed to the ground. It had thin spaghetti straps that were draped over her shoulders. The fabric was soft to the touch and felt cool on her skin, but she felt comfortably warm. A gentle breeze blew the bottom of the dress and she noticed that her feet were bare. She smiled as she recognized the soft cool feeling of the thick, green grass between her toes. For a brief moment, she was reminded of her childhood summers.

Abby became aware that she stood at the top of a hill and could see a shallow valley spread out beneath her. It seemed an ocean of grass separated her from the next hill where the storm raged. She was safe for now, but soon the storm would overcome her. She slowly turned in a circle, looking for a place to find shelter from the storm. Behind her, in the next valley, there was a small cabin surrounded by several large trees. She looked behind her and there was a flash of lightning. She shielded her eyes from the bright light as a horrendous boom of thunder followed and shook the air around her. Abby knew that she was almost out of time when the first drop of rain hit her on the cheek. Sometimes rain felt good on your face, but this rain almost seemed to sting. There was something very sinister about this storm and Abby knew that it was time to leave. A second raindrop landed on her shoulder followed by the third and then a fourth.

Abby pulled up her dress a bit, turned, and ran toward the small cabin in the valley. As she ran, she realized that she enjoyed the feeling of running on the plush grass beneath her feet. The thought of enjoyment in that moment made her laugh.

"Here I am, about to be overrun by a terrible storm, and I'm enjoying the softness of the grass," Abby laughed to herself.

That is the thing that I love about you the most, a voice said.

Abby continued to run toward the cabin, but looked to the left and right wondering where that voice had come from.

"Who said that?" Abby inquired.

I press on toward the goal to win the prize for which God has called me heavenward in Christ Jesus, the voice said.

Abby recognized those words, but couldn't quite place where she had heard them. Abby continued to run and the rain continued to fall. She looked behind her in time to see a flash of lightning crash into the top of the hill where she had stood just moments ago. The thunder followed immediately and just about pushed her to the ground. Abby was almost to the cabin, but she was beginning to get wet. She could feel wet hair against her face and the dress beginning to stick to her body. She ran and ran, but felt like she was barely closing on the cabin. Lightning crashed closer behind her and she stumbled, but steadied herself so as not to fall. For a moment, she wondered if she was going to make it.

Therefore, my brothers, you whom I love and long for, my joy and crown, that is how you should stand firm in the Lord, dear friends! the voice said louder.

Abby had no idea who was speaking to her or where the voice had come from, but the words gave her strength. She released her hold on her dress and ran, as a sprinter would have, with her arms pumping harder and harder. In a moment, the gap between her and the cabin closed and she was finally under the cover of the porch at the cabin and out of the rain. She didn't know who lived in this cabin, but decided that it was best to knock. Abby knocked on the door twice and lighting crashed once again, this time into one of the large trees that sheltered the cabin. The thunderous boom shook the entire cabin and tossed Abby against the door.

Rejoice in the Lord... the voice said. This time the voice sounded more familiar to her.

"Please, let me in!" Abby screamed as she began to bang on the door.

Do not be anxious about anything... the voice answered. Abby felt a shiver run through her body. Her body seemed to recognize what her mind hadn't yet come to understand.

"Please, let me in!" Abby screamed again, and continued to bang on the door.

I can do everything through him who gives me strength, the voice said. Abby's eyes widened as she finally realized whose voice she heard.

"Ford?" Abby said questioningly.

Abby, please come home, the voice said.

Abby smiled and knew that everything was going to be okay. She grasped the handle of the door and turned the knob. As the door swung open, the entire room was filled with light. At first, Abby had difficulty making out any of the shapes that she saw.

"Hey, Baby!" she heard Ford say. Above her she could see the face of her beloved husband come into focus. She felt his hands around hers. She could see tears in his eyes.

"Ford," Abby squeaked.

"Yes, Babe, it's me," Ford replied.

"Where am I?" Abby asked, hearing her voice get stronger.

A few more shapes came into focus and Abby began to recognize them as a doctor and a nurse. She felt the pillow against her head and became aware of the IV that was in her arm.

"You're gonna be okay, Sweetheart! You're gonna be okay!" Ford exclaimed.

She now recognized that the tears he had were those of joy. She smiled and he smiled back. "I love you!" Ford added.

CHAPTER 6

Nigel

He inhaled deeply and took in the fresh air that came off the lake. He shook his head at the wonder that he had witnessed over the past month. The sun was going down and the lake was so calm that it mirrored the sky. Nigel could see two sunsets converging upon one another, one in the air and one on the lake.

"God is an incredible painter, isn't he?" Tia asked.

After witnessing the destruction of the explosion that he set over a month ago, Nigel found that he could no longer *do the will of Allah*. Somewhere deep inside him, he realized that everything he had done was completely wrong. He had asked himself, "What kind of god would demand that you kill innocent people?" His answer had been a firm, "Not one that I want to worship." His instructions had been to drive south, back to the compound near Detroit, but instead he had gone a different direction. Nigel had driven around aimlessly for a while and had slept in the van on that first night. During that night he dreamed of water and he saw the face of an angel. In the dream, he saw himself on the beach by a very large lake. He was sitting in the sand watching the sun go down, when he saw her. She seemed to appear out of nowhere. When he awoke, he knew that he had to find that lake and hopefully that angel. The next day he began driving. He didn't have a plan and didn't know where he was going, but soon he found himself on a secluded country road. The road was slightly curvy and was surrounded by trees on either side. As he came around a corner he saw that he had found the lake from his dream. The water was blue and the sun sparkled off the soft ripples. There were cabins on the lake side of the road and trees on the other side of the road. Nigel could see people in the water and in their back yards. It seemed that everyone was enjoying their summer. At first he was confused that so many people could be completely at ease, with everything that was going on in the world. He guessed that because war hadn't come to the shores of the United States, to most Americans it still wasn't real. As he drove, he saw a campground beside the water, so he decided to pull over and take a look. At the time, he hadn't known where he was, but this place turned out to be a State campground on the northern side of Houghton Lake. Growing up in Detroit, he never knew that this magnificent lake had only been a couple hours away.

At first he was a little concerned about going up to the campground office to get a pass for the day. He hadn't been watching the news and wondered if he had been identified as the bomber. Finally, he decided to risk it and figured that if he got caught, well then he must have deserved it. In the end, the DNR officer hadn't batted an eye toward him. He got his pass and went to his assigned campsite. Nigel didn't have any camping gear and planned to simply sleep in the van again that night. He remembered getting out of the van and walking toward the beach. The sun was shining and a few people were out.

Nigel took off his shoes and socks and walked in the sand. The sand was clean and felt warm. He couldn't remember ever walking barefoot on a beach. As a child, he had never left the city of Detroit and so he never had the opportunity to walk on the beach and enjoy the hot summer. He lamented at everything that he had missed during his childhood. He rolled up his pant legs and stepped into the water. The water was cool and refreshing. The late summer heat had kept the water from being cold, even this far north. After a few moments he decided to go back and sit down on the sand. He leaned back bracing his body with his hands behind him and closed his eyes. He could feel his face warm as the sun shone down on him and he felt the warm breeze move across his face. He took a deep breath and was amazed to find that the air smelled so clean. Never before had he smelled such clean air.

"Hey there," a soft voice spoke.

Nigel opened his eyes and sat up and found that the voice belonged to a woman. At first her face was shrouded in the sun and Nigel couldn't see her features. But then she moved a bit to the right and her angelic smile came into view. Her hair was dark with highlights, which she wore in a long ponytail. Her dark brown eyes sparkled with something that Nigel just couldn't place. Maybe it was happiness, or maybe it was something else. Her skin was tan, partly because of her Asian heritage and partly from exposure to the summer sun.

"Hi there," Nigel responded.

"My name is Tia," she said extending her hand.

"Nigel," as he returned the handshake.

Tia spoke with a nondescript American accent and Nigel would soon discover that she was the daughter of a South Korean immigrant and a natural born American with European descendants. Her mother had immigrated to the United States in her early 20s, so that she could attend the University of Michigan. Her mother had met her father at a fraternity party during her junior year and they had immediately hit it off. A year after graduating from college, the pair had gotten married and Tia followed along nine months later.

Tia had grown up in the Ann Arbor area, but as her parents' careers grew, her family spent more time up north. Early on they spent their summers going to various campgrounds throughout northern Michigan. Later, her parents bought a home on the northern shoreline of Houghton Lake. Tia spent every summer there with her family until she graduated from college. This past Spring, Tia had walked through the graduation ceremony at Central Michigan University and was planning to spend the summer hiking around the state of Michigan. She had started in

Ludington and headed north to the Sleeping Bear Sand Dunes, but somewhere along the way she was called to go to Houghton Lake. The night before Nigel arrived, she sat by her campfire and prayed that God would show her why He had brought her to this campground. It would be weeks before Tia would share that story with Nigel, but she knew the moment that she saw him that he was the reason that she had ended up in Houghton Lake.

Nigel smiled at the memories that went through his head. Out of habit, Nigel almost replied *Allahu Akbar*, but caught himself and simply said, "Yes, God is an amazing painter."

"How do you feel about lunch?" Tia asked.

"It's one of my favorite meals!" Nigel exclaimed with a smile.

Tia smacked him playfully and said, "No, how do you feel about getting lunch now?" She knew that he was teasing her, but she loved it none the less.

"Yeah, T, let's go get some lunch." He had begun calling her *T* shortly after meeting her. Their connection was so strong and he had already fallen hard for her.

CHAPTER 7

Samantha

Summer in New Mexico could be difficult at times. Today the temperature was 110 degrees, but it was much cooler under the shade of the covered porch. Sam sat in her favorite chair with a glass of lemonade in her hand wondering how much longer they had.

According to the research that her lifelong friend, Ford, had done, it seemed like the second seal found in the Book of Revelation had already been opened. That prophecy came true when Iran made a move to conquer the Middle East. Daniel 8:4 had been clear that when Iran, the Persian ram, charged toward the west, the north, and the south, no one could stand against them. Just over six months ago, Iran had done just that. This prophecy coincided with the opening of the second seal of the Book of Revelation and the rider on the red horse. Over the past several months, Iran moved to control Syria, Iraq, Lebanon, and all of the Arabian Peninsula. Initially, the world stood by and watched as almost every country in the Middle East fell. Israel was the only country to stand tall, but mostly because Iran hadn't made a move toward them yet. For Sam, it was sometimes overwhelming to think about. Deep in her heart she knew that she was living in the last days, but she didn't like to think about it.

Just then the phone rang. As Sam reached for the phone she got a bad feeling in her stomach. Caller ID told her that it was her mother in Michigan.

"Hi, Mom," Sam answered the phone.

"Dear, I'm sorry to tell you this, but it is time," her mother said calmly. She talked slowly, as if to hold back her emotions. Several months ago, Sam's father had been diagnosed with stage-4 prostate cancer and his health had deteriorated by the day. Unfortunately, by the time the cancer was discovered, it had metastasized outside of the prostate. He had chosen surgery and, for the most part, it had been successful. However, since the cancer had already moved beyond the prostate, additional treatment was necessary and her father chose to have chemotherapy. The chemotherapy turned out to be unsuccessful. The combination of his advanced age and poor health didn't give the doctors much hope of a full recovery. At the time, Sam had been relieved that her father made it through the surgery, but the family wasn't given much hope that he would live much longer. With the chemotherapy only making him sicker, they decided that they would spend his last days enjoying as much time together as they possibly could.

"Samantha, Hospice visited today and your father is getting worse. It's time to come home," Sam's mother announced.

"I will be on the next plane to Michigan," Sam answered.

"Bye, Mom, see you soon," she added.

"I love you, Dear."

"I love you too, Mom."

Sam hung up the phone and the tears began to flow. These past several months had been an emotional rollercoaster. First there were the terrorist attacks, then her dear friend, Ford, had almost lost his wife because of another attack, and now her father was about to die. War had erupted throughout the world and Sam knew that it was only a matter of time before things would get really bad. With her dad on the verge of passing, it was all that she could take. She was thankful that her father had accepted Jesus as his savior and soon would be with God, but the pain was almost too much to bear.

Chapter 8

Zack

The world had changed so much in the last several months since the New Year's Eve terrorist attacks, but not much had changed in Wyoming for Zack. He spent the last several months living his life as he had for the previous twenty years, but lately his life of solitude was starting to get to him. Often he would find himself staring off into the distance and daydreaming about having a family. Since the death of his wife so many years ago, he had not allowed himself to become close with anyone. His best friends lived thousands of miles away from him, Ford in Michigan and Sam in New Mexico. He longed for companionship.

He walked into the bathroom and looked into the mirror. He was surprised by what he saw there. He was beginning to look like an old mountain man. His hair was far too long and his beard was unruly. He made a decision in that moment that he was going to go into town and get a haircut. It was time to find a little civilization.

After showering and cleaning himself up, he hopped into the truck and began the twenty minute drive into town. The village of Hulett, Wyoming was small, but it had everything that he needed; a grocery store, a bar, a restaurant, and, of course, a barbershop.

Zack pulled up and parked on the street in front of the barbershop. It had the old style barber pole outside, but several years ago it was upgraded to include styling for both men and women. Zack sat in his truck and could tell the shop wasn't too busy.

"I gotta do something different," he said to himself, and then he got out of the truck and walked up to the shop. As he opened the barbershop door, the bell clanged and it made him smile. The bell reminded him of simpler times. There was an older gentleman sitting in the back getting his hair cut by a man in his mid-sixties.

"Christin will be with you in a minute," the barber said.

Zack sat down in a chair and picked up the latest issue of Popular Mechanics. On the cover was a picture of a DIY wind generator. He flipped through the magazine, not really interested, but needing something to do.

"Can I help you?" came a voice that, to Zack, sounded like heaven.

Zack looked up from his magazine to see a beautiful woman walking toward him. She had a striped apron on over a light blue tank top and navy blue shorts. She had a white towel draped over her shoulder and she was carrying a pair of scissors. Her hair was brown with streaks of blonde and auburn that she wore in a ponytail. She put the towel on the counter along with the scissors and patted on the chair, beckoning him to sit. She smiled, and Zack immediately noticed the drastic contrast between her bright white teeth and her red lipstick. He stood there frozen for a moment and then finally walked over and sat down.

"Hi, I'm Christin."

"Zack, I'm Zack."

For some reason, Zack felt his face flush. It had been far too long since he'd last talked with a woman this beautiful. Christin shook a cape and laid it across Zack's body. He subconsciously straightened it as she tied it around his neck.

She slowly spun him around to face the mirror and asked, "So what are we going to do today? It looks like it's been a while." She smiled a bit.

Zack looked at her reflection in the mirror. She was bent down with her face next to his. Her green eyes were so dazzling that he couldn't say a word. He sat there with his eyes frozen on hers.

"Strong and silent, eh?" she said as her smile broadened.

"Uh sorry, it's just that," he paused, "I don't get out much."

Christin laughed and said, "That's okay."

Zack was overwhelmed by the sweetness of her laughter and the glimmer in her eyes.

"Let's start with a shampoo and then go from there," Christin said.

"Okay."

Christin slowly spun him back around and leaned his chair back so that his head lay in the sink. She gently pulled his hair from under his neck and into the sink. He heard the water start and in a moment she was rinsing down his hair. She took care not to pull it or get water in his eyes. She pulled shampoo through his long hair and began massaging his scalp. Zack couldn't recall ever feeling so good. He could have laid there for days. Finally, she rinsed out the shampoo and applied conditioner. She had said that normally she wouldn't apply conditioner to a man's hair, but because his was so long she thought it would be best. When she was finally done rinsing out the conditioner, she sat him up and patted down his hair with a towel to remove some of the moisture.

"So what should we do?" Christin asked.

"Huh?" Zack wasn't sure what she meant. He was so mesmerized by her that he forgot why he was there.

"How would you like your hair cut?"

"Oh, I don't care. Surprise me. It's far too long. Keep the beard, but feel free to trim it if you like."

"Oh, I'm definitely keeping the beard!" She smiled at him in the mirror.

Christin finished combing out his hair and began to make strategic cuts. It had been a while since his hair was short and he wondered what he would look like. After twenty minutes or so, she spun him back around so that he could see himself in the mirror. His hair was short on the sides, but a couple inches long on top. She styled it more than he normally would have, but he thought that it looked good. His beard had also been trimmed considerably, yet it was still quite full. In the mirror, his eyes moved toward hers and her smile broadened.

"So, what do you think?"

"I like it," he said as he ran his hands over the back of his head.

Still looking into his eyes, she moved some of the hair on the top of his head a bit.

"You clean up pretty good. I think I deserve a drink."

He smiled a bit and thought, *She just asked me out, didn't she?* That thought gave him a little confidence.

"Yes, you definitely deserve a drink. What time do you get off?"

"Well, you were my last cut of the day. I need to clean up a few things, but I should be ready in about 20 minutes."

"Okay, I have a few other errands to run, so I'll be back to pick you up in a while."

"Sounds great!" she said with a smile as she carefully slid the cape off of his body.

Zack got up and paid and then, before turning toward the door, he said, "I'll see you soon."

He couldn't get over how pretty she was. She smiled and walked back to her chair and that was when he realized that she was wearing cowboy boots.

That's it, I'm in love! he thought with a smile as he walked out the door of the barbershop.

Chapter 9

Christin

Christin stood watching as Zack walked out the door of the barbershop. She admired his broad shoulders. She knew that he was older than she was, but she didn't really care. He seemed like a nice guy and all they were doing was going out for a drink. There weren't a lot of good prospects in Hulett, especially for a single mom in her late thirties.

"Uncle Hank, I'm going to clean up and then call it a day."

The older barber looked up from his customer briefly and said, "Do you know who that is?"

"Yes, his name is Zack."

"Yes, he lives out on the old Branson ranch west of town. He is sort of a recluse. I've never heard anything bad about him, but then again I haven't heard anything good about him either. He keeps to himself mostly. Anyway, just be careful."

"Thanks, Uncle Hank, I will. We are just going to go down to Willie's Bar and Grill for a drink. I'll check in when I get there."

"Okay, Dear," he said and began cutting the man's hair in front of him.

Zack's timing was perfect. She had just finished cleaning up and removed her apron. She bent down to grab her purse and her hat.

"See ya, Hank!"

"Be good, Christin," Hank said with a smile. He knew that she would be good, but he liked to tease her a bit.

"Oh, I will be," she said with a smile and turned and walked out the door, making the bell sound its familiar ring.

Outside, Zack was just getting out of his truck and was coming around to meet her.

"Hey, Zack!" she exclaimed with a smile. "It's a beautiful day, let's walk."

Zack smiled and nodded, "Okay."

He turned toward the bar which was only two blocks away, spread his right arm wide, and grabbed his black cowboy hat with his left hand, making a tipping motion and beckoning her forward. Christin slightly tipped her light brown cowboy hat and feigned a curtsey with a smile.

Inside, Christin's stomach began to churn. She hadn't gone out on a date in a long time. Having a teenage daughter made it difficult to date. Christin knew that she needed to be careful, and finding the right guy to be around her daughter had been difficult. She didn't want her daughter growing up and making the same mistakes that she had made. Early on, Christin had always gone for the bad boys. She tried to be good, but there was something about a rugged man that turned her on. The problem had been that earlier on these rugged men had always been jerks and full of themselves. She always found it difficult finding a rugged man who was also a good man. Zack seemed like he might fit the bill, but she wasn't going to get too excited too quickly.

When they arrived at the bar, Zack opened the door for her and motioned her inward.

Okay, there's one point, for being a gentleman, she thought.

The bar was nice for a small town. It wasn't fancy or anything, but it was clean and not too dark inside. On the weekends, they had a local band that played classic rock and country, and you could count on seeing the same crowd every night. On occasion, there would be tourists who were in the area to see Devil's Tower, or to play golf, but they never stayed around too long.

When they walked in, the bartender waved and said, "Hey, Christin!" The bartender had graduated a year behind Christin and, of course, they knew each other. "How's Lizzy?"

"Hey, Missy, she's good. She's over at Ellie's right now."

"Hey, Zack," Missy said. Of course she knew Zack as well. They had gone out on one date seven or eight years ago. At the time, Zack wasn't ready to date, but one night after having a few beers at the bar, he had asked her out. She was more than happy to go.

"Hey, Missy." Zack saw Christin look over at him questioningly, but didn't say anything. Instead, he motioned her over to a table away from the door.

It wasn't too hot yet, but the air conditioning felt good to Christin. She sat down and put her purse and hat on the chair next to her. Zack sat in the chair across from her and put his hat on the remaining chair.

"So how do you know Missy?" she said and immediately regretted asking the question.

Great, now he thinks you're jealous! She thought to herself. *Well, you kind of are.* She was surprised by that thought.

"Missy and I went out once, several years ago. Just one date. I just wasn't ready to date at the time," he said almost nonchalantly.

"Oh," she said and paused now feeling somewhat guilty about asking.

"How do you know her?" Zack asked.

"She and I grew up in Hulett. She graduated a year after me. Believe it or not, my twentieth high school reunion is coming up in a couple weeks. I'm not sure why we are even having one since there were only twenty three of us in my class and most of us are still here."

Christin looked at Zack who seemed to be calculating the age difference.

Great, now I've basically told him how old I am! She thought. She was trying to think of another question to ask when Missy came up to the table with menus and drink napkins.

"What can I get you to drink?" Missy asked as she put a menu and napkin in front of each of them.

Zack, of course, deferred to Christin with a smile.

"I would like a Budweiser," Christin said.

"Me too," Zack replied.

"Great, I'll give you a minute to look at the menus," Missy said before turning and walking away.

"I wasn't really hungry before, but I am now. Let me buy you dinner as well," Zack suggested.

"Okay, I could use a little bit to eat."

They sat in silence looking at the menu. Christin had thought about getting an order of chili fries, but then thought about him watching her eat them.

Onion rings sound good, she thought. *Yeah sure, then you'll have great breath.*

As she continued to struggle with what to eat, she had the feeling that Zack was looking at her. She slowly lifted her eyes up over the edge of the menu and saw that he was looking straight at her. He had a little smirk on his face as if he knew the internal struggle that was going on inside her. She lowered the menu a bit and met his eyes. She couldn't help but smile.

"What?" she asked.

His smirk turned into a smile and he simply said, "Oh nothing," and went back to his menu. His smile seemed to get bigger, as if he knew some secret that he wasn't going to share with her. Her smile grew larger and she shook her head.

Screw it! I'm getting onion rings. It's not like he's going to kiss me anyway, she thought to herself.

She put the menu down and decided that she would give him a taste of his own medicine and started staring at him. She had a chance to look at him quite a bit while cutting his hair, but there in the bar she had a better opportunity to look at his face. He was definitely older than her, but not by much she thought. He was in great shape, probably in better shape than most guys she knew.

You so have the rugged look that drives me crazy! Please don't be a jerk, she pleaded with Zack inside her head.

She had difficulty determining his eye color in this light, but she thought they were hazel or possibly grayish blue. It was almost as if they changed color based on the light. His beard was very full and surprisingly lacked any gray. Most of the guys she knew were almost completely gray. She was admiring his firm jaw when he finally looked up at her. She felt her face flush and immediately she looked away.

Missy saved the day once again by bringing their beers.

"What can I get you to eat?" Missy asked.

"I'm just going to get the onion rings. Can you bring the spicy ranch dressing with that?" She noticed Missy's eyebrows raise up a bit as if she was surprised that Christin would order something that would certainly wreak her breath.

"How about you, Zack?"

"I would like the BBQ burger," he said with a smile, knowing all too well that the onion rings on that burger would wreck his breath and the BBQ sauce would be a complete mess. Missy had the strangest look on her face as she wrote down their orders.

"Okay, it will be right up," Missy said, as she turned and walked into the kitchen.

He obviously isn't out to impress me either, Christin thought.

Zack took a drink of his beer and then said, "I was going to get something less messy, but I figure you should see me the way I am. I also figured you weren't going to kiss me on our first date anyway." His confidence seemed to be growing by the minute.

Date! Christin thought. *Oh my gosh, this is a date!* Her heart began to race and she was sure that her face had become even redder then it had been earlier. She was trying her hardest to not smile, but she just couldn't help it.

"So, who's Lizzy?" Zack asked.

Oh my gosh! Oh no. she thought. But then she realized that if he didn't like her because of Lizzy, then he definitely wasn't the right one for her.

Chapter 10

Christopher

The sun was shining and the temperature was in the mid-seventies. Christopher sat under an umbrella at an outdoor cafe in downtown Manhattan. He was reviewing the contents of a folder on his next case when Sara arrived. Christopher stood to embrace her and held her for a moment before they said anything.

"Hey, Chris, sorry I'm late."

"It's okay, I was just reviewing our next case," Chris said with a smile and thought, *every time I see you, you take my breath away.*

Sara and Chris began dating shortly after the New Year's Eve attacks. They hadn't officially announced their relationship to leadership within the CIA, but Chris' immediate supervisor was aware of it. He had suggested to Chris that they keep their relationship low key when at

Langley and not be too overt about it when in public. It was difficult not to show his love for Sara in public, but it somehow made it fiercer in private.

"Before we get into that case, I would like to share something else that I found out recently," Sara said. "Is that okay?"

"Sure."

"Okay, so it's about you know who," Sara said.

"Okay," Chris replied. Since the Paris terror attacks, he and Sara had been investigating a man that the Islamic world called the Mahdi. According to Islamic eschatology, the Mahdi would come during the end times. It was said that he would come and lead the Islamic world during the end of days.

Chris and Sara hadn't been officially sanctioned by the CIA to find this Mahdi, but it seemed to consume both of them. So far, they hadn't let their search get in the way of their official case work, but soon they would have to let Chris' boss know what they were doing. Shortly after the Paris attacks, they had run down all the leads from the data they found in Ed's files. Ed had been a member of Chris' team in Paris and it turned out that he had been working directly for the Mahdi all along and was the mastermind behind the Paris attacks. Ed died shortly after the attacks when Sara shot him while defending Chris.

"Well, as you know, the trail went cold after we ran down all of the leads that we got from Ed's files," Sara said. Her disdain for Ed was apparent, as she pretty much spat out his name in disgust.

"But I found something just yesterday that I think might help us!" Sara exclaimed. "I think the path to the Mahdi goes through Turkey."

"Well now, that is interesting," Chris said. More and more he found himself being led by God. Sara had brought him to Christianity through her passion for Jesus and just last month Chris had committed himself to Christ. Ever since that moment, he felt God's hand, in everything that he did.

Sara wondered about his comment but said nothing. She knew that Chris would explain everything very soon. She looked into his eyes and couldn't help but feel love for him. Before he became a Christian, she found his love for her to be nothing like anything she had ever felt from another man. He loved her fiercely as she did him, but after he became a Christian his capacity for love seemed to increase exponentially.

"Interestingly, our next case takes us to Turkey." Chris revealed. "I have booked us a flight that leaves tomorrow for London. As you know, all commercial flights in and out of Turkey have been cancelled for the foreseeable future. From London, we'll be taking a military aircraft to Istanbul, Turkey.

"God leads us in mysterious ways," Sara said.

"Yes He does. So what else do you have?" Chris asked. Chris waved to their waiter and asked for their bill.

Sara was about to speak when the waiter came back with the bill and thanked them for stopping for lunch. Chris quickly threw down enough cash to cover the bill and motioned for them to get up.

As they walked down the street toward his parked car he said, "I'll go over the next case in the car, but first tell me what you found." Sara could tell that he was excited to learn what she had discovered.

"Okay, when we were sifting through the stuff that we found in Ed's lair, one particular document raised a red flag for me. At first I didn't think it was anything until I saw an article about the United Nations the other day. I found the article on an obscure Internet news website, and it mentioned an address for the United Nations Headquarters here in New York City." Sara paused for a moment as if she was collecting her thoughts.

"That address sparked a memory. It was as if I had seen that address before. At first, I thought *Of course I have seen that address*, but then I realized that I had seen it in the documents we recovered from Ed's hideout in Paris. Last night I was up until 2:00 a.m. going through stacks and stacks of paper when I finally found it."

Chris had stopped walking and was listening intently to Sara's story when a car backfired, causing both of them to jump. Chris scanned the street and saw a small puff of smoke floating upward over the traffic. Lately, he had been more jumpy than usual. He shook his head and turned back to Sara.

"Let's get to the car before you continue," Chris said. "Something feels weird and I want to get out of here and on our way."

"Okay."

Chris consciously grabbed Sara's hand and they continued walking down the street to the car. When he held Sara's hand he was able to forget about everything else that was going on in the world. The world was on the brink of war, but right now none of that mattered to him. He was with the love of his life and his commitment to Jesus had finally filled a hole in his heart and made him complete. He had never been happier and didn't think anything could change that. At least that is what he thought. Soon his world would be turned upside down and his faith would be tested.

Chapter 11

Sara

Sara looked out the window and watched the city go by as Chris drove them toward the airport hotel. She hadn't continued the conversation that they started at the cafe. Something in the wind had changed and she felt an overwhelming shadow go across her heart.

For a long time, Sara believed that the Mahdi, this elusive person that she and Chris were searching for, was the same person as the Antichrist. Islam and Christianity had been at odds for over 1300 years and would continue to be so, until the coming of Jesus. The Mahdi was the Islamic savior, a false messiah. Jesus was the Christian savior, the true Messiah. Islam had their own version of Jesus, who would come and declare that Islam was the true religion and that the Mahdi was their messiah. This Muslim Jesus would perform miracles and would cause many to fall away from

Christianity. This Muslim Jesus was known as the False Prophet in Christian eschatology. According to Islam, there was an entity who would come against the Mahdi, this was the ad-Dajjal. Sara always found it interesting the Christian eschatology and Islamic eschatology were virtual opposites of each other. The Mahdi was similar to the Christian Antichrist, the Muslim Jesus was similar to the False Prophet, and the ad-Dajjal was similar to Jesus.

Chris finally broke the silence, "So what does the United Nations have to do with this?"

"I think that the U.N. might be their next target," Sara said.

"Why?"

"Well, the document that I found in Ed's papers indicated that it was on the list of targets. But with Ed out of the picture, I wonder if their plans got delayed."

"So why do you think the U.N. is their next target?" Chris asked.

"Well, the general assembly is coming up soon and it seems to me that if you wanted to create utter chaos in a world amidst a war, take out the only body that might have a shot at cooling things off," Sara answered.

"Hmmm, that makes sense."

Sara was silent for sometime before saying, "I just wish we had time to get over there before we head to Turkey."

"I wish we could postpone our trip to Turkey as well, but Langley was pretty fired up to get us over there. It seems that there is some faction in Turkey that is pushing hard for an Islamic government, and they want us to see if we can find out who is in charge," Chris stated plainly.

This was the case that Chris started to mention earlier. Sara stared at him intensely and wondered what was going on. The current leader of Turkey had consolidated more power to himself, but hadn't completely moved away from their secular government.

"My suspicion is that the one in charge of this faction is our boy the Mahdi," Sara said.

"Yes, you are probably right," Chris replied, "but I sure wish I knew where to begin our search."

Sara and Chris sat in silence for the rest of the trip, and Sara began to wonder about the Mahdi.

Who is he? Where is he now? And how do we find him? she thought to herself. *I'm sure there is some scripture in the Bible that would help, but where do I start?*

For some reason, Sara thought of her friend, Michele. She smiled at the thought. It had been a while since she had heard from her. Michele and Sara had been college roommates and had spent the summer after their graduation abroad. Sara had mentioned Michele to Chris the first time that she spoke to him about the Mahdi. It was during their trip to Jordan where Sara first learned about the Mahdi. She and Michele had been rescued by some American men when they were cornered by Islamic radicals. The radicals had knocked Michele unconscious and the American men arrived just in time. As it turned out, the guy who patched them up took a liking to Michele and they started dating shortly after. They were married by the end of the year and Michele became pregnant almost immediately. Shortly after Michele learned that she was pregnant, her husband got word that he was to be deployed to Iraq. Two months before Michele gave birth to her son, the government notified her that her husband had died in combat.

Sara looked out the window of the government issued vehicle and wondered if she should contact Michele.

Why not! She grabbed her phone and began typing.

"Hey, Michele! How are you? I was sitting here thinking about you and decided to text. I hope that you are well! - Sara," Sara texted.

Sara looked over at Chris and smiled. He seemed to be concentrating hard while navigating the busy New York traffic. She noted how beautiful the city looked when the sky was blue and the air was clear.

bing

Sara looked at her phone and was surprised that Michele had already replied.

"Hey, Sara! I'm so glad you texted me. I was thinking about you too!! Strange! All is good here. What's new with you?"

"I am on my way to work. Are you still dating that new guy?" Sara asked.

Michele must have had a free moment because she replied right back. "Yes! Brian is his name. You need to come meet him. When do you think you'll have a chance to come to Michigan? I miss you!"

Brian! That's right. From what she had heard from Michele, he seemed like a good guy. Michele needed a good guy.

"I miss you too! I'm headed overseas for work tomorrow, but maybe when I get back I can stop by for a few days. I'll bet Jacob is huge!" Sara replied.

There was a long pause and Sara wondered if she would hear back from Michele tonight. Texting was so convenient, yet could create so much misunderstanding. A few more minutes went by and Sara decided that she would text Michele her question.

"Michele, one reason I texted you was because I have a question. It is about the Mahdi." Sara sent.

Almost immediately Sara's phone sounded.

"Ugh!" was all Michele said.

"Yeah, I know...it's a tough road to go down. But it's important. We keep finding connections between the Mahdi and the country of Turkey, does that make any sense to you?" Sara continued.

There was a short pause and Michele answered, "I'm not sure, but I know someone that I can ask. Brian's older sister is really into Biblical stuff and maybe she'll have an insight."

"I will be seeing her later today actually...very strange coincidence since she lives in New Mexico. Anyway, I'll talk to her and text back later tonight." Michele continued.

"Thanks Michele! Love you, girl!"

"Love you too, Sara!! Talk soon!"

Sara looked over to Chris and smiled. *Why Michele?* she thought, *Out of the blue, why would I think of Michele?*

"What time is our flight tomorrow?" Sara asked Chris.

"1:45 pm."

"Great! At least I can get a full night's sleep," she murmured. But sleep would be elusive for Sara that night. Something dark was coming and she could almost feel it.

CHAPTER 12

General Hasim

At the onset of Iran's invasion of the Middle East, General Hasim ordered their new Chinese-made Type 094 submarine be deployed into the Mediterranean Sea along with several other naval vessels. General Hasim was the leader of the famed Iranian Revolutionary Guard Corps (IRGC), and had been given almost complete control over the Iranian military by the Ayatollah. General Hasim had heard reports that the Ayatollah's health was failing and took it upon himself to ensure his ongoing control over the military. Hasim demanded that every general under his command pledge their allegiance to him. Those who objected mysteriously met their untimely demise by various accidents. After the first two deaths, most military leaders fell into line.

General Hasim had kept the launch of the new submarine a secret from the Ayatollah and no one but he and the submarine commander knew of its mission. The submarine was nuclear powered and had modern stealth technology, similar to the Chinese submarine that almost sank an American aircraft carrier at the beginning of the war. With the conquest of the Middle East virtually in hand, General Hasim decided that it was time to execute the submarine's true assignment and ordered it out of the Mediterranean Sea through the Straits of Gibraltar.

Six months prior, the world applauded when the IRGC mobilized throughout Iraq and began to push ISIS westward. Within the first month of the war, the IRGC had liberated all of Iraq from ISIS, with the exception of the Mosul region in northern Iraq. ISIS had been making plans to destroy a dam several miles up the Tigris River from Mosul, but the plan was foiled with assistance from Russian Special Forces. The destruction of the dam would have caused the Tigris river basin to be flooded all the way down to Baghdad and would have cost the lives of millions of civilians. ISIS in Mosul fell a week later and Iraq was completely liberated from ISIS within the month. Iran had succeeded, within a few months, where all others had failed over the course of many years.

The IRGC continued its march west into Syria a month after conquering Iraq. Iran soon controlled all of Syria, northeast of the Euphrates River. Iranian forces moved west through southern Syria and pushed ISIS toward Damascus. The Syrian government had been near collapse at the beginning of the war. They had been squeezed by both the Syrian rebel factions as well as ISIS. It was Russia's assistance that had almost completely removed the rebel threat early on. By the time Iran moved into Syria, the Syrian government had controlled the southwestern region including Damascus. ISIS was being forced east by the Syrians and the Russians, and west by the Iranians. Within a few months Iran had defeated the ISIS element in Syria.

Just last month, General Hasim declared himself to be the leader of both Iraq and Syria, but with everything else that was going on, the rest of the world took no notice. The Ayatollah's health continued to deteriorate and the General became even more emboldened.

Iran's invasion into the Arabian Peninsula had fared equally well. In the first two months of the invasion, Iran controlled the oil fields in Kuwait and had moved southward into Saudi Arabia. The Yemen government fell after several months of fighting against the Yemen rebel factions and the IRGC. The Saudi Arabian military seemed caught off guard when Iranian forces moved north from Yemen into southern Saudi Arabia. The IRGC advanced as far as the city of Khamees Moshait before they encountered any substantial resistance. It was clear to the Saudis that the Iranians were pushing toward Mecca, but with an army also pressing from the north through Kuwait, the Saudi Arabian military was overwhelmed.

At the moment, when it seemed that there would be intervention by other Arabian countries on the peninsula, like Qatar, U.A.E., and Oman, General Hasim surprised the world. Against the wishes of the Ayatollah, General Hasim launched a nuclear tipped ballistic missile from Shush, Iran. The five megaton nuclear bomb detonated over the coastal city of Ad Damman, which had a population of over 2 million civilians. The nations of the Arabian Peninsula surrendered and the rest of the world finally took notice.

In a short six months, the Iranian Revolutionary Guard Corps had successfully conquered Iraq, Syria, and the entire Arabian Peninsula. Islam's number one holy site of Mecca was now controlled by the Iranians for the first time since the death of Muhammad.

CHAPTER 13

Cheyenne Mountain, Colorado.

The President of the United States sat alone in his temporary office. It had been over six months since the attacks that destroyed a large portion of the White House and Capitol Building in Washington, D.C. His staff had done their best making this temporary office as comfortable as possible, including the portrait of President Lincoln that had been salvaged from the wreckage of the White House. The President sat in his chair staring at that portrait from across the room. He felt like he might know what President Lincoln experienced during his presidency. The United States was more divided now than during any time since the civil war of President Lincoln's era. The country had experienced violent conflicts around the topics of sexual orientation, race, wealth distribution, religion, and political affiliations.

The war overseas hadn't directly affected the people of the homeland yet, and until it did, people were unlikely to coalesce around a common front, and would continue to let their differences keep them apart.

The President reflected on the events of the past. He had been able to get Congress to fund the building of a wall along the southern border of the country, and construction had already begun. He had expended a lot of political currency to get it done. Prior to construction efforts being increased, there was a massive influx of illegal immigrants into the country. Even the threat of deportation didn't keep them out. The President also had successfully tripled the number of the Immigration and Customs Enforcement officers, and the sheer number of deportation hearings was jamming up the courts in the southern states. Three of the proposed twelve illegal alien detention centers that were in operation would soon reach capacity. Three others were scheduled to be operational in the next six months.

Terrorist activity within the United States had continued, but nothing on the scale of the New Year's Eve attacks. There were frequent mass shootings and bombings at various locations throughout the country, but the fickle media began to push the small terrorist activity to the background and out of the spotlight. The President knew that the situation was more dire than the media and the public believed, but without a major terror attack there wasn't much he could do.

Congress had voted against another war in the Middle East, so the United States pretty much stayed out of that war theater. Their absence had emboldened both Russia and Turkey, each of whom attempted to exert more leadership into the Middle East. Soon pressures mounted and Russia and Turkey found themselves at war. The thing that concerned the President the most was Iran's apparent conquest of Iraq, Syria, and the Arabian Peninsula. He had strongly denounced the use of nuclear weapons against Saudi Arabia, and called for strong sanctions against Iran. Most European countries followed suit and placed sanctions on Iran, as did the majority of the Sunni countries in Northern Africa. The sanctions didn't seem to have the desired effect as Iran controlled more than fifty percent of the world's oil production capability. China and North Korea were among the nations that didn't impose sanctions, and were publicly supporting Iran.

Russia, of course, supported Iran, but they were bogged down in a war against Turkey to their south and a war with NATO to their north. Sensing a conflict with NATO, Russia preemptively invaded the countries of Ukraine, Belarus, Estonia, Latvia, and Lithuania. Within months, Russia dominated many of the countries that made up the old Soviet Union. Poland, Romania, France, and England began engaging the Russians along the eastern border of Poland, along with other NATO countries. Germany, Belgium, and Spain were unable to provide much assistance since each was on the verge of civil war. The huge influx of Muslim immigrants from the Middle East created division within many European countries, but Germany, Belgium, and Spain had been affected the most. Rather than integrate with the native populations, the new Muslim immigrants created their own communities and in many cases they implemented Sharia law. These Muslim communities soon became no-go zones for police and military, and, as a result, the Muslims were able to create several strongholds. Eventually, these Muslim communities began to force their laws on neighboring communities and soon conflicts sprouted up everywhere. Most of these Muslim communities were made up of Sunni Muslims and were obtaining funding and arms from Turkey and Saudi Arabia. ISIS, after being forced out of the Middle East by Iran, began expanding its presence in Europe. Gun fights with local police and military soon escalated to large scale military battles. Not since World War II had Germany seen war on its soil.

The United States Congress would not declare war on Russia and limited the funding available for military incursions in Europe and the Middle East. The President of the United States did what he could with the powers that he had, but the terrorist attacks in New York and Washington, D.C. were pushing the country closer and closer to bankruptcy. The federal deficit would balloon over the next couple years just so the United States Capital building and the White House could be rebuilt.

The President shook his head knowing that it was only a matter of time before some tragic event would pull the United States into the war. The media had already begun labeling the ongoing war as World War III, but the President knew that it was only the beginning. With the United States and most Asian and African countries still on the sidelines, it could only get worse. With the wall almost built, he wondered what part Central and South America would play in the war, if any.

There was a knock on the door, followed quickly by the entrance of his Chief of Staff and the Vice President. The President had requested a quick meeting with his two top men before heading to the meeting of his Joint Chiefs.

"Hal, good to see you," the President said has he shook the hand of the Vice President. Vice President Harold "Hal" Jones was an old friend of the President. He and Hal were roommates for three years in college while they went to Penn State for their undergraduate degrees. Hal had joined the Army after college and worked his way up to Colonel before getting into politics. After basic training, Hal decided to go to the Army Airborne School and graduated top of his class. He later attended Ranger School and spent multiple tours in Iraq during the first Gulf War. After more than a decade of active duty, Hal decided to serve his country in a different way. He went back to his home state of Pennsylvania, ran for state senate and won. After his first term, he ran for an open seat within the United States Senate and won. It was during his second term as senator that the President picked him to be his running mate. The last twelve months had been the most challenging, but gratifying year as a public servant.

"Hello, Mr. President, it is great to see you, too," the Vice President replied.

"Jacob, what do you know about that problem that we discussed?" the President asked his Chief of Staff. Jacob Kolbe was younger than the President, but was a mover and a shaker in the party. Jacob had caught the President's eye four years ago when the President was only a senator. At the time, Jacob was functioning as the party whip and did a fine job of enforcing discipline within the party.

"Yes, Sir, I have some information that you might find interesting," Jacob replied and paused to collect his thoughts. He knew the President didn't like to wait, but he needed to be sure to deliver the message properly.

"Well?" the President asked.

"It seems that there is a credible threat to New York," Jacob said. He could see that the President was getting slightly irritated by his delays, but he had to get it right.

"Out with it!" the President demanded.

"It's the United Nations, Sir."

Jacob saw the Vice President perk up a bit at the mention of the United Nations.

"There has been recent chatter about an attack on the United Nations. With a session of the General Assembly scheduled to begin in two weeks, we have some heightened security concerns that need to be addressed."

The President and Vice President sat in silence as Jacob waited. The intelligence briefings had become almost unmanageable over the last several months. There seemed to be actionable intelligence emanating from every continent. The United States didn't have the money or resources to address them all.

"What about that other problem?" the President asked.

"I received word today that the CIA was dispatching a team to Turkey and that they should arrive there tomorrow. Their task is to assess any potential security concerns that there might be for the Turkish president," Jacob answered.

"Good. We can't afford a regime change now, right in the middle of the war. That would cause even more havoc over there, if that is even possible," the President said. There was a knock on the door, which was followed shortly with the President's secretary entering to let him know it was time for his meeting with the Joint Chiefs.

"Jacob, stay on top of these two issues for me and keep me posted," the President commanded, as the three of them stood and began walking to their next meeting.

"Sir?" Jacob said.

The President stopped midstride and turned to face Jacob. Jacob's complexion looked very pale, almost as if he were sick.

"Are you okay, son?" He found himself surprised by the use of the word *son*, but it seemed appropriate for some reason.

"Yes, Sir, well no, I'm not sure," Jacob replied. "There's one more thing and I'm not sure what it means."

The President could tell that Jacob was faltering, but his impatience got the best of him, "Out with it!"

"Sir, there is talk of a man over in the Middle East claiming to be Jesus."

"Jacob, it seems like every year there is some kook out there that says he is the messiah."

"Yes, Sir, but this person seems to perform miracles."

"Miracles, Jacob?"

"Yes, Sir, curing the sick, raising the dead, and um..."

"Yes!" The President's patience was about used up.

"Well, there are reports that he called down fire from the sky."

The President stared at Jacob for a moment.

"Fire from the sky?"

"Yes, Sir."

The President looked over to the Vice President in wonder and said, "Hal?"

The Vice President simply shrugged in disbelief. The President looked back at Jacob and said, "Any idea how long this *messiah* has been out there?"

"Not sure, Sir, but not long," Jacob replied. "With your permission, I would like to have a team look into this further."

The President shook his head in disbelief, but relented, "Okay, let me know what you find out." He patted Jacob on the back and said, "Okay, we have a meeting to get to," and they walked out of his office and down the hall.

As they walked, Jacob wondered why he had brought up all that stuff about the messiah. *If the President decides that I'm a nut job, I'll never work in this town again.* He shook his head and followed the President. *But something doesn't sit right. Something strange is happening and most people don't even realize it.* He decided then, that he would figure out what was going on. Even if it wasn't a priority for the President, he would figure it out.

CHAPTER 14

Santa Fe, New Mexico

The sun was going down as Dr. Stephen Weinstein finally flipped off his computer monitor. About six months ago he and his team had been pulled off their observation site near Santiago, Chile. At the time, they were monitoring the unprecedented eruption of two nearby volcanoes, Mount Tupungato and El Plomo. Dr. Weinstein's team travelled to Santiago in order to observe Mount Tupungato, which had been mostly dormant throughout modern history, but weeks prior to their arrival, the volcano had finally woken up. Seismic activity increased until the mountain finally blew its top. Dr. Weinstein and his team had recorded some of the best geological data in recent history, and with the eruption of Mount Tupungato, their trip was a success. That is, if you could call the eruption of a volcano a success, but the unexpected eruption of El Plomo had been the icing on the cake. Never before had scientists witnessed such an event. However, to his dismay, Dr. Weinstein and his team had been called home at the urgent command of his supervisor. At the time, the USGS thought that the Valles Caldera was about ready to erupt. The Valles Caldera is located just west of Santa Fe, New Mexico. As it turned out, by the time they got back to the United States, everything had calmed down in New Mexico.

Dr. Weinstein closed his briefcase and was headed for the door when the phone rang. At first he was going to ignore it, but something told him that he needed to take the call. He walked back to his desk and right after the fourth ring he picked up the phone.

"USGS, Dr. Weinstein speaking," he said.

"Stephen, it's Tracy," the caller announced.

"Hey, Tracy, what's going on?" Stephen asked.

"Well, I was bored and, acting on a hunch, I decided to head to Los Alamos to see if we could set up a few monitoring devices," Tracy answered.

Tracy was a senior member on Dr. Weinstein's team. She had been with him for almost ten years. It was pretty common for her to play her hunches, and often she was right.

"And what did you find?" he asked.

"The data is only preliminary, but I think it is worth watching. Valles is emitting methane at a rate that is just short of what we saw in Chile during the weeks prior to the eruption," she replied.

"Okay, get back here and we'll put together a plan of action. I'll put on some coffee and call the rest of the team. It looks like it's going to be a long night."

Chapter 15

Ford

It was evening and everyone was in bed. For the last several weeks, Ford found it difficult to fall asleep. Normally, it would take him twenty to thirty minutes before he slept, because he would always think through all of the next day's tasks. But this was different. It had become increasingly more difficult to sleep and when he fell asleep his dreams had become very disturbing. The previous night's dream had been especially vivid. He dreamed of a storm coming from the east. At first, the clouds had a dark red glow as if they were on fire. But soon the clouds darkened and became almost pitch black. They were filled with shapes like those of dark birds. The shapes rolled in and out of existence, as if to hide from Ford's sight. Their eyes would light up, anticipating the coming lightning strike.

Ford had no idea what the dreams meant, but there was more keeping him awake. Since Abby came home from the hospital, he felt more out of sorts than ever. The feeling he had was similar to the shudder he'd felt before the New Year's Eve attacks. However, this shudder was different. It wasn't as intense, but seemed to linger. The last shudder mirrored the quick attacks on his country, and he wondered if the next event would be more subtle, but longer lasting. He decided that tomorrow he would email Sam and see if she had any insight as to what his dreams meant. For now, he decided to get back to his research.

The second seal had been broken when Iran rushed out and conquered the Middle East. At the time, Ford had discovered a link between Revelation 6:3-4, Daniel 7:6, and Daniel 8:5-8. In Daniel 8:5-8, the prophet described a vision concerning the goat, with a prominent horn between its eyes, crossing the whole earth without touching the ground. This goat would attack the Persian Ram with great rage. The interpretation of this vision would explain that this goat was represented by the king of Greece. Additional research made it clear that this "king of Greece" was actually a leader from Turkey.

Ford suspected that the current leader of Turkey definitely fit the bill, as he had consolidated more and more power over the country of Turkey. The once secular government was moving toward an Islamic government almost daily. Not since the caliphate of the Ottoman Empire was abolished after World War II, has Turkey been ruled by Sharia law.

"What would make Turkey attack Iran with such rage?" Ford asked himself out loud.

What if Iran declared a caliphate?

"Yes!" he exclaimed, "That would do it!"

"Are you talking to yourself again, Dear?" Abby said from the other room. Ford had a habit of talking aloud when working through the details of his research.

He chuckled to himself and reply, "Yeah, sorry Hun!"

If Iran declared a caliphate, the entire Sunni population would be outraged. Iran was primarily of the Shia branch of Islam, which made up about 10% of the Muslim population. The majority of the rest was Sunni. Turkey, the de facto leader of the Sunni world at the moment, would have to do something. Was an attack on Iran by Turkey the next sign? And did this attack represent the opening of the third seal and the arrival of the horseman riding the black horse?

Ford looked further into Daniel 8 and read verse 8, *"The goat became very great, but at the height of his power his large horn was broken off, and in its place four prominent horns grew up toward the four winds of heaven."*

What if the original horn between the eyes of the goat represents the current leader of Turkey? Ford thought.

Daniel 8:8 says that this leader will succeed in defeating Iran (the Persian goat), but at the height of his power will be broken off and possibly killed. As Ford read on, he found that four prominent horns would grow up in place of the one that was broken. And out of one of the four another one would come. It would start out small, but would grow in power to the south and to the east and toward the Beautiful Land.

"Okay, so Turkey attacks Iran and defeats them, thus controlling the Middle East. Then the leader of Turkey would be replaced by four regional leaders, with one of the leaders being replaced by another leader," Ford murmured.

Looking back to Daniel 7:6, Ford found more evidence of these four regional leaders. Daniel 7:6 read, "After that, I looked, and there before me was another beast, one that looked like a leopard. And on its back it had four wings like those of a bird. This beast had four heads, and it was given authority to rule."

"But what countries will make up these regions?" Ford asked himself.

"They have to come from the list of seven beast empires."

Ford shuffled through some papers on his desk and found the list of beast empires. The list he had seen many times, but this time everything began to click in his mind.

Egypt
Assyria
Babylon
Medo-Persia
Greece
Rome
Islamic Caliphate

The first four empires are clear, as is the last one. It is the fifth and sixth empires, represented by Greece and Rome, that seemed out of place to Ford. Today, all of these empires, with the exception of Greece and Rome, are represented by Islamic countries. The list of the corresponding modern countries:

Egypt
Syria

Iraq
Iran
Greece???
Rome???
Islamic Caliphate

Greece is a predominantly Catholic country, as is Italy.

"This just doesn't fit," Ford exclaimed.

Ford got up and walked over to his bookshelf.

"I know there is a commentary on this subject that explains this oddity," Ford said as he looked for the book.

"Ah, here it is."

Ford first found the chapter on the Roman Empire. The Roman Empire began in 27 BC. At the height of the empire, it encompassed much of southern Europe, all of Turkey, most of Syria and Iraq, Israel, and parts of northern Africa. At 330 AD, the empire was divided between East and West, with Rome being the capital of the West, and Constantinople being the capital of the East. Early in the fifth century AD, Constantinople exceeded Rome both politically and commercially, and can be considered the primary capital of the Roman Empire. In 70 AD, the Roman Empire destroyed Jerusalem and the Temple, and over one million Jews were enslaved. In 132 AD, the Jews revolted again and were cut down. This time 600,000 Jews were killed. In 476 AD, the Western Roman Empire was deposed and Rome was sacked. Constantinople became the only capital of the Roman Empire. The Eastern Roman Empire continued to persecute Jews until the 9th century AD. In 1453 the Eastern Roman Empire finally fell to the Islamic Caliphate, which was called the Ottoman Empire. Constantinople was eventually renamed Istanbul when it became the capital city of the Islamic Caliphate. For almost one thousand years, the capital of the Roman Empire was Constantinople.

"Hmmm, I would say that is a clear argument for the sixth beast empire being represented by the modern nation of Turkey!" Ford exclaimed.

Ford scratched out Rome and replaced it with Turkey so that his list looked like this:

Egypt
Syria
Iraq
Iran
Greece???
~~Rome~~ Turkey
Islamic Caliphate

"So now all I have to do is figure out Greece," Ford said.

He flipped through the same commentary where he discovered the truth about the Roman Empire and found more information on Greece.

"Hmmm, Greece is predominantly a Christian country and historically didn't persecute the Jewish people," Ford mumbled. "Well, that is until Antiochus IV,"

"Maybe that's where I need to look?" Ford questioned out loud.

Ford perused the book and found that the Aramaic word for Greece is *Yavan*. He recalled the name Yavan from Genesis 10:4. Yavan is identified as the son of Japheth, who is the son of Noah. Genesis 10:4-5 reads "*The sons of Yavan:*

Elishah, Tarshish, the Kittim and the Rodanum. (From these maritime peoples spread out into their territories by their clans within their nations, each with its own language.)"

"Hmmm," Ford said to himself. He continued to read and found that it is the descendants of Yavan who are the people around the southern Balkan Peninsula and the west coast of Turkey. The countries that make up the southern Balkan Peninsula are Albania, Macedonia, and Greece.

"Well, Greece and Macedonia are almost entirely Christian and the Islamic population in Macedonia is primarily of Albanian decent," Ford explained to himself. "And only Albania is predominantly Islamic."

Ford continued to read, discovering that Phillip II of Macedonia reigned from 359-336 BC and he defeated the city-states of Athens and Thebes in 338 BC. His son, Alexander the Great, convinced him to control all of Greece and it was Alexander that expanded the Greek Empire east beyond Persia and south into Egypt. However, during this period, the Greeks were relatively cordial to Israel, going so far as allowing them to worship God according to their beliefs. Alexander ruled the Greek Empire until his untimely death in 325 BC. The period after his death is commonly referred to as the Diadochi, when rival generals of Alexander's fought for control of the empire. When the dust settled, there were four kingdoms centered around Macedonia, Turkey, Egypt, and Syria that came from the Greek Empire. The Seleucid Dynasty made up the largest section of the old Greek Empire and was ruled by Seleucus I Nicator. He made the city of Antioch the capital of his kingdom. It was Antiochus IV, the great, great, great, great grandson of Seleucus I, who began persecuting the Jewish people. It is the origins of Antiochus that will help identify the modern nation representing the fifth beast empire.

"History tells us that Seleucus I was most probably from the Illyrian tribes, which it turns out, are the descendents of the people of Albania," Ford read.

"So Albania is the modern day country that represents the fifth beast empire?" Ford questioned.

He picked up his list of the seven beast empires and scratched out Greece and replaced it with Albania, so that the list looked like this:

Egypt
Syria
Iraq
Iran
~~Greece~~ Albania
~~Rome~~ Turkey
Islamic Caliphate

Ford found it very interesting that every one of these countries is predominantly Islamic and that all of these countries are Sunni Muslims, with the exception of Iran, who are Shia Muslims. These two sects of Islam have been at odds since the death of Mohammad.

"So Iraq represents the ancient Babylonian Empire and Iran represents the ancient Medo-Persian Empire," Ford stated.

Going back to Daniel 7, Ford noted that the beast resembling a lion was represented by Iraq. The beast that resembled a bear was represented by Iran. The terrifying fourth beast is represented by the Islamic Caliphate.

"So the countries of Egypt, Syria, Albania, and Turkey represent the four headed beast that resembled a leopard!" Ford exclaimed.

Ford realized that all of these countries have a predominantly Sunni population. He also knew that the beast that resembled a leopard in Daniel 7 is closely related to the goat in Daniel 8. Ford wondered if it is possible that the divide between the sects of Islam is what will force the goat to charge at the ram furiously.

It was getting late and Ford's head was beginning to hurt. He stood up and looked out the window of his office and stared into the distance, letting his mind roam freely. The full moon provided just enough light for Ford to see the figure of an animal out near the edge of the forest. He wasn't certain, but part of him thought that it looked like a large goat. He shook his head and rubbed his eyes and when he looked out the window again, the figure had moved on.

"Was that really a goat?" Ford asked himself.

"No way!" he replied.

"Who are you talking to, Sweetheart?" Ford heard the voice of his beloved wife from the doorway.

Ford slowly turned around and smiled at Abby. He didn't answer the question. He simply looked at her lovingly.

"Come to bed, Ford, I'll help you fall asleep," Abby said with a playful grin on her face.

Ford raised his eyebrows and began shutting down his computer. Abby took his hand and lead him out of his office and into their master bedroom. As he prepared himself for bed and was about to turn off the light, he felt a small shudder. He wasn't sure what it meant, but in that moment he didn't care. He was with the love of his life and that was all that mattered.

Chapter 16

Samantha

When Sam left the car rental lot, she thought about how nice it was to be home. She surprised herself by associating the word *home* with Michigan. As she left the city and the terrain became more rural, the amount of green amazed her. The trees were green and lush, and the fields were full of green plant life. It had been a long time since she left Michigan for New Mexico and she had almost forgotten how beautiful Michigan was. As she drove north, she thought back to early that morning at the airport. She recalled saying goodbye to Rob and hugging him tightly. She hadn't wanted to let go of him, for fear she might lose him. The world was becoming such a crazy place. Back in New Mexico, Rob had kissed her on the cheek and whispered that he loved her. The memory of their goodbye made her smile. She and Rob were probably the happiest that they've been since they got married. Rob helped her get through everything that had happened the last several months. She didn't know how she would have ever survived without him.

Her hometown was pretty much the same as when she left. She made the turn at the light without even thinking about it. Her parents lived in the home that Sam had grown up in, and it seemed like she could probably get there with her eyes closed. She pulled into the driveway and put the car in park. She hadn't realized how nervous she was until she turned off the engine. Her stomach sank at the anticipation of seeing her father. Tears began to well up in her eyes as she tried to fight them off.

"Come on, Sam," she whispered to herself. "Be strong for Mom and Dad."

Taking a deep breath, she opened the car door and stepped out. The humidity was elevated. She had forgotten how muggy it could get during the summer in Michigan. Fortunately, the temperature was moderate in the high seventies, so the humidity didn't feel too uncomfortable. She looked around and wondered who else was there. A few cars were parked on the street, but there was no way of knowing if any of them belonged to her siblings. She took another deep breath and began walking up the sidewalk toward the house.

As Sam reached the porch, the door opened and she was greeted by her younger sister, Sonia. It made sense that Sonia was there, since she lived only a few miles away. It had been a while since she had seen Sonia, and to Sam's eyes she hadn't changed much. She was a little heavier, but still would be considered petite by most people. Sam was amazed that after having six children, Sonia was able to look so good. Sam smiled and embraced Sonia.

"Hey, baby sister," Sam whispered.

"Hey, big sister," Sonia returned.

When they released the embrace, Sam took Sonia's hands in hers and looked Sonia up and down.

"You are so pretty!" Sam exclaimed. "You amaze me."

Sonia blushed a little and said, "It's so good to see you, Sammy."

"How's Mom doing?" Sam asked.

"She's doing alright. Dad seems to be doing okay today too, but it's not good."

"Is anyone else here yet?"

"Ralph and Rebecca will be in later tomorrow and Brian is coming over later tonight," Sonia replied.

Sam nodded and took another deep breath. After exhaling, she reached for the door knob and entered her childhood home.

CHAPTER 17

Nigel

When Nigel woke, he could tell by the amount of light that shone through the tent that the sun was just starting to come up. He became aware of the soreness in his back. He wasn't accustomed to sleeping on an air mattress and he wondered how many more nights he could do it. Neither Tia nor he had a place they called home, so he wondered what they were going to do. He looked to his left and saw Tia sleeping next to him.

"You are so beautiful," he whispered to Tia while she slept. He needed to get up, but he knew if he moved too much he would wake her. He began thinking about the story that she had shared with him about her being called toward Houghton Lake. It was immediately afterward, that he told her how he felt like he was drawn toward Houghton Lake as well. Even though, at the time, he didn't know it was

Houghton Lake he was drawn to. He had shared his dream about the water and the angel. She had immediately blushed upon hearing him call her his angel. She didn't seem to realize just how beautiful she was. Tia had given God the credit for bringing them together. After years of following a god that only brought destruction, he had been reluctant to agree with her. Tia had said that Jesus was about love and not hate. She didn't believe that God and Allah were the same.

"How can they be the same?" Tia had said. "When one only wants the destruction of all non-believers, and the other only wants the salvation of all people."

Her arguments made sense, but he was still having trouble believing. He knew Allah was wrong and he knew that Islam had taken him down the wrong path. Still, Jesus was so foreign to him. He wasn't sure what to believe.

How long before they come looking for me?

Since meeting Tia, Nigel wondered how long he had before Ali would find him. He worried what they might do to Tia if they did find him. He vowed not to let anything bad happen to her. He deserved whatever punishment he received, but Tia was innocent.

"I love you, Tia," Nigel whispered. He had never voiced those words to her. He was afraid what her response might be. It seemed crazy to believe that he could fall in love with her so fast, but he believed his feelings to be true. Rather than get up, Nigel picked up the Bible that lay beside Tia and opened it up.

Chapter 18

Zack

"Uaagh!" Zack woke screaming. He found himself sitting upright in bed and covered in sweat. He took a deep breath and let his eyes become accustomed to the pre-morning light. He could tell that the sun would rise shortly and soon the room would be filled with the clean light of the morning sunrise. He switched on the lamp next to his bed. Normally, he didn't have any issue with darkness, but his dream had completely unnerved him.

In his dream, Zack found himself in the woods. He was with Christin and her daughter and possibly a few other people. They seemed to be followed by a group of beasts. They were humanoid, but not fully human. All had human bodies, but most didn't have human heads. Some had the heads of rams, others goats, some bears, while others had leopard heads. He could only see flashes of them as he ran through the woods and frequently looked back to see if they were getting closer. He was concerned that Christin and her daughter wouldn't be able to keep up with him. The dream continued as they raced through the woods. Ahead, he could see a wall and a light and he hoped that it would provide him with the shelter that they needed. As he closed in on the wall, he could see a gate. He yelled for the gate to be opened and then he heard a bloodcurdling scream. It didn't sound human at all, and it reminded him of the scream made by the beasts that the Nazgul's rode in the "Lord of the Rings" movie. There seemed to be an explosion and he was thrown to the ground, face down. A rush of heat and light debris slammed into his back. He rolled onto his back and before he could stand, a huge beast was upon him. The beast was fiery red, resembling a dragon like you'd see in a fantasy movie. But this dragon was different. Instead of one head, it had many. It had seven to be exact. And each one of them had their eyes trained on him. Zack had never been more terrified in his life and he was frozen stiff. The dragon looked at him intently for what seemed like days and in a sudden lunge came down upon him. The pain of its teeth into his flesh was unbearable and as he began to cry out in agony, he found himself back in reality. For an instant, he felt pain where the dragon had began feeding on his flesh. But it soon went away.

"Not sure I'll ever sleep again," Zack murmured to himself. "What the heck was that about?"

He brought his hands to his face and began to rub. He was hopeful that the memory would soon fade. But he knew that it wouldn't.

For as long as he could remember, he had been sharing his dreams with his lifelong friend, Sam. She always seemed to know what they meant. He decided that he would get up and email her the details now, before they became too fuzzy. He took one more deep breath and forced himself up out of bed.

"But before I do that, I need coffee."

Zack got up and walked into the kitchen and started the coffee pot. As he stood there, Christin came to mind. He just remembered that she had been in his dream. He had only known her for a short time, but he seemed to be falling for her. He shook his head.

"You sure are getting soft in your old age," he said to himself with a smile. *I really am falling for her, aren't I?* In that moment he decided that he needed to call Christin.

Chapter 19

Christin

Christin lay in bed thinking about Zack when the phone rang. She smiled when she saw that caller ID identified Zack as the caller.

"Hey there," she said softly, still smiling.

"We have to leave," Zack said somberly.

Christin's smile left her face and was replaced by a look of concern.

"What? I don't understand," she replied.

"Christin, I don't know if I can explain it without you thinking that I'm crazy, but deep in my heart I know that we need to leave this place and get to my friend's place in Michigan as soon as possible."

Zack went on to explain his dream and his plan to drive to Michigan versus fly. Something told him that it would be dangerous to fly and besides they wouldn't be able to bring everything that they needed unless they drove. It was a solid twenty four hours of driving from Hulett, Wyoming to Ford's place in Michigan. It would take them 2 to 3 days to drive there.

"Because we might not be coming back here, Christin," Zack said somberly.

"Zack, you're right, that does sound crazy," Christin replied.

"Yes, I know, but I know that I'm right," Zack said.

"Maybe, but I can't just pack up my life and leave. I like you. I like you a lot, but we've only known each other for a month or so," Christin said. "Besides, I can't uproot Lizzy like that."

"Christin, I like you a lot too, but deep in my heart, I know that I have to go," Zack said. "And I really want you and Lizzy to come with me."

"Sorry, Zack, but I can't come with you."

Zack felt his heart drop into his stomach. He truly had fallen for Christin hard, but he understood what she was saying. How could he expect her to leave with him?

"Okay, Christin. I will miss you. Damn! I will miss you!" Zack exclaimed. "I'll come by and say goodbye before I go. I have a few things I have to take care of here before I go, so it probably won't be until the weekend before I leave. If you change your mind, please let me know."

"I will. Thanks, Zack," Christin said. "You're a great guy! I will miss you, too."

Christin began to choke up, so she said a quick goodbye and hung up the phone.

Zack hung up the phone and just stared at it.

Chapter 20

New York

Ali watched as the Mahdi's private jet left the airstrip and headed toward Istanbul. Soon Ali would follow, but for now he had one more plan to carry out and one loose end to tie up.

Ali stepped into the stretch limo and sat down. As his driver closed the door behind him, he wondered how long it would take to find Nigel. The disappearance of Nigel had caught him off guard, and he was bound and determined to find him. All indications were that he was still in Michigan. Ali had sent several teams to search for him and he believed that he would soon be found.

Ali looked out the window and watched the city go by as he made his way to his apartment.

Back in his apartment, in lower Manhattan, Ali sat down at his desk and picked up the phone. A voice on the other end picked up after the second ring.

"Where do we stand?" Ali asked.

There was a pause and then the voice said, "Everything is going as planned. I believe that we'll be ready to go by the end of the week."

"Excellent," Ali replied, "Allahu Akbar, my friend."

Ali put down the receiver and stood up from the desk. He slowly walked to his window and peered out. He could see the Freedom Tower from a short distance. Not long ago, his Muslim brethren had changed the course of history by taking down the Twin Towers. The events of September 11th, 2001 would forever be remembered as the day the pendulum had begun to swing back toward Islam. Life in the United States and in the rest of the world, for that matter, would forever be changed.

His gaze left the newly built Freedom Tower and his mind began to wonder.

"Where have you gone, Nigel?" he said aloud.

Chapter 21

Christopher

Christopher looked in the mirror and splashed water on his face. Amazingly, he had slept great. The previous day's conversation with Sara had been strange. They seemed to be getting closer to knowing who the Mahdi was, but still they seemed so far away. Their little side project was nearing the point of obsession for them.

Thoughts of Sara came to mind as he stepped into the shower. He longed to be with her, but other than kissing they still hadn't been intimate. He and Sara agreed that it was best to wait until later. Sara hadn't used the M word, but he knew that it was in the back of her mind. It was definitely on his mind. As the warm water poured over his head, he decided then and there.

"I'm going to ask Sara to marry me," Chris said to himself.

The thought made him smile. He figured he had about forty minutes before he had to meet Sara downstairs. That might be just enough time.

In the room down the hall, Sara was in the bathroom combing her hair when the hair on her arms stood up. They were covered with goose bumps. She wasn't cold and didn't understand why that happened, but she could tell that it wasn't a bad thing.

"I wonder what Chris is doing?" she said aloud. Her feelings for Chris had grown more than she had ever imagined was possible. She knew that she was prepared to spend the rest of her life with him, and she knew that Chris loved her, but she didn't know where he stood on marriage. Sara was amazed at how quickly she had fallen in love with Chris. Never in her life had she ever fallen so hard.

Chris found himself hailing a cab and hoping that he had enough time. He knew that he might be a little late, but he didn't care. The cab took him about six blocks south and pulled over.

"$6," the cabby said.

"Here's a twenty," Chris said as he handed him the money. "Can you hang out here for a few more minutes. I won't be long."

"Sure, but hurry," the cab driver replied.

Chris ran into the store and was greeted by the store manager.

"How can we help you, Sir?" the store manager asked.

"Well, I know this probably sounds weird, but ..."

Sara was sitting in the lobby when she saw Chris come running through the hotel entrance. She looked at him questioningly. She could see the surprise on his face at seeing her there.

"Hi there!" Chris exclaimed, as he came up to Sara. He pulled her in and kissed her deeply. Sara could feel her heart begin to race and her temperature begin to rise.

"Hi," Sara breathed. She actually felt out of breath. Chris had literally taken her breath away and that made her smile deeply.

"Are you ready to go?" Chris asked.

"Sure," she replied as she picked up her bag. She had completely forgotten to ask where he had come from.

Chapter 22

Cheyenne Mountain, Colorado

Lieutenant Jason Chambers handed his credentials to the guard at the second check point that provided access to the main parking area outside Cheyenne Mountain's infamous NORAD command center. Just last week he had been assigned to his new position as a data analyst for NORAD, and he had a mixture of nervousness and excitement for his first day on the job.

Since the cold war ended in the 90s, the complex at Cheyenne Mountain had been used less and less. That is, until the events of 9/11. After the terrorists had taken down the Twin Towers and attempted to take out the Pentagon, the U.S. government began to upgrade the facility. After the New Year's Eve attacks in New York and Washington, D.C., efforts to increase the use of the facility had quadrupled. Every system had been improved and expanded, and a wing deep inside the mountain had been created for storing vast amounts of data collected by virtually all government agencies. The public had suspected, but hadn't fully understood, the scope of the data that its government collected on everyone. This facility housed data on what a person purchased with credit cards, what searches they performed on the Internet, what programs they watched on the television, and where they travelled on a daily basis. Most of the civilian population didn't realize that all of the *smart* devices they used on a daily basis, were reporting data to the government.

"Thank you, Lieutenant," the guard said as he handed back Lieutenant Chambers' credentials. The guard waved him forward as the gate opened in front of him.

Lieutenant Chambers drove slowly through the gate and progressed to the parking area where he would be met by his liaison. He grabbed his case and exited the truck. As he walked down the short row of vehicles, he saw a woman standing at the curb. She was tall and was dressed in her work uniform. As far as he could tell, she had dark hair and light brown complexion. He guessed she was either Native American or of Mexican heritage.

"Lieutenant Chambers," the liaison said as she extended her hand, "I am Captain Addison Hernandez."

"Nice to meet you, Captain," he returned, as he shook her hand. "I am very excited to start working for you, Ma'am!"

"Come with me Lieutenant and I'll show you your station."

Lieutenant Chambers followed the Captain to the last check point before entering the famed NORAD complex. A chill of excitement went through his spine and the doors closed behind him.

Chapter 23

Samantha

Sam followed her sister, Sonia, into the living room where her parents sat on the couch. They both looked old to Sam's eyes. Her father must have aged ten years in the last year or so. Her mother had fared better, but seeing her husband of fifty years slowly fade away had taken its toll.

"Hey, Dad," Sam said as she leaned down and kissed him on his cheek. He had lost weight, maybe twenty pounds or more. Sonia had told her that he wasn't eating very well these past few weeks.

"Hey, Sweetie," her father replied with a smile. His smile was still strong and loving. Sam had always been Daddy's little girl and she had always felt safe when he was around. Today wasn't any different. Tears began to build, but she fought to keep them at bay.

"Hi, Honey," her mother said as she came in for an embrace. Sam had been blessed with two loving parents and couldn't imagine being without either of them.

"Hi, Mom," Sam replied, as she returned the hug. Her mother's embrace was strong and Sam wondered if she would ever let go. Finally, her mother softened her hold on her oldest daughter. She grasped Sam's hands and looked her in the eyes.

"You are so beautiful!" her mother exclaimed. She let go of her right hand and grabbed Sonia's hand as well.

"Both of you are beautiful!" she added.

"Well, you know where they get it from, Dear," Sam's father said with a smile.

The three of them, Sam, her sister, and her mother, all looked lovingly on the man that they all loved dearly.

There isn't much time is there, God? Sam asked God silently. She already knew the answer to her question.

Sam sat down next to her father and gently grasped his hand. He smiled knowingly.

"Hey, Dad, how are you doing?" Sam asked.

"I'm alright," he replied. "Some days are better than others."

"How are you, Dear?" her father asked.

"I'm doing well. Rob and the boys are doing well also."

"Oh, that's good," he replied.

There was a moment of silence. Sam wasn't sure what to say next. Fortunately, the television was on to save them. As Sam expected, her mother and father were watching a conservative news channel when Sam arrived. The news of the day seemed to be all about the war that seemed to be raging everywhere except in the Americas. Sam knew that it was only a matter of time before it came to their back yard.

"I can't believe we are letting Iran get away with it!" her father exclaimed as he shook his head in disgust.

"I know that old president would have encouraged the rag heads to do what they are doing, but this new one I thought would be different," he continued.

"Dad!" Sam exclaimed. Her father knew that she didn't like him using derogatory language.

"What?" he asked with a smile.

"You know what!" Sam said in mock anger and then she laughed softly as she shook her head.

"But seriously, I don't understand why we allowed Iran to take over the Middle East," her father stated.

"Well, Dad, I think that we are still recovering from the attacks this past winter," Sam replied.

"Yeah, I know."

"I also think this might be God's will," Sam said.

"God's will?" he asked as he turned to face her.

"Yes, Dad."

"Well, how do you figure God would want all this to happen?"

"Well, you remember the prophet Daniel, right?" Sam asked her father.

"Yes, Dear, of course."

"Well, in the Book of Daniel, chapter 8, he prophesied that this very thing would happen," Sam stated plainly. "The Bible actually says that no one could stand against Iran, and that Iran would do as they pleased and become great."

"Well, I'll be," her father said.

There was more silence as her father turned back to the television and Sam's ears perked up as she heard the word *caliphate* spoken by the news anchor.

"It appears that the caliphate previously declared by the Islamic State has been denounced and a new caliphate has been declared by the Ayatollah of Iran," the news anchor announced.

Sam could not believe what she was hearing. Iran had declared a new caliphate. She wondered if Ford had heard already. Amazingly, several months ago, after the New Year's Eve attacks, Ford had told Sam that he expected Iran to declare a caliphate and that, as a result, the Sunni branch of Islam would rise up against the Shia branch of Islam found in Iran. This Sunni-Shia conflict had been prophesied later in Daniel 8, where this conflict had been symbolized by the goat in Daniel 8:5-7. As it turned out, the goat would cross the whole world without touching the ground and strike the Persian ram. This would result in the ram's two horns being shattered. In other words, the two power centers that are represented by the two horns would be destroyed. The leaders that represented these power centers in Iran were the Ayatollah and the Iranian Revolutionary Guard Corps.

"Dad, this is going to escalate into something even bigger," Sam said.

"Do you think?" her father questioned.

"Yes, Dad, I do."

Her father looked at her for a moment and then turned toward the television in silence.

Sam wondered how much more time her father had. For his sake, she hoped that he didn't have to endure the challenges that lay ahead for the rest of the followers of Christ. She turned away from her father as a tear escaped her eye.

Sam wiped her eyes and turned back to her father when the door bell rang.

Chapter 24

Ford

Ford was sitting on the couch watching the news after a long day working at the lodge when he heard the news anchor share the announcement that the Ayatollah of Iran declared a new caliphate, and named himself the Caliph.

"It was only a matter of time," Ford declared.

He grabbed the Bible that he normally had on the end table and opened it to Daniel chapter 8 verse 5, which read:

"As I was thinking about this, suddenly a goat with a prominent horn between his eyes came from the west, crossing the whole earth without touching the ground. He came toward the two-horned ram I had seen standing beside the canal and charged at him in great rage. I saw him attack the ram furiously, striking the ram and shattering his two horns. The ram was powerless to stand against him; the goat knocked him to the ground and trampled on him, and none could rescue the ram from his power."

It was pretty clear that the goat would prevail against the ram. The declaration of the caliphate by Iran would surely enrage Turkey and the rest of the Sunni world. The Turkish military was the largest in the Middle East. The United States had supplied Turkey with a multitude of airplanes and other military equipment for years. The Turkish Air Force was far superior to Iran's. Could the Turkish Air Force "cross the whole earth without touching the ground?"

The two horns of the ram were most likely represented by the Ayatollah himself and possibly the leader of the Iranian Revolutionary Guard Corps.

Does this mean that Turkey will assassinate the Ayatollah or at least stage a coup?

Will the leader of the Iranian Revolutionary Guard Corps be killed, or could that group be completely defeated?

Ford had so many questions. It was beyond time to get his family prepared. He would also have to notify Sam and Zack as well.

How much longer before Turkey launches their attack against Iran?

Chapter 25

Samantha

Sam and Sonia both converged on the front door together, but Sonia reached the door first. She opened the door to their brother, Brian, and his girlfriend, Michele.

"Hey," Sonia and Sam chimed in unison. Sonia hugged her brother and then turned to Michele.

"Michele, how are you?" Sonia asked as she hugged her.

Sam and Brian made eye connect and they both smiled. It had been far too long since she had seen her brother.

"Hey, Brian," Sam said as she gave him a big hug.

"Hey, Sis," he replied. They held the hug for a long time until Sonia cleared her throat.

"Sam, this is Michele," Sonia began, "and Michele, this is my big sis, Samantha."

Michele was the first one to speak, "Very nice to meet you, Samantha."

"It's very nice to meet you, too," Sam replied.

"Let's go into the kitchen," Sonia said as she closed the door behind them.

In the kitchen, Brian and Sam sat down at the kitchen table across from each other. Sam thought it was interesting that both of them sat in their *assigned* childhood seats.

I guess old habits die hard, Sam thought.

Sonia offered everyone a beverage before heading to the refrigerator.

"Just a glass of water for me," said Michele as she sat down next to Brian.

"Any beer in the frig?" Brian asked.

"I'm fine, Sonia, nothing for me," said Sam.

Sonia grabbed two glasses from the cupboard and set them down on the counter. Then she opened the refrigerator and pulled out a pitcher of cold water. After filling both glasses, she gave one to Michele and sat the other in front of the seat next to Sam.

"Thank you," Michele said as she picked up her glass.

"You are most welcome."

Sonia then went back to the refrigerator and after replacing the pitcher of water, she said, "Is Bud Light okay?"

"Sure," Brian replied.

Sonia produced a Bud Light, opened it, and sat it down in front of Brian.

"Wow!" Brian exclaimed. "Full service and everything."

Sonia playfully smacked his shoulder before sitting down next to Sam.

The conversation was mostly mundane topics. No one seemed to want to talk about the topic that was on everyone's mind. It was hard enough thinking about her father, let alone talk about it. Sam figured they would be talking about it soon enough.

As the silence was about to become awkward, Michele spoke up.

"Samantha, you know a lot about the Bible, right?" Michele asked.

Sam was a little bit shocked by the question. Apparently, Brian had been talking to Michele about her.

"Sure, what's up?"

"Well, strangely enough, just today my friend, Sara, texted me."

Sam sat there waiting for Michele to continue and after a moment she giggled a bit.

"That's a weird way to start a conversation," Michele said, picking on herself as she turned toward Brian.

Brian smiled and sort of shook his head a little.

"Anyway, my friend, Sara, texted me and asked me a question about the Mahdi," Michele stated.

Sam's eyes opened up wider as she felt a slight wave of energy go through her. She looked down at her arms and they were covered in goose bumps.

"You know who I'm talking about, don't you?" Michele asked Sam.

Never in a million years would Sam have thought that the Mahdi would be the topic of conversation at that table.

"I do know a bit about the Mahdi," Sam answered.

Michele nodded knowingly and paused before speaking again. Sam looked at Michele and could tell that she was unsure what to say next.

"Well, just today, my friend, Sara, asked me about the Mahdi. She was wondering what connection the Mahdi had with the nation of Turkey."

Sam sat in silence for a moment, partially because she thought Michele might have more to say, but primarily because she wasn't sure where to begin. She and Ford had talked about the Mahdi so many times. Part of her felt the story of the goat, in Daniel 8, was the relevant portion.

"Are you familiar with Daniel 8, from the Bible?" Sam asked.

"I've read some of Daniel, but I couldn't tell you what Daniel 8 is about," Michele replied.

"Daniel 8 talks about a ram and a goat," Sam began. "I know that probably seems irrelevant, but it isn't."

"Okay," Michele replied.

"The ram," Sam paused. "The ram represents the nation of Iran. Daniel prophesied that Persia, which is modern day Iran, would conquer the Middle East."

Michele seemed a little surprised that this 2500 year old prophecy was being lived out before their eyes.

"I see it in your eyes. You see that Daniel's prophecy has already come true in the last year," Sam noted.

Michele nodded, but didn't say anything.

"So this goat had a single prominent horn," Sam began. "It is prophesied to sweep across the whole world and strike the ram. The goat represents the nation of Turkey."

Sam could see the recognition in Michele's eyes and before she could continue, Michele spoke up.

"So is this goat the Mahdi?"

"No, there's more to the story," Sam replied. "The goat became very great, but at the height of its power, its horn was broken. It is important to know that, in Bible prophecy, a horn represents a leader or a king."

Michele nodded. Brian and Sonia also seemed interested, but said nothing.

"So this horn is broken and four more horns grew up in its place," Sam continued.

"So four kings will rise out of Turkey?" Michele asked.

"Close," Sam replied. "But I think what will happen is this goat will defeat Iran and will take over control of the Middle East. But when this single horn, this single leader of Turkey, is broken, the Middle East will be divided into four nations, each with its own king."

"Wow! But where does the Mahdi come in?" Sonia chimed in before Michele could say anything.

"Great question, but first I want to speculate about the identity of the goat with the prominent horn," Sam replied. "It is very possible that the current leader of Turkey is represented by this prominent horn. Earlier today, I heard on the news that Iran declared a caliphate."

"What's a caliphate?" Sonia questioned. Sam smiled at her younger sister's interest in the topic. She wondered what Brian was thinking as she glanced over at him. He seemed to be somewhat engaged in the conversation, but it was still hard to tell what he was thinking.

"Simply put, the caliphate is a worldwide Muslim confederacy. It includes one common government, military, and, of course, religion. The caliphate is ruled by a person called the Caliph. He is the supreme ruler of the caliphate. By declaring a caliphate, it is possible that Iran has angered the rest of the Muslim world," Sam said.

"So you think that Turkey will rush out and attack Iran, and that the single horn on the goat from Daniel 8 could be representing the current leader of Turkey?" Michele said questioningly.

"Exactly," Sam said, as she put her index finger on the tip of her own nose.

"Wow! That is crazy!" Michele exclaimed, both Sonia and Brian nodded in agreement.

"So what about the Mahdi?" Michele asked.

"Well, we have to read further into Daniel 8, specifically Daniel 8:9, which says," Sam said. *"Out of one of them came another horn, which started out small but grew in power to the south and to the east and toward the Beautiful Land."*

"So this small horn comes out of the four that grew up after the first horn was broken," Sam continued. "This small horn represents the Antichrist, who, as it turns out, is also the Mahdi."

Michele seemed to think a bit and before she could say anything, Sam spoke again.

"Let me summarize. The goat with the prominent horn, in Daniel 8, could represent the current leader of Turkey. It is probable that this leader would rush out and conquer Iran. You see, Iran follows the Shia branch of Islam, and pretty much the rest of the Muslim world follows the Sunni branch of Islam. These two factions have fought since the death of Muhammad. As we know, today Iran currently controls all of the Middle East, with the exception of Israel. At some point after Turkey conquers the territory controlled by Iran, the Turkish leader will die, assuming he is the prominent horn. Maybe he'll be assassinated, or maybe he'll just die. Who knows? Anyway, when this happens, there will be a power vacuum and as a result, four leaders will rise up and take control of various areas of the Middle East. We'll probably see a new Turkish leader, a new Iranian leader, a new Egyptian leader, and a new leader of the Arabian Peninsula. I suspect that this new Turkish leader will only be temporary, as the small horn, the Antichrist, the Mahdi, will rise up and takes control over Turkey. From there, he will begin his conquest of the Middle East and beyond."

Sam took a deep breath. She was amazed that she had recited all of that without referring to the Bible. She was really starting to understand all of this, more than she ever imagined.

"Wow," Michele said. "Just wow!"

"I know what you mean," Sam replied. "Some people think that it is crazy to think that all of this Bible prophecy is coming true. But here we are, witnessing all of it. I think people are crazy not to believe that it is happening right before our eyes."

Chapter 26

Sara

bing

Sara was putting her travel bag in the overhead compartment above her seat when she heard her phone. She looked at Chris, who was patiently waiting for her to take her seat next to the window. She smiled up at him before ducking her head and moving toward the cramped space next to the window. It was a little warm on the airplane and she raised her arm to adjust the airflow of the vent over her seat. Chris was just getting himself settled when Sara finally reached for her phone. The chime had reminded her that she needed to turn off her phone, but first she would find out who was texting her.

"Sara, I have news," was the text that she received from her friend, Michele.

Sara quickly typed the words, "What news? I only have a few minutes. The plane is about to take off."

Sara decided to leave her phone on a few more minutes while she waited for Michele's reply. She looked out the window and it looked like any other summer day in New York. When she turned toward Chris, she found him smiling at her. She smiled back and his smile widened. It was impossible not to smile when she looked at him. She was about to ask him what was on his mind when her phone chimed in.

"K, call me when u land. I have info. Where RU going?" was the reply she received from Michele.

Dang! Sara thought to herself. I wonder what Michele found out?

"What's up?" Chris asked.

"Oh, my friend, Michele, must have talked to her boyfriend's sister, because she has some information," Sara replied.

"Ok, will do. England. See ya!" Sara typed a reply to Michele, and then turned off her phone.

"What information does she have?" Chris asked.

"Michele's boyfriend has a sister who is really into end times stuff, and she knows a little bit about our friend," Sara replied, suddenly feeling like their conversation was being heard by others.

Chris nodded but didn't say anything. Sara looked at him and wondered what he was thinking. She was about to ask him what he was thinking when the captain notified the passengers and flight crew that they needed to prepare for takeoff. Within minutes, the 747 was in the air and over the

Atlantic Ocean. Sara wondered what the next few days would bring them. She wondered if they would come any closer to learning the identity of the Mahdi.

CHAPTER 27

Samantha

Shortly after cleaning up the dinner dishes, Brian and Michele left. Sam was in the kitchen sipping a glass of white wine and talking to Sonia when their mother came in.

"I really want to thank you two for coming," their mother said. She was smiling, but Sam could tell that her heart was heavy.

"Of course, Mom," Sam started.

"There's no other place that we'd rather be," Sonia finished.

Her mother grabbed Sam's hand and then Sonia's hand. Sam could tell that she was fighting back tears.

"He's so happy to see you two!"

Their father had fallen asleep in his chair right after dinner. According to their mother, he'd probably sleep on and off until the morning. He seemed okay to Sam, but her mother went on to explain that time was short. The Hospice worker had said that it could be weeks or months. Based on what she had seen today, Sam couldn't believe that it could only be weeks. Her father seemed much stronger than that.

Sam squeezed her mother's hand and smiled. "I plan to stay for a while." Sam couldn't bring herself to say what everyone was thinking. She had to swallow hard to keep the tears from flowing. There was a long moment of silence before Sonia stood up and announced that she had to go.

"I should probably go, too," Sam started. "I'll be back in the morning. Please let me know if you need anything."

Sam's mother hugged both of them and told them that they were loved.

Sam looked back at her mother standing on the porch and waved back. She summoned as much of a smile as she could before backing out of the driveway and heading toward her hotel.

Sam's home town was small according to most people who lived in large metropolitan areas, but it was big to her. The town had almost doubled in size since she left. She was amazed at how much traffic there was.

Her hotel room was nice, but not extravagant. She plopped down on the bed and looked up at the ceiling. It had the texture of a typical hotel room, what some people called popcorn ceiling. The bed was comfortable and she was beginning to nod off when her phone rang.

She sat up slowly and reached for her phone that was on the night table.

"Hello, Babe!" Sam answered. It was Rob. Sam had forgotten to call him after arriving.

"Forget something, Sweetie?" Rob asked in a playful way.

"Yeah, sorry, Hun," Sam started, "I got caught up in the nostalgia of coming home."

"No worries. I just wanted to make sure you were okay," Rob said. "How's your dad doing, Sam?"

"He seemed okay. Tired, but good. Mom says he has good days and bad days."

"I can only imagine," Rob said.

Sam sat there thinking about her father, almost forgetting that she was on the phone with her husband.

"Sam?"

"Oh, uh, yeah, sorry," Sam stuttered as she came back to reality.

"It's okay," Rob said with a pause. "I wish I could be there with you."

"Yeah, me too." There was more silence. The silence felt empty to Sam. She didn't feel like talking and she knew that Rob was struggling to find the words to comfort her.

"Rob, I'm pretty tired from the long day," Sam started. "I think I'm going to lay down."

"Okay, Sweetie."

"Sam?" Rob asked.

"Yeah?" Sam asked in reply.

"It's going to be okay."

Tears began to slide down her face. Sam swallowed hard, trying not to totally lose it. She was trying to reply when Rob spoke again.

"I love you, Sam!"

The lump in her throat moved as she choked down a sob.

"Babe?"

Sam heard Rob, but couldn't find her voice. She sat there trembling and choking down one sob after another.

"Lord, please give Sam the strength to be there for her mother and father. Please give her the strength to make it through this ordeal. Lord, let her feel your peace and love, and share it with the world. In Jesus Christ's name, I pray. Amen."

As her husband prayed for her, she felt a loving peace come over her. The tears that she was shedding for her mother and father, and for herself, came to an end. The heaviness that was in her heart was lifted and she felt totally invigorated.

"Rob!" Sam exclaimed. "You never cease to amaze me. Thank you!"

"It is amazing what God's love can do, isn't it?" Rob said.

"Yes. Yes it is."

"I love you, Babe," Rob said.

"I love you, too!" Sam replied.

She hung up the phone and lay back down on the bed. She smiled at her husband. She smiled at her Lord and savior, Jesus Christ. Only He could take away the pain she had felt earlier. Only He could take away the sins of the world. In that moment, Sam was reminded of the Gospel of Matthew, where in chapter 10, Jesus is sending out the disciples to preach to the world. It is a calling that Jesus was giving to everyone to go out and spread the word. It is also a reminder that we are to put God first, above everything else.

Chapter 28

Nigel

Nigel and Tia walked hand in hand through the maze of booths at the craft show. Craft shows weren't high on Nigel's list of things to do, but Tia seemed to enjoy them. This craft show was outdoors and so it was a little more tolerable for Nigel. He enjoyed being out in the sun.

Tia was looking through some large scarves that she would use as a wrap over her bathing suit at the beach.

"Gonna pick up another butt scarf, eh?" he asked with a smile.

"Stop!" Tia feigned mock disapproval before laughing.

Nigel looked her over quickly. She wore a light colored knee length skirt that clung to her loosely, flowing with her every move. The white tank top that she wore clung to her body, so as to give a hint of her curves, but was very tasteful.

He smiled and said, "I'm gonna go over to that booth with all the funny signs."

"Ok, I'll come over there when I'm done here," Tia replied.

There were a lot of different booths at the craft show. A person could buy homemade jams and jellies, yard decorations, home decorations, campfire wine holders, and many more items. As Nigel approached the booth that sold the signs, he noticed a man in the next row of booths looking toward him. Nigel made eye contact with him and the man looked away. The man seemed to move his point of interest to the hand carved statues in front of him. Nigel watched him a moment longer and finally moved toward the sign booth.

The booth had a lot of fun signs. Many of them reminded the reader that you weren't dressed appropriately if you weren't wearing sandals or flip-flops while up north.

Nigel stood there looking through the signs for a few more moments before Tia returned. She ran her hand across his back and slid close to him.

He returned the squeeze before asking if she had found the scarf that she was looking for. She smiled and took his hand.

"I think I'm done here. Do you want to head back?" she asked.

"Sure."

Nigel led Tia down the grassy aisle that led toward the parking lot. He looked over at her and smiled. A moment later, his peripheral vision caught movement to his right. He noticed a man looking at them. It was the same man as before.

Why is this guy looking at me?

Before he could answer himself, they were at the car. He pulled the keys out of his pocket and suddenly felt pain in his head before everything went dark.

Chapter 29

Tia

Tia was looking at Nigel when a strange man moved quickly up behind him. Before she knew it, the man hit Nigel on the head and Nigel was falling down. A split second later she was being roughly held by a man that she couldn't see. The man who had knocked out Nigel stooped and picked him up. He looked quickly to the left and to the right to make sure that he hadn't been seen and pulled Nigel into a nearby van.

Tia's hands were tied up before she knew what was going on and she was quickly thrown into the van after Nigel.

As the van moved down the road, Tia did her best to inspect Nigel, trying to see if he was okay. The kidnappers had also tied his hands and feet to make sure that he would not be able to move once he regained consciousness.

Because the van lacked windows in the back, Tia had no way of knowing where they were going. But based on the bumpiness of the ride, she thought that they might be on a county road versus the highway.

Why would anyone do this to us?

As far as she knew, she didn't have any enemies.

Was this random? Or was there some part of Nigel's past that he hasn't shared with me?

At some point, she realized that the road was smoother and their speed had increased. It was likely that they were on the highway now.

Where are we going?

She looked down at Nigel almost willing him to wake up.

Wake up, Nigel!

Nigel stirred, but didn't wake.

Tia began looking around the van, trying to formulate a plan for their escape. Besides Nigel and her, the van was completely empty and there wasn't a lot of light to see by.

Saheed sat in the passenger seat of the van driven by Mohamed. He watched the rural landscape pass by as they drove south. Their task had been to kidnap Nigel. Taking the girl had been Mohamed's idea. Saheed didn't like it, but Mohamed was in charge. Besides, if they had left her in the parking lot, the authorities would have been notified before they had a chance to get out of town. This way, it would be hours before anyone might notice that they were missing.

Saheed met Mohamed less than a year ago, while attending his last semester at the University of Michigan. Saheed was attending a rally sponsored by the Council on

American-Islamic Relations (CAIR) when he met him. Mohamed had boasted about being part of the team that had blown up the Super Bowl and Saheed had been impressed. Soon he began to attend secret meetings held by Mohamed. The purpose of these meetings was to identify targets and to recruit more members. After a couple meetings, Saheed discovered that Mohamed wasn't the one in charge, and that he was taking direction from someone in New York. Rumor had it that Mohamed's boss was the one that executed the New Year's Eve attacks and that gave credibility to Mohamed's group. It was believed that Mohamed's boss was named Ali, but that is all Saheed knew about the man.

Saheed had actually met Nigel once before. It was right before Nigel disappeared. Rumor had it that Nigel had been blown up in his last attack, but apparently Ali didn't believe it. So several teams were tasked to find him. Once Nigel was sighted, Ali asked Mohamed to pick a man that he trusted and go bring Nigel back to him. Saheed had been excited when Mohamed chose him, because there was a chance that they would get to meet Ali face-to-face if they were successful with the kidnapping.

As they drove down the freeway, he looked back through the small window into the cargo area. Nigel still looked like he was unconscious, while the girl was looking around frantically. Saheed shook his head.

Taking the girl was not a good idea.

Tia was just about to give up when Nigel finally opened his eyes.

"Ugh, what the..."

"Hey, Baby, how are you?" Tia asked.

"Oh man, my head is killing me, what the heck happened? Wait. Why am I tied up and where are we?" Nigel asked. Tia could see the terror rise up as his eyes widened.

"Nigel, try to stay calm, but we are in a van moving very quickly. You were knocked out and we were kidnapped."

"Oh crap, they found me!" The terror in his face scared her.

"Who found you?" Tia asked.

"Tia, I'm so sorry to get you into this mess," Nigel replied, not answering her question. "I knew that I should have gone further away from them. What the heck was I thinking?" he paused, suddenly only thinking about Tia. "Wait, are you hurt? Did they hurt you?" His eyes scanned over her body as he tried to assess her condition.

"Nigel, I'm fine. Scared, but I'm fine," Tia replied.

"Oh good. I'm so sorry, Babe," Nigel muttered. He was choking back tears. The emotion that came up in him as he thought about the possibility of Tia being hurt was so profound. It was all he could do not to sob in front of her.

"Why did you say, 'They found me?'"

"Tia, I haven't told you everything about me," Nigel replied. He dropped his head in shame and felt as if his heart was going to break. He so desperately wanted his past to be forgotten, but he knew that the time was now to tell Tia everything.

"Tia, I love you and I never meant to hurt you, but I was a completely different person before I met you," Nigel paused hoping and praying that Tia would forgive him for what he was about to tell her.

Lord, please don't let my past ruin my future. Nigel prayed for the first time to Jesus. He had yet to accept Jesus as his personal savior, but began wondering if now was the time. Tia had talked about Jesus almost on a daily basis and Nigel was beginning to like the idea of a God that encouraged love and not destruction.

"Tia, before I continue, there's something I need you to help me with. Our time is limited and I want to be on the right side of things," Nigel paused as he felt an incredible wave of emotion well up in him.

"Tia, please show me the way to God and help me bring Jesus Christ into my life!"

Chapter 30

Christopher

When the 747 touched down at Heathrow Airport, Chris looked over to Sara and smiled.

"I was thinking that you should call your friend back as soon as possible, but I think you should wait until we get to the hotel."

"I agree. I have a weird feeling," Sara replied.

"Our flight leaves tomorrow around 10:00 a.m., so we have a little time to relax. Let's get checked into the hotel and then go get some dinner."

After picking up their luggage, Chris waved down a taxi. On their way to the hotel, all Chris could think about was the ring that he just purchased for Sara. He wanted to propose to her after dinner, but there just wasn't enough time to get everything ready by then. So he decided that he would get everything ready before they left for Turkey. That way he could propose when they returned from Istanbul.

"What are you smiling at?" Sara questioned. She had obviously been watching him while they made their way across town.

"Oh, I'm just glad to be here with you," Chris replied with a smile. Sara squinted her eyes at him, knowing that there was something that he wasn't saying.

"Uh, okay," she conceded.

After checking into their hotel, Chris walked Sara to her room and then, instead of going to his room, he made his way down to the hotel desk where he set his plan in motion.

Chapter 31

Sara

In her hotel room, Sara sat on the bed getting ready to call Michele. Chris was up to something, but she couldn't figure it out. She knew that it wasn't bad, it was just strange. He never acted this way.

"Oh well, no time for a conspiracy, I need to call Michele," Sara whispered to herself and she began dialing Michele.

"Hello?" Michele answered.

"It's Sara."

"Hey, Sara, how are you?"

"I'm good. So what did you learn about the Mahdi?" Sara asked.

"Well, it's a long story, but I will try to remember everything."

Michele went on to explain what she had learned about Daniel 8 and how it was likely that Turkey would soon attack Iran and take over the Middle East. And that soon, the Mahdi would rise out of Turkey.

"So that is interesting," Sara finally said. "So the current leader isn't the Mahdi, but he could represent the single horn of the goat."

"Yes, I guess if we see Turkey attack Iran and conquer them, then that would be our sign," Michele replied.

"Yes, I agree, Michele. This is good stuff. So then we can expect the leader of Turkey to go away at some point and then the Middle East will be divided into the four regions, represented by the four new horns on the goat," Sara stated.

"Yep," Michele replied.

"Then out of Turkey will come another leader, and it is this leader that will be the Mahdi, the Antichrist."

"Yes, that is how I understand it," Michele replied. "I wish you could meet Brian's sister, Samantha, because she really knows this stuff."

"Yeah, maybe when I get back I'll come see you and see if I can meet Samantha," Sara replied.

After hanging up with Michele, Sara sat on the couch and thought through everything that she learned. She and Chris might have to put together a short list of those people who might be able to rise up and take control after Turkey conquers the Middle East, and it is split into four regions.

Just as she finished writing up her notes, Chris came through the door.

Chapter 32

Mahdi

The Mahdi arrived at the Presidential Palace shortly after his plane landed in Istanbul. The President had requested an emergency meeting with his Ambassador to the United Nations.

"Good morning, Ambassador," the check point guard said. "Please go on inside."

The Ambassador simply nodded and walked through the check point.

The Ambassador's name was Muhammad al-Malik. He was a handsome man who looked far younger than his actual age of fifty. Many thought that he could pass for being in the mid-thirties. Muhammad had grown up in Istanbul. He spent the last twenty years building his career as a politician. Educated in England and Egypt, he was fluent in more than six languages. His resume was impeccable, which made him a perfect candidate for the next prime minister of Turkey. Because of the recent death of the Turkish Ambassador to the United Nations, Muhammad had been promoted from Deputy Ambassador to Ambassador.

Muhammad rode the elevator down to the third basement level, which housed the President's situation-room. Upon exiting the elevator, he was escorted to the President's office by two security guards who never questioned his credentials. When he reached the President's office, a third guard quickly opened the door and ushered him into the spacious room.

"Muhammad, how are you, my friend?" the President of Turkey greeted him in the normal Turkish fashion.

"I am well, Mr. President."

"I appreciate you coming. We have some important things to discuss. You may have heard that the Ayatollah of Iran declared a new caliphate." The disgust on the President's face was matched by Muhammad's.

"Yes, Sir, I have."

"Well, I will not stand by and let those bastards try to claim leadership of all Islam," the President continued.

"That is good. How can I help?"

"I have set an attack plan in motion, and I think it is best that you stay in Turkey for some time. I'm not sure it will be safe in New York," the President stated.

"When does the attack begin?" Muhammad asked.

"I ordered the attack a moment before you arrived."

"Excellent, Sir."

Muhammad could barely refrain from smiling. Things were moving along quickly. It was only a matter of time before he would be in control of everything.

Chapter 33

Santa Fe, New Mexico

"Okay, here's the situation," Dr. Stephen Weinstein began. "Yesterday, Tracy observed high levels of methane emitting from Valles." He nodded to Tracy, suggesting that she take over the meeting.

"Do you guys recall the level of methane emission from Tupungato prior to it erupting?" Tracy asked the team. The majority of the team nodded in recognition and she continued.

"The levels we are seeing here are similar, and I think I'd like to set up equipment around the perimeter of the caldera to see if we can get a better idea about what is going on. The problem is, if Valles is about to go off, we are in big trouble. There really is no escaping a full eruption from Valles."

"Tracy, do you really think it's going to erupt?" Ben asked. Ben had been in Chile to witness Tupungato and was still fairly new to the field.

"Ben, I'm really not sure," she replied, "but if it's going to erupt, we need to make sure we give people enough time to get out of its way. Maybe with enough warning, they might have a chance."

The team heard her words, but everyone knew that an eruption from Valles would change the United States and the rest of the world forever.

Valles Caldera, New Mexico

A day later, the team found themselves spread out across the floor of the caldera. There were various mountains and hills within the caldera that were made by magma pushing the crust of the earth upward during the last 50,000 years. Valles measured 12 miles in diameter and satellite imagery showed a series of large hills along the northern perimeter of the caldera. The resurgent dome, which is called Redondo Peak, rises some 2,450 feet above the floor of the caldera and 11,258 feet above sea level.

Tracy stood at the base of Redondo Peak and looked up in awe. She knew that this peak was the creation of magma being pushed upward from inside the earth. She had witnessed many incredible things, but the power of the earth still amazed her.

"Hey, Ben and Cal, have you set all your instruments?" Tracy called over the radio.

"Yeah, I'm set and headed in," Ben replied.

"I have one more to set and then I want to check out something on the northern edge of Redondo," Cal answered.

"Okay, we'll see you back at the visitor's center," Tracy said.

The visitor's center was mainly used for the public, but on occasion, the team would use it as their base of operations for any experiments that they were doing. Tracy was about 20 minutes from the center and figured that Cal wouldn't be back for a couple hours based on his location.

"Hey Ben, I want to head back to the office and discuss our next steps with Stephen," she radioed to Ben.

"Okay, I'll come in and wait for Cal," Ben replied. "I'll see you later tonight."

"Thanks, Ben!" Tracy said.

"No Problem."

Tracy got in her truck and headed back to Santa Fe. Normally, the team would have met at their office in Los Alamos, but today Dr. Weinstein was at his office in Santa Fe. It was a 90 minute drive, so Tracy would have time to think.

Tracy couldn't remember when their team had been so busy. It seemed as if geothermal activity was increasing almost everywhere. There had been reports world wide of increased volcanic activity. The duel eruption in Chile was a perfect example. She had just turned onto highway 84 and was heading south, when she felt it. At first, when she felt the shimmy, she thought her old truck was acting up again.

But this was different. It was the trees along the road that made her understand what was going on. She slowly pulled the truck over to the side of the road and watched as the trees shook back and forth. Even though she had stopped her vehicle the shimmy increased. The earth was shaking and she knew that it was a big one.

All the traffic on the road around her also slowed to a halt. Some people got out of their cars, but most stayed inside them. Tracy grabbed her phone and began to dial.

"Tracy!" Dr. Stephen Weinstein exclaimed. "It's big. I think 7.0 and it looks like it's coming from Valles."

"Shit! Cal and Ben are still there."

"Where are you, Tracy?"

"I'm on the 84 about 40 minutes from you."

"Ok, hurry and get here as soon as you can."

"Stephen, I'm going to call Ben and Cal first," Tracy replied.

Tracy looked at her watch and realized that it had only been 40 minutes since she left the visitor's center. *Damnit, Cal is probably still on the mountain*, she thought to herself as she dialed him. The phone rang five times before going to voice mail.

"Cal, call me as soon as you can. I want to make sure you're okay," she said into the phone. She hung up and dialed Ben.

"Hey, Tracy, are you ok?" Ben asked. Ben was always concerned about everyone else. If she didn't work with him, she'd consider dating him. She shook her head and wondered why she had that thought.

"Yeah, I'm ok. How are you?"

"Things were a little rough here," Ben said plainly. "There is a bunch of broken glass and scared people, but everyone is okay. That was a big one."

"Stephen said it was a 7.0 and that it came from Redondo."

"Crap! Cal called me a few minutes before it hit, saying that he was going to leave shortly."

"That is not good."

"I'm concerned for him, Tracy."

"Yeah, me too. Let me call Stephen and find out what he wants us to do," Tracy said. "In the mean time, contact the rangers and let them know that we have a man out there. Maybe they can send out a search party."

"Okay, will do. I'll call you when I know something," Ben said.

"Thanks! Be careful, Ben!"

Tracy hoped that the instruments that they had just set had provided the team with some good data, but she was worried about Cal. She picked up the phone again and called Dr. Weinstein.

"Hello, Tracy!" Dr. Weinstein answered anxiously.

"Ben is okay, but we think Cal was out on Redondo when it hit."

"That's not good."

"I told Ben to see if the rangers could go out there and find Cal," Tracy started, "but what do you want me to do?"

Before Stephen could answer, Tracy continued, "I really want to go help find Cal, but my gut tells me that I should get back to the office and see if I can make any sense of the data."

"Tracy, I think you should come in. Ben and the rangers can look for Cal."

There was a pause on the line. Each of them knew the significance of that earthquake, but neither wanted to voice their concerns.

"Okay, I'll let Ben know and then I'll be back on the road," Tracy said. "See you soon."

"Be careful, Tracy!'

"I will."

CHAPTER 34

Cal

Cal was near the base of Redondo Peak in the heart of the Valles Caldera when he saw something strange. He had just hung up with Ben telling him that he wouldn't be long.

Cal walked up to a small shallow pond and immediately felt the heat coming off the surface. There were large bubbles slowly rising up from the bottom, which was only about three to four feet below the surface. There were some geothermal sites within the caldera, but the heat of the surrounding desert generally evaporated most of the water sources. Cal held out an instrument with the intention of measuring the temperature of the water, but as he approached the small pond, the heat was far too intense for him to get close. The air temperature about fifteen feet from the edge of the pond was approaching 180 degrees and he couldn't get any closer. He had been in this area many times and didn't remember this pond. It was the type of thing that the team would have mapped. Granted, it was a small pond, but probably big enough for someone to have noticed it before. He wasn't sure how it had escaped them.

Cal grabbed his phone, but before he could make a call, a seismic tremor threw him to the ground. Looking up from the ground, he saw the side of Redondo Peak shaking as well. Small rocks and pebbles began to fall. Looking toward the pond, he could see large ripples on the surface as the earth shook everything in sight. Still on the ground, he picked up the phone and began to get on his feet. The shaking began to intensify and soon staying on the ground seemed to make the most sense. The ripples on the pond became small waves and the small rocks became larger rocks. Only fifteen feet from the pond, he decided that he should attempt to crawl further from the peak and the scalding hot water. Then suddenly, the earth moved like he'd never experienced before. There was a loud crack and then a rumble as a boulder the size of a car fell from the face of Redondo above. Cal had no time to react, but as the boulder fell, he knew that it was going to miss him. As relief settled in, there was a tremendous splash and Cal was overwhelmed by gallons of scalding hot water. Immediately, searing pain rushed through his entire body and Cal let out a scream that would have struck terror into the heart of the bravest man. Cal's vision went blind as his eyelids were burnt off of his face and soon pain was the only sensation that he knew. Barely audible above his own screaming, Cal heard another loud crack. He had no time to even imagine what created the sound before a huge boulder slammed into him and his world went completely dark.

Chapter 35

Cheyenne Mountain, Colorado

Lieutenant Jason Chambers had only been on the job for a couple of weeks. He was working diligently at his desk when the first lockdown alarm rang. At first he wasn't sure what he should do. It was 15:00 hours when the sirens went off and the room was filled with swirling red lights. He was more than 1,000 feet below the surface of the mountain and had no idea what might be going on outside. He looked over at Captain Hernandez, who had been working on the terminal across from him, and could see concern on her face.

"Let's go, Chambers," Captain Hernandez commanded.

Lieutenant Chambers locked his keyboard and followed her down the hall. People were filing out of rooms on either side of the hall and were headed toward the security station. Lieutenant Chambers recalled something about the evacuation plan that he was given when he was going through his orientation his first day at work. It said that just past the security station, there was a shelter where all personnel could go in case of a lockdown alarm.

They passed the security station and turned right down another long hallway. At the end, he could see everyone passing through a doorway. There were armed guards on either side of the door, and even though he had been in the military for several years, the sight of armed guards outside this room, along with the unknown cause of the alarms, put him in a state of unease.

The room, cavern actually, was expansive. There were terminals in various places, but mostly there were tables where most personnel sat and waited.

"Chambers!" his captain urged.

She led him to a set of terminals on the wall to the right of the door.

"Let's see what's up."

She sat down, began typing a series of keystrokes, and soon she was in a program that he'd never seen before.

"This is the Alpha-Matrix program," she said. "It will let us discover the source of the alarm."

A few keystrokes and mouse clicks later and there it was. Apparently, there was seismic activity south of them in the northern section of New Mexico. He wasn't sure if he was supposed to be reading over her shoulder, but he did it anyway.

"Hmmm, it looks like it is coming from west of Santa Fe," Captain Hernandez said. "I wonder what's there?"

"Captain, I think that is the Valles Caldera," he replied.

Lieutenant Chambers had spent his childhood in Albuquerque, New Mexico and had always had an interest in earthquakes and volcanoes. When he was in high school, he had convinced his parents to take him to visit Valles during spring break of his senior year. When most of his friends were either going to Texas, Arizona, or Mexico for fun in the sun, he wanted to visit a volcano that had been dormant for more than fifty thousand years.

"What is Valles Caldera, Lieutenant?" his captain asked.

"Well, Ma'am, a caldera is like a volcano, except it is larger. A caldera covers a larger area and doesn't have the telltale mountain peak like a volcano," Chambers answered. "Yellowstone National Park is actually on top of one of the largest calderas in the world. That is why it has so much geothermal activity, like geysers and such."

"I have heard about hot springs near Santa Fe, but never anything about volcanoes," the captain said.

"Ma'am, the Valles Caldera has been dormant for almost 50,000 years."

"According to this data, there was a 7.0 earthquake," the captain said.

"Ma'am, why would an earthquake almost 400 miles away cause us to go into lockdown?"

"That is an excellent question, Lieutenant," she replied.

Chapter 36

Santa Fe, New Mexico

Shortly after 5:00 p.m., Tracy arrived at their main office. Looking to the west, toward Valles, she didn't see anything out of the ordinary. She wasn't sure what she was looking for, but she hoped that Ben and Cal would be okay.

Inside, she went to the laboratory and found Dr. Weinstein staring at his computer. He seemed mesmerized by whatever it was he was looking at.

"What have you found?" Tracy asked as she stepped up behind him.

"Oh, ummm, I'm not sure yet. Gosh, I didn't even hear you come in," Stephen answered. "How are Ben and Cal?"

"Ben is fine for now, but still no word from Cal."

"Okay, well, look at this," he said pointing toward the computer screen.

"I see methane levels are slightly raised, as are sulfur levels. Sorry Stephen, but I can't make sense of any of this."

"I know, right?" Stephen replied. "It just doesn't make any sense."

There was silence while he seemed to organize his thoughts.

"You see, Tracy, everything that I see here points toward an eruption," Stephen stated. "Everything is there except the plume."

"What does this mean?"

"I don't know, Tracy," Stephen said as he ran his hand through his hair in frustration. "I really don't know."

Cheyenne Mountain, Colorado

Captain Addison Hernandez was still looking through the Alpha-Matrix system to determine the cause of the lockdown, when over the loud speaker was heard, "All clear. I repeat, all clear." And then there was silence. Hernandez looked up at Lieutenant Chambers questioningly and then logged out of the system.

"Let's get back to the lab and continue with our work," Hernandez commanded.

"Yes, Ma'am."

Captain Hernandez and Lieutenant Chambers walked out of the large room and back down the hall with the hundreds of other people who worked at the Cheyenne

Mountain facility. When they were almost to their lab, Chambers spoke up. "What do you make of all that, Ma'am?"

"Shhh," Captain Hernandez scolded as she looked around wildly.

Lieutenant Chambers hadn't known the captain very long, but her reaction seemed very strange to him. They went to their respective terminals and began working on their current project, just as if nothing had happened.

Around 17:00 hours, the captain came over and slipped Chambers a small piece of paper. On it were the words:

> *Say nothing*
> *Smokey Joes at 21:00 hours tonight.*
> *Destroy this.*

With that, she excused herself for the day and left. Chambers looked at the piece of paper one more time before running it through the shredder. Clearly something was bothering the Captain and he had no idea what it could be. He packed up his case, logged out of his computer, and left the office.

Chapter 37

Nigel

The van that held Nigel and Tia arrived at the compound in Detroit sometime after nightfall.

Saheed came around to the side door of the van and opened it slowly. He grabbed Tia by the arm and pulled her out of the van. He expected a struggle, but didn't get one. She seemed almost calm.

Mohamed grabbed Nigel roughly and got no resistance from Nigel either.

"What's your deal, Nigel? Don't you know what is about to happen?" Mohamed said loudly.

"I don't fear you, Mohamed."

Mohamed drove his fist into Nigel's stomach, buckling him down on to his knees. Tia made a short squeal of fear.

"Take the girl and put her into a cell," Mohamed commanded.

Saheed nodded and took her away.

"We have a phone call to make," Mohamed explained as he lead Nigel in the opposite direction that Saheed and Tia went.

"What have you done?" Ali Basharat asked.

Nigel looked at the computer screen and into the face of Ali and said nothing. Ali motioned with a nod and Mohamed punched Nigel in the side of his head. Pain seared through his face and his ears began ringing. Nigel had been tied tightly to the chair so that he could neither move his hands nor his feet. Otherwise, he surely would have fallen to the floor.

After a short moment Ali spoke again.

"This is the last time I will repeat the question. What have you done?"

Nigel looked directly into Ali's eyes and said, "Do your worst. I am not afraid."

Ali motioned again to Mohamed. Nigel winced, thinking another strike to his face would occur. After a moment, he looked to his left and right wondering where Mohamed had gone. As he was about to speak to Ali, Mohamed came in, pushing Tia roughly in front of him. He threw her down on a chair to Nigel's left, and tied both her arms and legs down to the chair. Nigel couldn't get a good look at her from the angle where he sat, but he thought that maybe she had been roughed up a bit. A piece of duct tape made it impossible for her to make a sound.

Mohamed forced Nigel's chair around so that he could look directly at Tia. He noticed that her skirt was torn high up on her thigh, revealing her tan legs. There was a small tear at the bottom of her tank top. Anger flared up and Nigel screamed at his capture.

"I'm going to kill you all if Tia is harmed."

"Tia, huh? Sexy name," Mohamed spat. At that, Nigel attempted to move so violently, that he almost fell.

From the computer, Ali said, "I guess we'll have to change our strategy."

As if given a command, Mohamed grabbed Tia's shirt near her chest and took out a knife. He cut through the fabric of her shirt down about six inches revealing part of her bra.

"Wooo, what a nice piece of ass you have here, Nigel. If I had more time I would most certainly spend a little time with her," Mohamed said sinisterly.

Tia began to show real signs of fear. The calm that she once had was completely gone. Nigel's anger turned to fear. The last thing he wanted was for Tia to get hurt.

"What do you want from me?" Nigel pleaded.

"I just want to know what you've done," Ali repeated.

"I don't know what you mean," Nigel said.

"Why didn't you come back after your last mission?" Ali asked.

Nigel slumped and shook his head. He looked at Tia and pleaded to God for help.

Jesus, Lord please help us. I know that I've done some bad things in my life, but Tia doesn't deserve this. Take me instead and let her go.

In that moment, Tia's demeanor began to calm again, and a peace swept through Nigel's body. Nigel also realized that neither of them would survive the night, but he felt peace, knowing that they would be together on the other side in heaven.

Nigel lifted his head to the Lord and said, "When these things begin to take place, stand up and lift up your heads, because your redemption is drawing near."

If eyes could smile, Tia's did in that moment. She recognized Nigel's words to be a direct quote from Luke 21:28. Tia lifted her head as well.

"What the hell are you talking about?" Mohamed screamed.

"Mohamed, shut your mouth!" Ali commanded.

"Sorry, Sir," Mohamed humbly said.

"It's worse than I thought, Mohamed. Nigel has been corrupted by this infidel," Ali said solemnly. "Nigel, you had a lot of promise and you did a lot of amazing work for Allah. But now it isn't your redemption that is drawing near, it is your destruction."

Nigel and Tia remained still with their heads lifted up toward the sky.

"Mohamed, end her!" Ali command. His voice of pure evil.

Mohamed grabbed Tia by the chin and sliced her neck from left to right. Tia was dead before she had a chance to feel much pain.

Nigel, on the other hand, felt as if his heart had been cut in half. He watched as blood emptied out of her neck, down her chest, and onto the floor. Her head hung down and Nigel knew that she was dead.

"Lord, why?" Nigel screamed toward heaven. And then he remembered something that Tia had said to him shortly after bringing him to Christ in the van on their way to the compound.

Nigel, my love, we will be tested. Trust in Jesus regardless of what happens to us, regardless of what happens to me. I love you and Jesus loves you. This life is only a journey toward our final destination with God.

Tia's words reverberated through his head and his calm was restored.

"Allah is your lord," Ali said.

Nigel paused a moment and the words came to him.

"No, my faith is in Jesus Christ. I will never do the will of Allah again. My love for Christ is my redemption," Nigel replied. "Jesus Christ is Lord," Nigel added with a smile.

"So be it," Ali said, and motioned to Mohamed.

Mohamed grabbed Nigel's chin and sliced through his throat. There was searing pain and then wetness on his neck and chest and then calm. The room began to fade as life left his body. Darkness surrounded him for a moment and then there was a light. And then he was with his angel once again and he was surrounded by the love of God.

CHAPTER 38

Turkey

At 5:00 a.m. local time, 20 mid range bomber/fighter aircraft began leaving Incirlik Air Base located in Adana, Turkey. Many were F-16s developed in the United States. From Incirlik, these aircraft could reach Damascus in less than an hour and Baghdad in just over an hour. Other targets included Beirut, Lebanon, Mosul, Iraq, and Cairo, Egypt, as well as other areas controlled by the Iranian military. The timing of these attacks would be critical to the success of the military campaign.

In the Persian Gulf, a dozen cruise missiles were ready to launch from an oil freighter. These cruise missiles were pointed at Tehran, Iran, Riyadh, Saudi Arabia, and Shush, Iran, as well as other Iranian military installments in the Middle East.

Just before dawn, the first bomb was deployed in Aleppo, Syria. The F-16 was piloted by Sahid Muhamod and his rank was equivalent to Captain in the United States Air Force. Sahid grew up in a small Turkish border town not far from Aleppo, and had traveled there on several occasions. The civil war in Syria had drastically changed the landscape throughout Syria, but it had dramatically affected Aleppo. Once a thriving metropolis of more than 4.5 million people, the estimated population was now less than a million.

When Sahid deployed his payload of four E61 tactical nuclear weapons on Iranian bases throughout the city, he knew that life would never again be the same.

As he launched his aircraft up and away from the bomb locations, he saw a series of bright flashes behind him. Shortly after, the sound of the four bombs hitting their targets reached his ears and his heart broke. As he continued to turn his aircraft back toward Incirlik, he saw four large mushroom clouds growing toward the clouds. It looked as if the entire city was on fire. He was suddenly horrified by the destruction that he delivered to the people of Aleppo.

What have I done?

Similar incidents occurred at Iranian military installations near Damascus, Baghdad, Mosul and other locations throughout the Middle East. The destruction at Aleppo had been a warning to the world that Turkey would do anything for control over the Middle East.

On the oil freighter in the Persian Gulf, crews rushed to remove canopies that covered several Tomahawk missile launchers. The order had been given to deploy five cruise missiles. Each missile was targeted for specific key Iranian military installations throughout Iran. Two other missile launchers were also unveiled. These were capable of launching mid-range Inter Continental Ballistic Missiles, also known as ICBMs. Each of these missiles had a payload of a ten megaton nuclear warhead. When the order was given, one missile sped toward Tehran, Iran, with its target being a midlevel burst over the palace where the Ayatollah resided. The second missile sped toward Shush, Iran, where the leader of the Iranian Revolutionary Guard Corps was believed to be. This blast would occur very close to the surface minimizing the blast radius, but virtually ensuring that the entire bunker would be obliterated.

Within a matter of minutes, the coordinated nuclear attacks on Iranian military installations throughout the Middle East would leave Iran defenseless and leaderless against the invasion that would follow.

Chapter 39

Iran

The Ayatollah sat in his favorite chair in his reading room. He had been an avid reader his entire life. Prior to the Iranian Revolution in 1979, he was able to read books at the local library. Afterward, getting his hands on books was difficult until he began to rise up in power. Now he had access to any book he could imagine.

The book that he was currently reading was the Quran. The current verse spoke of fighting for the cause of Allah. This particular verse gave him pleasure. He enjoyed seeing the destruction of infidels throughout the world, but especially in the United States of America.

After recently declaring a new caliphate and making himself the new Caliph, he knew that there would be grumbling from the Sunni world, but he expected them to fall in line, especially after what Iran had so recently accomplished militarily. They had proven that no force could stop them.

Not even the Great Satan, the United States of America.

He smiled at the thought and then began a fit of coughing that lasted for over ten minutes. His health had continued to fail and he knew that he didn't have a lot more time, but he took pride in the fact that he had accomplished what hadn't been done in a very long time.

I have conquered the Middle East and my reign is now supreme.

Just as this thought began to fade, his military advisor came bursting into his reading room.

"Sir, you must come with me!" the advisor exclaimed.

"What is it?"

"I will explain on the way to the bunker," the man said as he began to lift the Ayatollah into his wheel chair.

The advisor was virtually running down the hall, pushing the Ayatollah toward the only place he thought would save the religious leader's life.

"Sir, we are under attack!"

"Attack! Who can attack us?" the Ayatollah asked. He seemed to puff out his chest in pride.

They rounded a corner where the elevator to the bunker lay open. The military advisor got the Ayatollah into the elevator and yelled, "Go!"

Immediately, the elevator began to make the 200 foot decent, but they were too late. The explosion of the 10 megaton nuclear warhead over the capital city of Tehran vaporized much of the surface of the city, including the palace where the Ayatollah was. The elevator had only dropped 20 feet when the elevator shook violently. Flames burst through the ceiling of the elevator and a split second later the elevator car began its free fall. If the flame hadn't killed everyone on board, then the final crash at the base of the elevator shaft finished them off.

The first horn of the Persian Ram was broken.

General Hasim was at the command center in Shush when he got the word that the Turkish government had began its attack. Already 100 feet below the surface, General Hasim felt invulnerable. That is, until word came in that Tehran had been hit and was virtually destroyed.

"Sir! Tehran is gone!" his second in command declared.

"We can assume that the supreme leader has been killed," the General replied.

"Issue the martial law protocol. I will take command for the Ayatollah until his situation can be validated," the General added.

"Yes, Sir."

"Then get me a status on ...."

The explosion rocked the bunker and the General never had a chance to finish his sentence before he and everyone at the secret base in Shush was vaporized.

The second horn of the Persian Ram was broken.

Chapter 40

Addison Hernandez

Captain Addison Hernandez wasn't one to get shaken by most things. Inner city living had that effect on you. Either you were tough as nails and made it out, or you weren't and it ate you alive. Growing up in the worst part of Detroit had almost finished her off. She saw her younger brother die from a gunshot wound as a result of a gang fight. Her younger sister was lost when she started hanging around the wrong people. She had been expelled from high school as a freshman for dealing drugs. Last Addison heard, her younger sister was turning tricks to support her meth habit.

Addison blamed herself for the shortcomings of her siblings. Her father had left when she was only five. She could barely remember him, which was good, because most of what she remembered was of the fights he had with her mother. Her mother tried to raise her children alone, but had to work two jobs just to make ends meet. At the age of eight, the responsibility of the younger children fell upon Addison. Without a strong parental influence, it only made sense that her younger siblings would go down the wrong path. When she was a senior in high school, her mom became distant. Addison believed the loss of her brother had been the catalyst for her mother's changes. She would spend 12-14 hours working and then come home and drink herself to sleep. It was all that Addison could do to get through high school and get out of town.

In her last month of high school, Addison had gone to a presentation by the local Air Force recruiter. Her mother cried when Addison told her that she was going to join the Air Force, but she didn't try to stop her. Her mother also knew that the Air Force would be Addison's only way out of the life that she was in.

She had been in the Air Force for almost twenty years. While in the Air Force, Addison was able to take college credits and eventually earned her bachelor's degree. This allowed her to move from an enlisted soldier to an officer, which expanded her potential for the future. She often wondered where she would be if she hadn't attended that presentation from the recruiter in high school.

For some reason, the lockdown had shaken Addison. She had remained calm throughout most of it, until Lieutenant Chambers began talking about it.

Why would they lock us down for an earthquake almost 400 miles away?

Smokey Joe's BBQ

Addison arrived early and found a quiet spot near the back of the restaurant bar. This place was always pretty quiet on Tuesdays, which is why she chose it. She ordered a Bud Light and waited for Lieutenant Chambers to arrive.

She wasn't sure what she was going to tell him, but she had to tell someone. Just then Lieutenant Chambers arrived and she waved him over.

"Jason. Can I call you Jason?" Addison asked, but continued without waiting for a reply. "I know that this is maybe a little strange and I wanted to apologize for my behavior earlier today."

"No problem, Captain."

"Listen, I know that it goes against all your training, but please call me Addison," she started. "I don't want people knowing that we are military."

"Okay, Captain, uh, I mean Addison," Jason was visibly uncomfortable calling his commanding officer by her first name.

A moment later, there was a commotion at the bar. Everyone there seemed to be extremely interested in the news program that was on.

Jason slowly stood and made his way over to the bar, just in time to hear the most frightening thing he could imagine.

"...reports are coming in of multiple nuclear explosions throughout the Middle East," the news anchor announced.

Addison joined Jason and, after a few more moments, grabbed him by the arm.

"We have to get back to base. It will be on lockdown soon, if it isn't already. We need to find out what is going on here."

"Yes, Ma'am...uh, Addison."

When Addison and Jason arrived at their base, it was a buzz of activity. They had made it back just in time, because a moment after they got in through the last check point, the base went on complete lockdown. It would be a long time before either of them would be leaving.

Chapter 41

Christopher

Chris woke to the sound of an alarm coming from his phone. Based on the amount of light in the room, he knew that it was still night. He rubbed the sleep from his eyes and reached for his phone. It was roughly 7:00 a.m. and the alarm coming from his phone could mean only one thing. Something had gone terribly wrong. He keyed his password into the phone and read the secure message.

HOME

Translation: abort whatever mission you are on and get back to Langley as soon as humanly possible.

Chris knew that Sara received the same message and would be knocking on his door very soon. He hopped out of bed and rushed to get dressed. Fortunately, his bag always remained packed when he was on the road.

A few minutes later, he was ready and at the door to his room when Sara's knock came.

"Hi, Sara. I made a call and a car will be here to pick us up shortly."

Chris looked at Sara. She wore no makeup and had thrown her hair into a ponytail.

Beautiful!

He couldn't wait to wake up next to her every morning. Even without any time to get herself ready, she was amazingly beautiful.

"Ok, I'm ready. Do you have any idea what is going on?" Sara asked. They hurried down the hall toward the elevator.

"I don't, but in my entire career, I have never received that code." Chris paused as they reached the elevator and pushed the call button.

"It must be bad," Sara said just as the door to the elevator opened. Fortunately, the elevator car was empty.

"Yes. It must be bad."

Chris didn't say another word. He thought about all of the plans that he made the previous evening after arriving at the hotel. He had planned a private dinner where he would propose to Sara overlooking the Thames. This was to take place after they returned from Turkey. Now he wondered what would happen.

I guess my proposal will have to wait.

They arrived at Heathrow Airport shortly after 8:00 a.m. local time and found their way to the hanger that held the aircraft that they were supposed to board. Originally, the aircraft was supposed to take them to Istanbul, Turkey, but upon arriving they discovered why they wouldn't be going there today.

Chris and Sara were greeted by a tall man in a dark suit. He asked them for their identification one last time before escorting them aboard the C-20 Gulfstream. Once seated, he began to brief them.

"My name is Agent Wilson. Instead of going to Istanbul, we are taking you two back to Langley. There has been an incident in the Middle East," Wilson said.

"An incident?" Chris questioned.

"Yes. Information is still coming in, but what we know so far is that just over 90 minutes ago, Turkey launched a massive military strike against Iranian military assets throughout the Middle East."

"Okay. What exactly do you mean by massive?" Chris questioned. Sara just remained silent and let Chris talk.

"Well, all the details aren't yet clear, but it seems like Turkey launched 10-20 tactical nuclear warheads and at least 2 large nukes."

"Holy shit!" Chris exclaimed. Since meeting Sara, Chris had used less profanity, but the circumstances seemed to call for it in this occasion.

Agent Wilson didn't offer any additional information, so Sara spoke up.

"The two large nukes...do you know where the targets were?" Sara asked.

"One hit the center of Tehran. The blast radius indicates that it was upwards of a 10 megaton warhead. Initial estimates are more than 2 million casualties. We believe that most government installations there have been incinerated and it is likely that the Ayatollah is among the casualties."

"Whoa," Sara said somberly.

"How about the second nuke?" Chris asked.

"That one is a little less clear. It seems to be in a remote area near the city of Shush, Iran. Shush has a small population of maybe 50,000 people. This bomb was also detonated much closer to the surface."

"Wow! That is a big bunker buster," Chris responded.

"Yeah, that's what we thought," Agent Wilson replied.

"Are we aware of any military base in the area?" Chris asked.

"There have been rumblings, but if it was a base and it was important enough to deserve a 10 megaton nuclear warhead, then we seriously dropped the ball on that one," Agent Wilson replied.

There was silence for a bit while everyone contemplated the future.

"We were hoping to leave in 10 minutes, but it seems like we have a delay due to a problem with the airplane. It looks like we might not be able to leave for another few hours."

"Agent Wilson, is there anywhere we can sit and get some coffee? It looks like it's going to be a long day," Chris asked.

"Yes, come with me."

In a small cafeteria, Chris and Sara found some coffee and a little breakfast.

"While we're sitting here, let's go over some possibilities for the Mahdi," Chris suggested.

"Sure, do you have any ideas?"

"Well, what do we know about him?" Chris asked.

"One, it is believed that he is a descendant of Mohammed," Sara stated. "I also heard that he is a man in his 40's. At least when he arrives he is. No telling when he *arrived*."

"Okay, so not a lot to go on so far," Chris said with a smile.

Sara heard his joke and lightly punched him in the arm.

"I'm not done yet, Silly," Sara said with a smile. "I have some notes in here, hang on," she said as she went through her bag.

"Okay, so he also has black hair and it is said that he will be handsome. Here's another one, he is well built and of medium stature. His hair is black and will fall to his shoulders. He will also have a thick black beard. It is said that his teeth are white and he has a mole on his cheek." Sara continued.

"Where did you get all this info?" Chris asked.

"It was from a website about the Mahdi I found a while ago," Sara answered. "This one is really strange. It says that the mark of the prophet, Mohammed, will be between the shoulders of the Mahdi. I wonder if that is the mark of the beast?" Sara wondered aloud. "Wait, there's more. The mark will be round like a pigeon's egg."

"Seriously? This sounds ridiculous," Chris exclaimed.

"It all comes from the hadiths that make up the texts of Islam," Sara explained.

"Okay, so what do we know?" Chris asked.

"He has black hair, a black beard, he is well built, handsome, in his 40's when he arrived, and he has a mark between his shoulders that is round like a pigeon's egg," the last item Chris said with a chuckle.

"Yeah, not a lot to go on," Sara agreed. "But maybe I can find more out there. I've been a little busy lately."

"Let's focus on what is going on in Turkey right now and see if we can identify anyone in their government who might match the description that we have of him," Chris said.

Just then, Agent Wilson came in and said that they were almost ready to board their airplane.

"We'll brief you on everything once onboard," Agent Wilson said.

Chapter 42

Sara

The briefing lasted only forty five minutes and afterward no one said much. Sara looked out over the ocean as their transport plane took them *home*.

Why would Turkey launch this attack?

Sara thought back to her recent conversation with her friend, Michele. She had told Sara that it was likely that Turkey would attack the Middle East soon and that the Mahdi would follow soon. Sara reached into her bag and pulled out her Bible. She opened up to the Book of Daniel, chapter 8, and read verses 5-7.

"*As I was thinking about this, suddenly a goat with a prominent horn between his eyes came from the west, crossing the whole earth without touching the ground. He came toward the two-horned ram I had seen standing beside the canal and charged at the ram in great rage. I saw him attack the ram furiously, striking the ram and shattering his two horns. The ram was powerless to stand against him; the goat knocked him to the ground and trampled on him, and none could rescue the ram from his power.*" - Daniel 8:5-7

Chris sat next to her going through some mission documents. She smiled as she admired his rugged good looks. He didn't realize how handsome he was and that made him even more attractive. He seemed to sense her staring at him and slowly turned to meet her eyes. His smiled broadened and she couldn't help but smile back.

"What's up?" Chris inquired.

"I was thinking about what my friend, Michele, said to me about the Mahdi."

"Okay?" he questioned.

"Well, let me read to you from the Book of Daniel," she said and then read verses 5 through 7 from chapter 8.

"Okay, I'm not sure exactly what all that means," he surrendered.

"Yeah, I know, it is a little complicated. But from what Michele learned from her boyfriend's sister, it seems to be predicting what just happened over in the Middle East."

"Sorry, Sara, I just don't see it."

"Well, according to Michele, the goat represents the nation of Turkey. The single horn on the goat represents Turkey's leader." Sara paused a moment and moved the book closer to him, pointing to the words *suddenly a goat with a prominent horn between his eyes came from the west, crossing the whole earth without touching the ground.* See this, a massive air strike could be how the goat, Turkey, crossed the whole earth," Sara said.

"Yeah, but they hardly crossed the whole earth," Chris argued.

"But think about this scripture from the view of the reader in 700 BC. Their view of the whole earth was vastly different. From their point of view, isn't it possible that going from Turkey to Iran is crossing the whole earth?" Sara asked.

"Yeah, I guess you have a point there," Chris replied. He seemed to be contemplating the scripture.

"So what is this about the two horned ram?" Chris asked.

"Well, if you recall, the two horned ram represents Persia, or in this case, the modern nation of Iran," Sara replied.

"Okay, so the two horns are?" Chris asked.

"Two leaders I guess."

Sara seemed confused as well, but then it was like a light bulb turned on over her head and her eyes lit up.

"Who are the two leaders of Iran?" Sara asked.

"There is only one leader, and that is the Ayatollah," Chris replied.

"Sure, he is in charge of the government, the religion, and the military, but look what is going on, or at least was going on, until Turkey attacked. There was a military general from the Iranian Revolutionary Guard Corps who declared himself the leader of Iraq and Syria. There have been rumors that the Ayatollah's health has been declining and who better to step in for the country during a time of war than the hands-on leader of the military?" Sara asked.

Chris seemed to contemplate what she just said.

Sara didn't wait long to continue her argument.

"Look, earlier in the scripture where the two horned ram is described, it says that one horn was longer, but then the other grew up later. It is almost implying that the second horn will take over power at some point. It could be argued that this second horn is the military leader of Iran, who has grown up while the Ayatollah's health wanes."

"I guess that makes sense, but we really have no proof," Chris replied.

"True, but look what has happened," Sara started, but paused to gather her thoughts. "Tehran is destroyed, and it is presumed that the Ayatollah is among the casualties. There is the first horn of the ram that is broken."

"Yeah, okay, what about the second horn?" Chris asked.

"Right, you said it yourself. That second nuke was a bunker buster. What if there was a secret military base near Shush and that is where the military command center was?" Sara asked.

"The second horn would be broken. That is, assuming that he died in the attack," Chris answered.

"A 10 megaton bunker buster?" Sara questioned.

"Yeah, nothing survives that," Chris answered. "But this is all just guessing. We need better answers. I can't just walk into the Director's office and plop the Bible down on his desk and point to these verses. He'd have me thrown out of the building."

"Yeah, you are probably right. I wonder if there is anyone who is close to the Director who would listen to us and maybe go to bat for us," Sara said. "Who do we know in the agency that is Christian?"

"Gosh, that's like finding a needle in a haystack, Sara."

"Yeah, you're right. But maybe it's time that we brought our research on the Mahdi to the Director. Maybe it's time to put together a list of possible candidates," Sara replied.

Chris contemplated their conversation.

"We have some time. Let's think about all of this before we get home and come up with a plan," Chris said.

"And pray on it," Sara replied.

"Yes, I agree, let's pray on it."

CHAPTER 43

Ali

Ali Basharat was strangely saddened because he had to kill Nigel.

"Nigel had such great promise," he said aloud. "The American whore ruined him."

"Excuse me, Sir?" his driver questioned.

"Nothing. How long?"

"We are arriving now, Sir," the driver replied.

Ali's limousine arrived at the private airport entrance reserved for diplomats and other VIPs. It would only be a few moments until his airplane would depart and he would be on his way to Turkey.

"Thank you, Allahu Akbar," Ali said.

"Allahu Akbar," his driver repeated.

On board his airplane, Ali dialed his phone one last time before departure. The phone was picked up on the other end after just one ring.

"Sir?" the voice said.

"Are we ready?" Ali asked.

"Yes, Sir. We await your command."

"Ok, proceed, and may Allah be with you," Ali said.

"Allahu Akbar," the voice said.

"Allahu Akbar," Ali repeated.

As he hung up the phone, Ali looked out the window in time to see the airplane begin its ascension into the sky. Things were moving along perfectly according to the Mahdi's plan.

Allah has blessed us.

Chapter 44

New York City

Dabria sat at the wheel of the commercial bus, waiting for her command to leave. She had come to the United States more than four years ago on a student visa. She spent the first three years attending Yale University. She did well the first two years taking Pre-Med classes. For the most part, she had become Americanized. She went to parties and dated boys. It wasn't until her third year, when she met Ahmed, that things started changing for her. He was similarly Americanized, but soon became radicalized by some Syrian refugees who he met at a local mosque. Ahmed began talking to Dabria about everything he learned, and eventually convinced her to go to the mosque with him.

It only took a few months for Ahmed to radicalize her and convince her to quit school and help with their cause. It had been the backlash that she received after the past New Year's

Eve attacks that convinced her that America didn't like Muslims. She had seen many friends get hurt in various scuffles. She herself had been harassed multiple times.

Officially, Dabria's student visa expired the minute she decided not to continue her education. She had been living as an illegal alien for more than six months.

As she sat in the bus, she wondered how Ahmed was. He was in a dump truck behind her waiting for the command to leave. She thought about what she was about to do and found solace in the fact that soon she would be with Allah. She also found it ironic that her name, Dabria, meant *Angel of Death*. Ahmed had said that her name was pretty appropriate for what she was about to do.

Just then, the leader of their cell waved her out the door. Dabria put the bus into gear and began driving out of the warehouse. Her trip would take about 30 minutes during normal traffic. She looked into her rear view mirror and saw that both of the other buses followed her out of the warehouse.

Chapter 45

New York City

The captain of the oil freighter joined Ali's group after his brother had been killed by Americans a few years ago. He was tired of their arrogance. He knew that some innocent people would die today, but he found comfort in the Quran, which said that all infidels were unworthy and must convert or die.

His freighter moved down the East River and would reach its target in about 30 minutes.

Asu started flipping switches and adjusting dials in preparation for departure. Asu was an ex-Syrian Air Force helicopter pilot who arrived in the United States, on a refugee visa, a few months prior to the New Year's Eve attacks. Most of his family had been killed in the Syrian civil war, but the loss of his wife and infant son had pushed him over the edge. He blamed the United States and the previous American President for not intervening earlier. Apparently, some red lines could be crossed. His purpose for coming to America was to continue the assault on the infidels.

The commander on the field gave him the signal to proceed and he pressed the button that started the blades spinning. Soon he was in the air and on his way to his death. To Asu, death was the quickest way to Allah and he was more than ready to go. He had already lost everything and nothing else to live for.

"Allahu Akbar," Asu said aloud.

Chapter 46

New York City

Dadria drove the bus east down E 45th Street. As she reached the corner of 1st Ave., she accelerated the bus. She was fortunate that she had a green light, otherwise things may have turned out differently for her.

She was surprised how easily the gate in front of her peeled away in front of the bus. She swerved right and stomped down on the accelerator.

"Allahu Akbar!" she screamed as her bus rammed into the United Nations Building, which detonated upon impact. More than 100 pounds of C4 blew a hole in the western wall of the building, breaching the inner assembly hall.

The second bus driven by Ahmed, penetrated deeper into the building and detonated a huge amount of blue napalm, which incinerated the rear portion of the assembly hall.

Chapter 47

United Nations Building, New York City

The General Assembly meeting was scheduled to begin in less than an hour, and most diplomats and dignitaries were already in the United Nations Building in New York City.

The United States Ambassador to the United Nations was chatting with his French counterpart.

"Strange that the Turkish Ambassador is absent," the U.S. Ambassador said.

"Yes, considering everything that is going on, you would think he would attend such an important meeting," the French Ambassador replied.

"Katia, so how is Pierre and the children?" the U.S. Ambassador said.

Katia had been married to her husband for more than ten years and had three young children.

"They are doing great. Right now they are vacationing in Colorado," Katia replied.

"Bad time for this meeting, I guess," the U.S. Ambassador said.

"Yes, but..." Katia said as the building shook from the first explosion.

It was the second explosion that threw both of them to the ground. The entire rear wall of the assembly hall exploded and filled with fire.

Katia ran over to the U.S. Ambassador and beckoned him to follow her.

"Come on!"

He struggled to get up, but finally did, and the two of them ran toward the podium at the front of the hall.

"We'll use the Secretary General's private entrance to get..."

That is when the ceiling exploded. Flames and debris landed among them. They both dove for cover and Katia was surprised that they were still alive.

The U.S. Ambassador bent over and grabbed Katia's hand to help her up and suddenly another explosion rocked the building. Still holding the U.S. Ambassador's hand, Katia found her way to her feet.

"Come on," she said. Suddenly, she realized that the Ambassador wasn't connected to his hand anymore. She gasped and dropped the hand of the Ambassador and looked left to see the dead body of the Ambassador among the rubble.

She was about to scream in terror when another explosion tore through her body and death took her.

Chapter 48

New York City

Asu was approaching his target when he saw the first bus explode. Shortly after, the second bus disappeared into the United Nations General Assembly Building and detonated. As he neared the dome on top of the building, he saw an oil tanker in the East River. On deck, the crew was uncovering what looked like a dozen missile launchers. A brief smile appeared on his lips before he screamed out *Allahu Akbar* and then crashed his helicopter into the building, forcing the detonation of the C4 explosive and blue napalm.

The oil freighter captain had given the signal to launch the missiles and within minutes they were uncovered and deployed. Thirteen in all, each missile found its target, which was the river side of the United Nations General Assembly Building. He saw smoke billowing from the opposite side of the building. The roof was covered in flames from the helicopter attack and now the eastern wall was riddled with large holes from which fire and smoke were billowing out.

Ali, his commander, said that the first three attacks should be enough, but that his oil freighter would be the insurance to finish the job. Not only was his freight full of oil and gasoline, but there was almost a ton of C4 explosive, and a ton of what Ali called *blue napalm*. Blue Napalm was a thick blue liquid that was virtually undetectable by conventional bomb sniffing dogs and electronic equipment. When detonated, it would quickly expand into a foamy substance and a second charge would ignite the foam. The resulting blast was 100 times more explosive than the original napalm used in Vietnam.

The captain held the detonator in his hand. He took a deep breath and closed his eyes. He hoped that his family would be proud of him.

"Allahu Akbar!" he yelled as he pressed the detonator.

After a moment, the captain opened one eye and wondered what had happened. He opened the other eye and began shaking the detonator. He violently pressed the button again and nothing happened. He feared that he wasn't worthy of Allah's blessing and, in desperation, he pressed the button one last time.

The explosion was so huge that it took out windows more than ten blocks away. The concussion crumbled the east wall of the General Assembly building and flames spread across the entire width of the East River, catching a few boats that were passing by on fire.

Jack and his wife, Linda, were driving through the Queens Midtown Tunnel in their old station wagon. Linda was mad at him again. He was just thinking that she probably was done with him for good this time.

"Linda, I'm sorry," Jack apologized.

Linda continued to look forward, not acknowledging him at all.

"Listen, Babe, I know that I'm a dumbass, but what am I supposed to do?"

Linda looked over at him with a look showing that she agreed with his assessment that he was a dumbass.

"Babe..." Jack started. And that is when the ceiling of the Queens Midtown Tunnel collapsed upon them.

Chapter 49

Cheyenne Mountain, Colorado

The President was sitting with the Director of Homeland Security discussing the border fence construction when his Chief of Staff came into the office.

"Sir, there has been another attack."

"Where?" the President asked.

"The United Nations General Assembly Building, Sir."

"Jacob, are you kidding me?" the President asked.

"No, Sir."

"What is the extent of the damage?"

"Complete, Sir."

"Complete? What do you mean by complete, Jacob?" the President asked.

"Sir, the entire building has been destroyed. Sir, most of the Assembly is among the casualties," Jacob added.

For a brief second, the President had forgotten that the General Assembly was supposed to happen that day.

"Oh my God!"

For the first time in his memory, Jacob saw fear on the President's face.

"Do we know how it happened?"

"Sir, it seems like it was a four pronged attack," Jacob said. He then proceeded to brief the President on the details of the attack.

Washington, D.C.

The Vice President sat in his office at the U.S. Naval Observatory in Washington, D.C. He was going over the President's most recent memo regarding the military contingencies if the United States was pulled into the war in Europe and the Middle East, when suddenly his secret service personnel burst into his office.

"Sir, we have to go!" the agent in charge commanded.

The Vice President immediately grabbed the folder containing the information that he was reading and his laptop and stuffed them into his briefcase and followed the agent out the door.

"What is going on?" the Vice President asked.

"Sir, there has been another attack and we need to evac you immediately."

"An attack? Where?" the Vice President questioned.

"Sir, it's the U.N."

The Vice President and his secret service detail quickly moved to a military helicopter that was waiting on the rear lawn. It was a rarity that the Vice President would travel via helicopter, so Hal knew that the situation was dire.

As they boarded the helicopter, the Vice President asked the agent in charge what details he had.

"Sir, I don't know a lot, but it sounds like the U.N. building has been destroyed."

"Destroyed?" the Vice President exclaimed. "Where are we headed?"

"Sir, our evac plan is to get you up in the air and out of D.C. as fast as humanly possible. We should have you to a DC-10 at Ronald Reagan in less than 30 minutes."

Chapter 50

Christopher

Chris and Sara were talking about possible candidates for the Mahdi when the co-pilot came out of the cockpit and gave them the bad news.

"Sir, there's been an attack in New York and we are being diverted," the co-pilot stated.

"An attack? Where?" Chris asked.

"Sir, we are not completely sure, but we think it was at the U.N. building."

"The U.N?" Chris asked as he looked over at Sara. Sara's eyes were wide with surprise and concern.

"Yes, Sir. The U.N. We are being diverted to Detroit and should arrive there in approximately 3 hours," the co-pilot continued.

"Thank you," Chris said. With that, the co-pilot excused himself.

"Oh my gosh," Sara said.

"We can't seem to get ahead of this," Chris lamented.

Sara couldn't think of anything to say. They both sat there in silence and finally Sara blurted out.

"Why not divert us to Washington?" Sara asked.

"Well, it's possible that other threats exist," Chris replied.

"But we need to get to Langley and find out what to do next."

"Yes, Sara, I agree. But something tells me that Detroit is the right place for us to go."

Sara looked at Chris in confusion. Chris turned away and began staring down the aisle of the airplane.

Why would we go to Detroit? he thought to himself. *And why does it feel right?* he added.

The airplane carrying Chris and Sara landed in Detroit Metro Airport later in the afternoon and the temperature was still quite warm. Chris grabbed their bags and followed Sara down the aisle toward the exit. He watched the subtle sway of Sara's hips and smiled.

What an amazing woman I have been blessed with! he thought to himself.

As Sara turned the corner, she spun her head around to look toward Chris. Her hair seemed to flow in slow motion from side to side. It reminded him of those shampoo commercials where models would fling their hair.

Sara returned his smile and continued down the causeway into the terminal.

I have to ask her soon, otherwise I am going to explode.

Once in the terminal, Chris and Sara sat down to confirm their plan.

"So you want to go see your friend, Michele?" Chris asked.

"Yes. I think it would be a good idea to talk with her further and possibly talk to her boyfriend's sister," Sara replied. "I can't think of any other reason for us to be diverted to Michigan."

"It really doesn't make any sense. There are so many other places that we could have been diverted to," Chris confirmed.

"According to GPS, it is just over two and a half hours to Midland," Sara said. "It's a small town with a population of just over 40,000 people. I've been there a couple of times to see Michele, but it's been a few years," Sara added.

"Okay, let's get over to the car rental counter and make our way there. Maybe you can call ahead and make sure she knows that we are on our way," Chris replied.

Chapter 51

Sara

"Hi, Sara," Michele answered.
"Hey, Michele, guess what?"
"What?"
"I'm in Detroit."
"What? Are you coming to see me?"
Sara could hear the glee in Michele's voice.
"Yes, we'll be on our way shortly. I'm guessing we'll be there just before 10:00 p.m."
"We?"

Sara smiled. She hadn't told Michele about Chris yet. Life had been busy. Michele knew that she worked for a government agency, but she didn't know that she was a CIA agent.

"Yes, I'm with a work associate."

A work associate? What the heck am I saying? Sara thought.

"Can you recommend a good hotel there?"

"Sara, there are a lot of options now. I would recommend the Residence Inn by Marriot near the mall."

"Okay, I'll give them a call on our way up."

"How are you, Sara?" Michele asked.

"I'm good. We have a lot to talk about," Sara replied.

'A lot' is an understatement. Michele will know that Chris is more than a work associate almost immediately.

"Yeah. I miss you so much!" Michele exclaimed.

"Me too! But I also want to talk to your boyfriend's sister," Sara added.

"Okay, I will be talking to her a little later and we'll set aside some time. Brian's Dad isn't doing too well. I don't expect him to last more than a couple of weeks," Michele added.

"I'm so sorry," Sara consoled.

"Yeah, he's such a nice guy. His entire family is here and they are spending quality time together. Samantha, that's Brian's sister, has been here a few days. Their dad has gone from walking through the house unassisted to using a walker in just the last couple days," Michele added. "I fear he'll be bedridden soon."

"So sad. Cancer?" Sara asked.

"Yes, prostate cancer. The doctors took it out, but didn't get it all. It's such a shame."

"Are you sure Samantha will want to talk with us?"

"Yes, I think she will. She is pretty passionate about the Bible. I'm assuming you're going to ask her about end times stuff?" Michele asked.

"Yes, more about the Mahdi, too."

"Is this work related?" Michele asked. "I thought you worked for the Commerce Department," she continued.

"Yes, sort of, but not really. I'll explain when we get there."

"Okay, drive safe, Sara. We'll see you soon."

"I'll text you when we get to the hotel and then we'll set up a time to talk tomorrow. Love you, sister!"

"Love you too, Sara."

Sara hung up just as Chris was walking over to her with the car keys.

"All set?" Sara asked.

"Yep, the shuttle will take us to the car."

"Okay, sounds good."

"Are you okay, Sara?" Chris asked. He could see the strain on her face.

"Yes, I am. My friend's boyfriend's dad is dying and he doesn't have much time. It just makes me sad."

Chris came up and hugged her.

"He's one of the lucky ones," Chris replied, as he embraced her.

"Yes, I suppose you're right. At least he won't have to deal with all of the persecution that is coming," Sara replied.

Chapter 52

Ford

Ford and Abby woke up to the news about the war in the Middle East and couldn't believe their eyes. Every news outlet was broadcasting stories about nuclear war in the Middle East.

"This is what you've been talking about, isn't it?" Abby asked. Her face was pale with fear.

"Yes."

Ford was speechless. He couldn't believe his eyes.

A moment later the phone rang and Abby answered it.

"It's Tom! He wants to talk to you!"

"Tom, how are you?" Ford asked.

"Dad, this is insane. What is going on?"

"Tom, how quickly can you get packed and on the road?"

"I have my go-bag ready. But where am I going?"

"Tom, listen carefully. Do you recall the map package that I put together for you and the route that I believe will be the best for you getting home to us?"

"Yes, of course," Tom replied.

"Good. Air travel might be difficult and potentially impossible in the next few days."

"Dad?"

"Tom, it is about 20 hours of driving under normal circumstances. Take I-44 and get thru St. Louis, Missouri as quickly as possible. The Mississippi River may become a choke point very soon. That is a 9 hour trip!" Ford exclaimed. He paused to catch his breath so as not to create a state of fear for Tom.

"Dad?"

"Yes, Tom?"

"I'm scared."

"Yes, Tom, I understand. Faith will get you through this. And hopefully, we are just overly cautious and nothing will change here in the United States, but we need to stay on guard and be prayerful."

"Okay. Thanks, Dad."

Ford could almost feel the calm flow into Tom.

"Fill your car with as much food and water as you can in the next 30 minutes. Take your go-bag and anything else that you think you might need and then leave. Start making your way here."

"Okay. Love you, Dad."

"I love you too, Son!"

"Tell Mom that I love her, too."

"I will put her on so you can do that yourself." Ford handed Abby the phone and tears began to trail down her face.

"I love you too, Tom. Hurry home!" she exclaimed before hanging up the phone. Ford moved to Abby and held her in his arms. He could feel her tremble slightly.

"I love you, Abby. Tom will be safe."

Ford tried to stay current with the news of the war in the Middle East, but he had more preparations to make at the lodge. Around lunch time, while watching television, the news anchor broke in.

"This just in! There were multiple explosions reported at the United Nations Building here in New York. Details are sketchy, but terrorism is believed to be the cause."

Abby suddenly stiffened, "We have to call John. He went to town an hour ago."

"I'm on it, I will get him home," Ford replied.

"Hello?" John answered his cell phone.

"John, where are you? I need you to get home as soon as possible."

"What's up, Dad? Is everyone okay?"

"Yes, John, everyone is okay, but I need you home like now. I'll explain everything when you get here. Drive normal, don't speed."

"Okay, Dad, I'm on my way. I'll be there in fifteen minutes or so," John replied.

John was hanging out with his girlfriend, Gwen. They were both going to Michigan State University in the Fall and had been dating since halfway through their senior year in high school. Gwen was a nice girl that both Abby and Ford liked a lot. John and Gwen had just picked up lunch and were sitting at a picnic table in the city park.

"Gwen, I have to get home. My Dad is acting weird again."

Gwen smiled. She liked both of John's parents and knew that John thought that they were both a little strange, especially his dad. She leaned over and softly kissed him.

"That's okay, I need to be home soon anyway," Gwen replied.

Gwen had listened to John's dad talk about the end of the world on a couple of occasions. He was passionate about the subject and was definitely knowledgeable as well. In the past, she had picked up the Bible and read several of the passages that he quoted. She wanted to talk to John's father about it more, but John never seemed interested.

As they drove toward her home, Gwen looked over to John and wondered, *Do you follow Jesus?*

Ford hung up the phone and told Abby that John would be home soon. He needed to contact both Sam and Zack. They needed to know what was coming next.

Chapter 53

Samantha

It was evening when Sam's phone rang. The caller ID told her that it was Ford. Ford usually used email to communicate with her, so a phone call usually meant it was urgent.

"Hi, Ford," Sam answered.

"Did you see the news today?"

"Yes, I can't believe that Turkey nuked Iran. Do you think this is the fulfillment of Daniel 8?" Sam asked.

"Yes, exactly."

"So what do you think will happen next?" Sam asked.

"My guess is that both horns of the Persian Ram have been broken. I believe that one horn is the Ayatollah and the other is possibly a military leader, but I really don't know. However, the next part of that scripture says that the goat will trample the ram. My best guess is a ground invasion, into the

Middle East, by Turkey," Ford answered. "I also expect that the current leader of Turkey will be removed from power, probably assassinated in the near future.

"The scripture says that the goat becomes very strong and, at the height of his power, his prominent horn will be broken off. I think this means that the leader of Turkey, the prominent horn, will be removed. But this will happen at the height of his power, so the entire Middle East must first be conquered by Turkey," Ford continued.

"So what does this mean for us?" Sam questioned.

"The conquest of the Middle East by the Persian Ram ushered in the rider on the red horse, from the book of Revelation. This rider was supposed to take peace from the earth. Many parts of the world are currently at war. Only World War II was bigger. I expect that war will continue to expand throughout the world."

"Ok, but what about the goat?" Sam asked.

"The conquest of the Middle East by Turkey will usher in the rider on the black horse. The black horse will bring famine, pestilence and suffering. Difficult times are coming."

"What do we do?"

"Sam, I think it is time for us to prepare for the possibility that world food and water supplies will become scarce. People will become desperate and potentially dangerous. I also believe that Christians will be severely persecuted by the servants of Satan. In the Middle East, Muslims will persecute Christians at an alarming rate. First we need to make sure all our loved ones are saved. We need to be prepared to make sacrifices, and there is a chance that we'll lose people."

"Ford, this is crazy. I'm here in Michigan with my parents. My dad is dying. Hospice is saying that it could be a week or two before he passes. I was planning to stay until he is gone to help mom with everything, but Rob and the boys are back in New Mexico. What should I do?"

Ford could hear the pain and anguish in Sam's voice.

"I'm sorry to hear about your dad. Staying with him is important. Can Rob and the boys come to Michigan?"

"I don't know, Ford. Rob is so busy with work right now. And I don't think he's completely on board with all this stuff."

"Sam, let's pray on it and talk tomorrow. I don't know exactly what to do. I did tell Tom to come home though."

"Wow, he's in Oklahoma, right?"

"Yes, that's right. I told him to drive here versus fly," Ford said. Ford wasn't sure if he should go on, but finally did. "I don't think air transportation will be very feasible soon. I think they will limit flights. I also think they might consider setting up choke points to limit movement around the country," Ford continued.

"Seriously?" Sam asked.

"Yes, but I really don't know. I hope I'm being super conservative, but martial law is a distinct possibility."

"Okay, Ford, like you said, let's pray on it and talk tomorrow."

"Take care, Sam."

"You too, Ford."

Ford looked at his watch. Seeing that it was 6:00 p.m., he hoped that Tom would cross the Mississippi River by 8:00 p.m. He decided that he would call him after he talked with Zack.

Chapter 54

Zack

Zack's phone rang.
"Hello?" Zack asked.
"Hey Bro, it's Ford."
"What's up, man?"
"I'm going to get right to the point. I know you're not all about this end of the world stuff, but I am really concerned about what is going on in the Middle East," Ford said.
"Yeah, that's some crazy shit," Zack said and then paused.
There was almost an awkward silence between them for the first time in their lives. Ford sensed that Zack had more to say, and Zack could tell that Ford was waiting for him to continue.
"Listen, Ford. I had this crazy dream the other day. It was weird, but afterward I had the feeling that I need to get over to Michigan with you," Zack continued.

"Wow, that's exactly what I was thinking!" Ford exclaimed.

"I tried to convince Christin to come with me, but she said that she couldn't uproot her daughter and leave at the spur of the moment," Zack said.

"Christin is your new girlfriend, right?"

"Yeah, we've only been dating for a month and I guess that isn't enough time to follow her crazy boyfriend to Michigan," Zack said with a nervous laugh.

"I'm not sure what to tell you. I can understand her uncertainty about such a move. It's hard to take in all this and I'm the crazy one who researches this stuff all the time," Ford said.

Zack laughed, but didn't say anything.

"You're a good man. I hope and pray that Christin and her daughter will be safe," Ford said.

"Yeah, me too. I like her a lot, man."

Ford smiled and said, "That's awesome, Dude. So when do you think you'll get here?"

"I am going to leave the day after tomorrow. I have a few things that I need to take care of first. Maybe I can convince Christin to come with me in that time. Anyway, it's about a three day trip, so I should be there in five days or so. I plan to take the northern route through the Upper Peninsula."

"Good idea. Okay, Zack. Keep me posted on your progress and we'll be ready for your arrival. Drive safe and we'll see you soon. Love ya, Brother."

"Love you too, Ford."

Ford couldn't believe that he had talked with Zack for almost two hours. It was close enough for him to call Tom, so he dialed the phone.

"Hello?" Tom answered.

"Tom, how is your progress?"

"I just passed Saint Louis, Missouri. I plan to drive another two hours or so and then stop," Tom answered.

"Awesome, I'm glad you have gotten a lot closer. I don't know if you heard the news about the United Nations building in New York, but there was another attack."

"Oh man, no. I've been listening to music."

"That's okay, but maybe you should keep the radio tuned to whatever news station you can pick up. Things are progressing quickly."

"Okay, I will do that."

"Tom, do me a favor and text me when you stop and let me know where you are, okay?" Ford asked.

"Sure, Dad. I love you, Dad. Tell Mom for me too, okay?"

"Will do, Son. I love you, too."

Chapter 55

Ali

Somewhere over the Atlantic Ocean, Ali received word that the attacks on the United Nations were a complete success and he decided to call his master.

"Well done, Ali," the Mahdi said over the phone.

"The mission couldn't have been more successful, Mahdi," Ali replied.

"What is your ETA?"

"It looks like we'll be landing in Istanbul in about three hours, Sir."

"Great. Come to the palace as soon as you can. We have a lot of work to do," the Mahdi replied.

"Allahu Akbar," Ali chimed.

"Allahu Akbar," the Mahdi answered.

Chapter 56

Santa Fe, New Mexico

"Stephen, Cal still hasn't reported in. The forest rangers have been searching for quite some time. We found his Jeep near the northern edge of the Redondo. He last reported that he was going to investigate something out that way, but we can't find any sign of him," Tracy said.

Stephen could hear the concern in her voice.

"Tracy, I will make a call to the local police and see if they can help with the search, but right now I need you here."

Tracy made a confused face. It was as if she couldn't believe that he was going to leave Cal out there on his own.

"I know what you're thinking, Tracy, but trust me, it is more important that you stay here."

"Why?" Tracy questioned.

She hadn't meant to express so much distain, but she was pretty angry with Stephen because he seemingly wanted to abandon Cal.

"Listen, Tracy. I think that Valles is on the verge of going off," Stephen said plainly.

He saw her anger turn into confusion, with maybe what was a little excitement and fear. No human had ever witnessed a caldera eruption.

"Are you serious? Well, of course you are. But how do you know? I mean it seems impossible," Tracy stammered.

"Yes, it does seem inconceivable, but very possible," Stephen answered. "All the data we have points to an eruption. The only problem is that I don't know when, where, and to what extent. That is why I need you here to help me."

Stephen seemed to gather his thoughts before continuing.

"Because if this is really happening, millions of people could potentially die and we need to alert the authorities," Stephen continued.

Chapter 57

Zack

In the morning, Zack headed into town to collect a few things and to arrange with the post office to hold his mail. He felt a little silly doing it, but he thought it was a good idea, in case he ever came back.

"How long will you be gone, Zack?" the post office worker asked.

"Probably a month or so, Helen," Zack replied.

"Okay, I'll put six weeks down."

"That will be perfect. Thanks, Helen."

Helen was in her late 60's and had been working at the post office for as long as Zack could remember. She was always cheerful and very personable.

"So where are you going? If I may be so bold."

"I'm headed to Michigan, to visit some friends that I haven't seen in a very long time."

"That is nice. Did you hear the news about New York?"

"Yes, I did. Helen, we live in scary times. Do be careful."

"Oh, Zack, I'm not worried. All that crazy stuff is so far away. No one cares about Hulett, Wyoming."

Zack smiled, but didn't say anything.

"Okay, you are all set. Have a great vacation and drive safely."

"Thank you, Helen. I'll see you later," Zack replied, knowing in his heart that he probably wouldn't.

After leaving the post office, Zack walked a block down to the barbershop where Christin worked. When he opened the door, the bell rang and Christin looked up from the head of the lady whose hair she was cutting. Her smile turned down before she recovered and smiled again.

"I'll be done in a few minutes, Zack," Christin said as she went back to cutting the lady's hair.

Zack picked up a magazine from the table in front of him and pretended to leaf through it, but he spent most of his time taking in the view of Christin.

Man, you are beautiful!

He could hardly believe that he was going to leave her. It was killing him to even think about it. How would he ever say goodbye.

Christin finished up with her customer and came over and sat next to Zack.

"Hi," Christin said.

The way she said it, she meant more than a simple greeting.

"Hi there," Zack replied.

"Did you come to say goodbye?"

Zack could see her eyes well up with tears and it broke his heart.

"Christin, I don't want to leave you," Zack started.

He could feel a lump growing in his throat. He wasn't one who normally shed a tear, but he thought today might be different.

"I'm leaving tomorrow morning and I just wanted to see you again."

"I wish you wouldn't go. I think we have a really good thing going on here."

"I know! We have a great thing going on. But something big is about to happen and I have to go. I sure wish you'd come with me."

"Zack, I can't."

A tear rolled slowly down her cheek. Zack moved slowly to wipe it away and felt her tremble at his touch. Suddenly, she jumped to her feet and started toward the back room.

"Christin, wait!"

Zack followed, ran up, and caught her from behind. Christin stopped and turned. Tears were streaming down her face. Her eyes were red and puffy, and yet Zack thought she was the most beautiful woman in the world.

"Christin," Zack whispered.

He brought her closer into him and she buried her head into his chest. They held their embrace for the longest time. After a while, Zack pulled back slightly and kissed her on the forehead.

"Leaving you is going to kill me, but I think staying here might kill me as well. My heart is breaking because I have to go. You call me if you need anything, and I will be here."

Zack bent his head down slightly and Christin looked up to meet him for a kiss. Zack held her head gently as they kissed. There was so much passion in that one kiss that Zack almost changed his mind. But before he could, Christin pulled away.

"Bye, Zack!"

With those words, Christin turned and ran into the back room. It was as if the air had left the room, because Zack couldn't breathe. He felt the lump in his throat get thick and then a tear rolled down his cheek. Only when his wife died, so many years ago, had he felt pain anywhere close to the pain that he felt. He turned and walked slowly out the door.

clang

The bell rang one last time for Zack.

Chapter 58

Samantha

Sam left the hotel around 9:00 a.m. and drove to her parents' house. When she arrived, the hospice worker was just leaving.

"How is he doing?" Sam asked the hospice worker.

"He is resting right now, but we are in the last stages. I'm sorry, but he doesn't have much time left."

The message hit Sam hard and she had to fight hard to hold back tears.

"I'm sorry," the hospice worker added.

"I thought that he had a couple more weeks?" Sam asked.

"Yes, so did I, but things have progressed faster than I first thought."

"Thank you for everything that you've done for my dad and my family. We couldn't have made it through this without you."

Sam instinctively gave the woman a hug. Sam needed a hug and wished that Rob could have come with her.

"You are very welcome. Your dad is a very nice man. You and your family are lucky to have him."

She smiled and left.

Sam took a deep breath and opened the door. When she got inside, she walked to the living room and found her father lying in a hospital bed. She knew that they were bringing a bed in today, but was surprised that he was already in it.

Sam's mother was sitting next to her husband and smiled when she saw Sam.

Sam walked over to her and bent down to hug her.

"How's he doing, Mom?"

"He's fine, but he is going fast."

A tear escaped her mother's eyes and Sam had to clench her jaw to hold back her own. She wanted to be strong for her family, but inside her heart was breaking.

The previous night, Michele had asked Sam if she could meet with her friend, Sara. Apparently, Sara had questions about the Mahdi. Sam didn't know what Sara did for a living, but found it strange that she wanted to talk about such things. Sam agreed to meet them for lunch after she had a chance to see her father. Talking to Sara might help keep her mind off the state of her father's health.

"Mom, where is Sonia?"

"She went to the store to get some things. She said that she'd be back in a couple hours. I think she just needed to get away for a bit," her mother replied.

"She has done so much. She deserves a break. I'm so proud of her," Sam replied.

"Yes, she has been great."

"Hey there, Kiddo." Sam's father said.

Sam got up and gave her father a kiss on his cheek.

"How ya doing, Pops?" Sam asked.

"Strong as an ox and stubborn as a mule," her father replied in a raspy voice.

Sam smiled, but a tear trailed down her cheek.

Sam spent the morning talking to her father. He would doze off on occasion and she would just sit there and stare at him. Wondering how such a strong man could have been beaten down by such a crappy disease.

Her mother spent a lot of time in the kitchen. She was probably just staying busy. Sam could smell cookies baking in the oven.

When Sonia got back, Sam could tell that she had been crying.

"You okay, Kid?" Sam asked her little sister.

"Yeah, just got here a minute ago and had a little moment," Sonia replied. She feigned a smile and walked into the kitchen to join her mom.

Sam followed and the smell of snicker doodle cookies caressed her nose.

"Mmmmm. That smells soooo good!" Sam exclaimed.

Her mother was just taking a batch of cookies off of the cookie sheet. Sam and Sonia stared at them as their mother slowly placed them on a paper towel that lay on the counter.

After the last one was placed, their mother looked up at them and said, "Well, okay, you can have one."

She smiled broadly and the girls each grabbed a warm snicker doodle.

"Oh these are so good!" Sam exclaimed.

"Sooo good!" Sonia repeated with a little cookie crumb falling out of her mouth.

The little crumb landed on the floor and the three of them broke down with laughter. It was minutes before they all calmed down.

"Hey, what's going on in there?" came the voice of Sam's father from the other room.

The girls went in, followed by their mother. The man smiled as he saw them.

"How about a cookie for me?" he said.

His wife smiled at him and pulled a cookie off of a plate that she had brought in with her. She knew her husband well. They adjusted his bed so that he could sit up better and their mom gave him a cookie. His first bite was big, probably more than he could handle. A lot of crumbs fell out of his mouth. Sam could tell that he was having trouble eating the cookie, but was enjoying it none the less.

"Sooo good!" the man said.

The three girls giggled a little. It was a good day.

Chapter 59

On the road

After travelling most of the day, Tom had decided to stop in Terre Haute, Indiana. He stayed the night in a Motel 6 and got back on the road early. He had driven a few hours when he received a call from his dad.

"Hey, Dad, just passed Indianapolis," Tom said as he answered the phone.

"Great, you are making great time. You should be home by dinner."

Chapter 60

Christopher

Chris and Sara pulled up to Sam's parents' house around noon. When they got out, Sara rushed over to her friend, Michele, and gave her a big hug. Chris smiled and grabbed the pizza that they were going to share for lunch.

Chris walked up and introduced himself to Sam as Sara and Michele continued to hug.

"Hi, I'm Chris."

"Sam."

"It's very nice to meet you. Maybe we can start lunch while these two love birds hug," he said with a chuckle.

Sara looked over to him and gave him a goofy look and reluctantly let go of Michele.

"Michele, this is Chris," Sara said.

"Hello," Michele said, as she shook Chris' hand.

"It's nice to meet you."

"Sara, this is Brian's sister, Samantha," Michele said.

"Hi, nice to meet you," Sara replied.

"It's nice to meet you, too. Please call me Sam."

Sam led them over to an outdoor dining table that had a large umbrella over it.

"Is this okay?" Sam asked. "There's a lot going on inside."

Everyone was happy to eat outside and enjoy the warm summer afternoon. The four of them ate while Michele and Sara played a little catch up. When everyone was almost done eating, Sam spoke.

"So you want to learn about the Mahdi?" Sam questioned.

"Yes, we do," Sara replied.

"So what do you know?" Sam asked.

Sara went on to talk about how there was evidence that the Mahdi and the Antichrist were the same.

"But that is about all we know," Sara finished.

Sara was reluctant to share any information that might be considered classified, so she left out the part where she and Chris thought that the Mahdi might be behind some of the terrorist attacks that occurred a few months ago in New York, Paris, and Nashville.

"Well, my friend, Ford, is the real expert on all this stuff, but I agree with your connection between the Mahdi and the Antichrist. But there's more information that is relevant to things happening today," Sam said.

Chris and Sara looked at one another, but said nothing. Sam noticed their look, but went on.

"Are you familiar with the book of Daniel in the Bible?" Sam asked.

"Sure," Sara replied and Chris nodded.

"Well in chapter 8, there is a reference to a ram and a goat. The ram represents the nation of Persia, or modern day Iran. This scripture describes the events that took place six months ago when Iran conquered the Middle East," Sam said. She recognized the surprise in the faces of both Chris and Sara, so she paused a moment.

"There is evidence that the goat represents the nation of Turkey. This goat starts out with a single horn. This horn represents a king or leader who will lead the nation of Turkey against Iran, and conquer the Middle East. It talks about how this goat will cross the entire earth without touching the ground and in the end will trample the ram," Sam added. "I think what we are seeing in the Middle East right now is reflective of what the goat is prophesied to do in chapter 8 of the Book of Daniel."

Both Chris and Sara had looks of amazement, and just sat there in wonder. Finally, Sara spoke.

"That is crazy, I mean amazing. Is there more?"

"Sara, there is more. The scripture goes on to say that the single horn of the goat will be broken and that four other horns will grow up in its place."

"So what does that mean?" Sara asked.

"If you recall, I said that a horn represents a king or leader. My friend, Ford, believes that the first horn will be removed from office. Maybe he'll get assassinated or maybe just die, but in any case, he will go away. His removal will cause a little bit of chaos and four regional leaders will rise up and take control over their respective regions," Sam said.

Sam paused and waited for questions, but when none came, she picked up her Bible and opened it up to the book of Daniel and continued talking.

"Here is where it gets interesting. In verse 9 of chapter 8, the Bible says, *Out of one of them came another horn, which started small but grew in power to the south and to the east and toward the Beautiful Land. It grew until it reached the host of the heavens, and it threw some of the starry host down to the earth and trampled on them. It set itself up to be as great as the Prince of the host; it took away the daily sacrifice from him, and the place of this sanctuary was brought low. Because of rebellion, the host of the saints, and the daily sacrifice were given over to it. It prospered in everything it did, and truth was thrown to the ground.*"

Sam saw their confusion and smiled.

"Yes, I know exactly how you feel," Sam started. "Basically, this says that another leader will rise out of one of these four regions and grow in power. This leader will grow to the east and to the south. The regions where the four leaders will rise up are most likely Turkey, Iran, Egypt, and the Arabian Peninsula. Only the leader from Turkey can grow to the east and south to conquer the Middle East. It is likely that this new horn will come from Turkey."

"So this new horn, will conquer the Middle East?" Chris asked.

"Yes, but more importantly, is the last part of that scripture that ties this horn to the Antichrist. There is a lot of scripture that depicts the Antichrist doing these things, but this scripture is the only one that helps us identify Turkey as the nation that the Antichrist will most likely emerge from," Sam replied.

Sam could see the wheels turning in Chris' head, and she began to wonder what it was that Chris and Sara were trying to discover.

Almost sensing Sam's thoughts, Chris looked up and scanned the area before beginning to talk.

"What I'm about to say is potentially classified, but you seem to know more than us already," Chris started. "Sara and I work for a government agency and we have been investigating a person that we believe orchestrated all of the New Year's Eve attacks. My gut tells me that this person also is responsible for the attacks at the U.N. that just occurred."

Michele seemed surprised, but Sam didn't show much expression.

"Prior to coming here, we were on our way to Turkey to investigate a potential government coup d'état. A coup d'état, is when elements within the government attempt to overthrow the existing leader and take control. We believe that the person behind it is the man referred to as the Mahdi," Chris said. Sam raised her eyebrows a bit, showing her surprise.

"So if I put two and two together, it seems like this Mahdi, who is also the Antichrist and the small horn, is potentially getting ready to take out the first prominent horn on the goat," Chris said as he tapped his finger on the verse in the Bible indicating as much.

"Wow, we truly are living in the end times," Michele said in awe.

Chris, Sara, and Sam all nodded in recognition of that truth.

"I really wish that you guys could meet my friend, Ford, because he knows so much more about all this," Sam said.

"Sam, I believe the reason we are in Michigan right now is to meet you and Ford. After the attack on Iran, our mission was aborted and we were headed back to New York. But the attack at the U.N. caused our flight to be diverted. There are a number of places to divert us that make more sense than Detroit. I believe God sent us here for a reason," Chris said.

Sara smiled at how far Chris had come with his beliefs.

"How far away is your friend?" Chris asked.

"Only an hour or so," Sam replied and smiled. She really didn't think that she'd have time to see Ford while she was in Michigan, but maybe she would have a chance. But then she realized that she couldn't leave her father.

"Listen, my dad doesn't have much time, so I can't leave right now, but I can contact Ford and see if he can meet with you," Sam said.

"Okay, sorry about your father, but we really appreciate you helping us out," Chris replied.

"We'll head back to the hotel. Give us a call when you hear back from your friend," Sara added.

"I will," Sam replied.

After saying goodbye to Sam and Michele, Chris and Sara drove back to the hotel. Chris was amazed at the things that he witnessed and how God seemed to be guiding him. And then he started to think about his planned marriage proposal that seemed to continue to get pushed off. He had a moment of self doubt and he began to pray.

Lord, please guide my path. I love Sara and want to spend the rest of my life with her. If that is your will, please show me what you want me to do.

Chapter 61

Samantha

After Chris and Sara left, Sam went into her parents' house to see how her father was doing. Sonia and her mother were sitting in the living room talking quietly while her father slept. His breathing was slow and weak. His health seemed to worsen by the minute.

How much longer do we have with him.

Sam sat down in a chair on the other side of the room and pulled out her phone. She decided that she would text Ford and see if he had time to meet with them tomorrow.

"Hey, Ford. What's up?" Sam texted.

Ford wasn't the best at returning texts, so Sam was surprised when he replied almost immediately.

"Hey, Sam. Just working around the house. Hoping that Tom gets home soon."

Sam recalled Ford telling her that his oldest son was traveling back to Michigan from Oklahoma. Ford had asked him to come home because he was worried about events that would follow the bombing of the United Nations building. Sam wished she were home with her family, but she felt compelled to stay with her mother until her father passed away.

"Are you available to chat with some friends sometime in the afternoon tomorrow?" Sam replied.

"Sure, it would be great to see you, Sam."

"Actually, I won't be coming. My friends need to talk to you about end-times stuff. Sorry, but time with my dad is short. He will be gone soon," Sam continued. A tear slid down her cheek and she was thankful that her father's bed blocked the view to her mother and sister.

"Sorry to hear about your dad. Please keep me updated. I am more than happy to talk with your friends. Just have them meet me at the Lodge."

"Okay, Ford. Thank you!"

"No problem, Sam. I will pray for you and your family."

"Thanks. I wish I could come see you too," Sam replied.

Later in the afternoon, Sam stood by her father, holding his hand, hoping she would have another chance to talk with him, but his breath seemed labored and rough.

Sam's mother came up behind Sam and put an arm around her.

"Hi, Mom."

Her mother didn't say anything, but after a while she spoke.

"You know, your father and I had a great conversation last night. His speech was labored and I could tell he was in pain, but we spoke."

A tear ran down her mother's cheek and Sam's stomach jumped and her heart ached.

"He is ready to go, Sam."

At those words, Sam shook as she struggled to choke back her tears. A small squeak left her throat and tears began to flow. She hadn't had much time to process everything that was going on and it all hit her in a rush. In that moment, her father squeezed her hand. It was as if her father knew that she needed him. His eyes opened slightly and he whispered.

"Sammy."

"Hi, Daddy."

"What's...the matter?" he asked. He struggled to say the words.

"I just love you, Daddy," Sam replied.

Her father seemed to fall back asleep and his hand loosened slightly. Sam didn't know what she was going to do without her father. He was always a strong man and to see him like this almost broke her. She was about to turn and leave the room when his hand tightened around hers.

"Love...you...too...Sammy."

Her father's voice was raspy and horse. It was barely a whisper, but the words were clear. She had heard her father say that he loved her many times, but deep in her heart she knew this was the last time.

She couldn't choke back the sob that rose up from her heart. Tears began to flow in a stream down her face. Her mother's squeeze tightened on her shoulder and she lightly kissed Sam's cheek.

They both stood there, arm in arm, looking down at the man that they had loved for a lifetime. Sam knew the time was close and prayed.

"Lord, Jesus, only you know the date and time, but when that time comes, please accept my father's soul into heaven so that he may experience your complete love and be with you forever. Lord, please fill my family with love so that we may endure the days to come, and that we may all have the strength to follow your word. In Jesus Christ's name, I pray, Amen."

"Amen," her mother responded.

"Amen," her sister answered from behind.

In that moment, both Sam and her mother felt her father relax his hand. He took one more breath and was with his savior.

The three women stood around the man that meant so much to them and held each other. Sam wished that the rest of her siblings had been there to see their father pass. It was heart wrenching, but Sam felt blessed.

A half hour later, Brian arrived to say goodbye to his father before the funeral home took him away. Ralph, Sam's older brother, and Rebecca would both be there the next day. There was a lot of work to do, but Sam needed to call home and talk to Rob. She needed her husband now more than ever. Sam decided to head back to her hotel and make the call.

"Hello," Rob answered.

Sam choked up and couldn't speak.

"Hello, Sam. Are you okay?"

Sam whimpered and tried speak again.

"Rob..."

Rob could hear his wife sobbing on the other end of the line and felt helpless.

"Oh, Babe, I'm so sorry," Rob consoled Sam.

"Rob...he passed."

"I'm so sorry, Honey."

"Thanks, Rob. Sorry I lost it there."

"Oh, don't be sorry. He was a great man. He was lucky to have such a great family."

"Yeah, we were all lucky. I have the best family in the world. I have the best husband in the world, too."

There was silence on the other end of the line.

"Rob?" Sam asked. "Rob?"

In Albuquerque, Rob heard his phone go dead. Then he heard a rumble in the distance. He stood up from his living room chair and looked out the window that faced the north. What he saw brought a look of terror to his eyes.

CHAPTER 62

Santa Fe, New Mexico

Dr. Stephen Weinstein was on the phone with the park ranger when everything started to shake.

"His last reported location was near Redondo Peak..." the park ranger started, but then the phone went dead and all Stephen heard was a dial tone. Then books and other materials began falling off the wall.

From the other room, Tracy began yelling.

"It's happening! It's happening!"

Dr. Weinstein ran into the other room and looked at the computer screen that Tracy was staring at.

"Oh my God!" Dr. Weinstein exclaimed. "Call everyone!"

Tracy picked up the phone and dialed and he did the same. Dr. Weinstein placed a call to his boss in Lakewood.

Lakewood, Colorado was where most of his superiors were stationed. His immediate supervisor was named Dr. David Cook and he answered the phone on the first ring.

"Dr. David Cook here," David answered.

"David, Valles is going off," Dr. Weinstein said solemnly.

"Oh shit!"

"Yeah, I only have minutes. You probably have 60 minutes before the blast wave reaches you. That is, if it gets that far. I don't know exactly how bad this is, it just started."

As Dr. Weinstein was talking, an alarm began to sound on David's computer.

"Stephen, I just got a warning. The sensor near Redondo just registered more than 10 on the Richter scale before going off line."

Stephen was silent for a moment. He knew what that meant. He looked at his watch and two minutes had gone by since the rumbling had started.

"David, I have to go. Call everyone that you can. Be safe!" Stephen exclaimed.

"I will. Good luck!" David replied.

Stephen picked up the phone and called his wife who would be at his home in Santa Fe right now. The phone rang once before his wife answered. She sounded worried.

"Stephen, what is going on?"

"Honey, it's happening. I'm sorry. I just wanted to let you know that I love you," Stephen whispered.

"I love you too, Stephen. How much time do we have?" she continued.

"Minutes, Dear."

His wife was silent on the other end of the line. He could hear muffled sobbing and his heart began to break. Stephen looked over at Tracy and he could tell that she was calling her loved ones as well. He hoped at least she had been able to call someone outside the blast radius.

Stephen listened to his wife sob on the other end of the phone before it went dead. He looked at the telephone receiver for a moment before slowly putting it down. He looked up to see Tracy doing the same thing.

"It's been an honor, Tracy," Stephen whispered.

"Stephen. Yes it..."

The room exploded and everything was enveloped in flames. Tracy and Stephen never felt a thing.

Chapter 63

Cheyenne Mountain, Colorado

Jason was sitting at his desk when all hell broke loose. A warning siren began blaring and all sorts of lights began flashing everywhere. Addison came rushing out of her office and came up to Jason.

"Jason, there has been a huge geological event. It looks like the epicenter is the Valles Caldera. How big would such an eruption be? Are we in danger?" she asked.

"Captain, when you say huge, what do you mean? What did it register?" Jason asked.

"It said 10+. Is that even possible?" Addison asked.

"Ma'am, we need to get into a secure bunker. We are going to get hit hard. I don't know how much time we have, but I'm guessing it is less than an hour before it gets here," he replied.

"Come with me, Lieutenant!" she commanded.

Captain Addison Rodriquez and Lieutenant Jason Chambers ran down the main corridor until they reached a section that was labeled *Top Secret Clearance Only.*

"Ma'am, we can't go in there!" Jason exclaimed.

Addison ignored him and swiped her security badge causing the light to turn green and the door to unlock.

Jason stared at her but said nothing as he followed her down another hall. The hall looked to be more than 100 yards long and there seemed to be an elevator door at the end of it. As they were racing down the hall, a group of men came crashing through a set of double doors. They turned right toward the elevator. Only fifty yards away, Jason thought that he saw a man that resembled the President of the United States. Still running beside Addison, he asked her the question.

"Is that..." Jason began.

"Yes!"

"You knew?"

"Yes, now hurry up!"

The President and his security detail reached the elevator and doors opened immediately. The secret service team quickly ushered the President inside and closed the door. Four of the men in the President's security detail turned and faced away from the elevator.

Addison and Jason were about 20 yards away from them when all four drew their weapons and the one in charge issued a command that they stop.

"Halt!" the secret service agent commanded.

Addison and Jason stopped only about 10 yards away. Addison wasted no time before she spoke.

"Listen, we need to talk to the President!"

As if anticipating her request, he shook his head no.

"It is a matter of national security!" Addison said sternly.

"The President is in the bunker. No one goes in and no one comes out."

Addison slowly began to move forward and continued to speak.

"Listen, we have important information about what is going on out there. None of us are safe here," Addison said calmly.

"Do NOT advance another step or I will be forced to put you down!" the agent in charge commanded.

Addison stopped moving forward and looked at her watch.

"Listen. Here is the situation. According to our data, it looks like the Valles Caldera has just erupted."

The agent didn't quite seem to understand.

"A caldera is like a volcano, but bigger. They are sometimes called super volcanoes," Addison explained.

"The blast radius of Valles is most likely...Lieutenant, what is the radius?" Addison asked Jason.

"Ma'am, it could potentially reach as far as Denver." Jason replied.

"Denver?" Addison asked.

"Yes, Ma'am, Denver!"

Addison turned to the agent in charge and let that sink in before speaking again.

"Cheyenne Mountain is about 50 miles closer to the caldera and is most certainly in the initial blast radius. Anyone not in a secure bunker will most likely not survive the initial blast. What happens next, Lieutenant?" she asked Jason.

"After the initial blast, the air will be filled with ash. No telling how much, but we can probably expect tens of feet here. Anyone who survives the initial blast will likely choke to death within minutes, due to the amount of ash in the air," Jason explained, and paused to let that sink in. "This eruption is like nothing humankind has witnessed during our history."

The lead agent seemed exasperated. He most likely had loved ones within the blast radius. He seemed to calm himself and holstered his firearm. The other three agents holstered their weapons as well.

"I'm sorry, but even if we wanted to get into the bunker, we can't. It can only be opened from the bunker below, by someone with the right clearance."

Addison looked at her watch and was depressed to see that they probably only had minutes before the blast would reach them.

"Jason, let's go."

Addison turned away from the elevator and began walking. After about ten steps, she stopped and turned.

"I know a place that we might be able to get to where we might have a chance to survive," she said to Jason and the other four men.

The lead agent looked at her and stared.

"The abandoned missile silo in Section C!" she exclaimed.

The lead agent seemed to understand.

"How certain are you about this blast reaching us?" he asked.

"99 percent," Jason replied.

The agent turned to his men and spoke.

"Guys, I know this is highly irregular and we were trained to never leave our post, but I think circumstances exist that were never expected. If this blast reaches us, going to the silo might be our only chance," the agent said. "I want you to know that regardless of what you choose, I will support your decision. You can go with the Captain or you can stay here at your post," he continued. "With me," he added reluctantly.

All three of the other agents indicated that they would stay with their leader.

"Okay, good luck guys!" Addison said as she turned and ran.

After running what seemed like miles, Addison came to another secure door. She anxiously swiped her card and was rewarded with a strong beep and a red light. Jason could tell that she was nervous and knew that time was running out. She took a deep breath and swiped the card again. This time the green light came on and the door unlocked.

The hallway behind the door only went about 50 yards before there was another elevator door.

"This is it," Addison said as she pushed the button.

She and Jason stood there a few more minutes before the door opened. They rushed inside and Addison pressed the only button on the console.

"Looks like a one way trip," Jason joked.

The elevator began descending and had only gone about 30 feet when the blast hit the base. Even though they were partially underground and somewhat protected by the mountain, the explosion was tremendous. The elevator car continued to descend, but then slammed against the wall of the elevator shaft. Both Addison and Jason were thrown against one wall and then they fell to the floor as the elevator car caromed back. There was a loud moan coming from above them. It was as if the cables holding them, more than 500 feet above the floor of the elevator shaft, were screaming in pain. Another sound, one that was even scarier, rushed downward toward them. Jason recognized it to be the sound of flash fire pushing downward.

The elevator car was buffeted by the wave of fire, some of which blasted through the vent in the ceiling. Jason saw the column of fire hit the floor and expand out, engulfing them both. Addison began to scream in agony, but their pain didn't endure long before the cable finally broke, plummeting them to a certain death at the bottom of the elevator shaft.

Chapter 64

Rob

Shortly after Rob's phone call with Sam had been interrupted, Rob looked out the window and saw the initial eruption from the caldera. The huge eruption matched how he imagined a nuclear explosion might look. The ash cloud vented upwards to a height that he could not fathom. He also saw the ash, lava, and flame expanding outward from the center of the eruption in every direction.

Rob knew that his time was limited. He decided that he would pray. He prayed for his family and friends and for all those who would be affected by this catastrophe. He could only imagine how many people would be killed.

Probably Millions?

After thanking Jesus for his incredible life and recognizing that he would soon be with God, he looked up and smiled.

"I am ready, Lord!"

The sound of the coming explosion grew until it was louder than an oncoming locomotive. And then there was silence.

Death had taken Rob and he felt no pain. And then he was with God.

Chapter 65

Cheyenne Mountain, Colorado

The President and his Chief of Staff sat in the command center waiting for a call to go through to the Vice President, who was currently cruising at 36,000 feet in Air Force Two. Neither said a word and finally there was an answer on the other end of the line.

"Mr. President?" the Vice President answered.

"Hal, there has been an event," the President said.

"Yes, Sir, we just got word."

"Hal, we don't have a lot of time. Where are you right now?"

"Sir, we are somewhere over Kentucky. With the attack on the United Nations, the secret service wanted to get me to a secure location. With the White House still out of commission, we decided to head to Cheyenne. We figured that was the most secure location right now."

The President's heart fell into his stomach.

"Hal, you have to turn that plane around. The Valles Caldera just erupted and soon the sky will be filled with ash. They are telling me that the ash cloud may go as far East as North Carolina, which seems crazy, but none the less, you need to get the plane out of the sky!" the President exclaimed.

Hal turned to the agent sitting next to him and told him to relay a message to the pilot to turn the plane around.

"Sir, what is going to happen to you?"

"Hal, go to Camp David, then assemble the cabinet and get them into the bunker. It is time to enact the 25th Amendment. I'm not sure if we are going to survive the blast."

"Sir, it has been an honor. We'll send a team as soon as we are able."

"Thanks Hal, but the honor has been mine. Okay, get moving. You have a lot of work to do."

"Thank you, Mr. President."

The President hung up the phone and looked over to his Chief of Staff.

"Jacob, we don't have much time. Let's see what we can do to get more people down here," the President said.

"Sir?" Jacob replied.

The President didn't waste any time answering, but turned to one of the analysts who was monitoring the event that occurred in New Mexico.

"Lieutenant, how much time do we have?"

"Sir, we have maybe 15 minutes."

The President got up from his chair and turned to the secret service agent in charge.

"Okay, Meyers, call your boys upstairs and see who they can round up in the next 10 minutes. Tell them the elevator will be there in 10 minutes and leaving in 11 minutes."

"Yes, Sir!"

Agent Meyers immediately called the agent in charge upstairs and soon learned that no personnel were within range to be saved.

"Sir, it's just my four men that can be saved. All other personnel are 15 minutes away at the closest."

"Send up the elevator. Let's get those boys out of there."

"Yes, Sir!"

Agent Meyers immediately sent the elevator and called up to the other agents.

We are cutting it close! Agent Meyers thought as he looked at his watch. Five minutes had already elapsed from when the Lieutenant told them they had maybe fifteen minutes.

It was three minutes later when the elevator door opened, revealing the four secret service agents who had been upstairs.

"Sir, it's here!" the Lieutenant exclaimed.

A moment later, the entire room shook and the lights went out. Even 1000 feet below the surface, inside a bunker that could survive a direct strike from a nuclear warhead, they felt the impact of the exploding caldera.

The President looked upwards in the dark, patiently waiting for the ceiling to come down on them and prayed.

Please, God, let us make it through this. I have more good work to do for you.

The President's response came quick as the emergency lights turned on and the shaking subsided.

"Thank you, Jesus!" the President exclaimed.

Chapter 66

Samantha

Sam looked at her phone and redialed Rob's number, only to hear a busy signal. Dropped calls were less common than they used to be, but the dropped call didn't worry her at all. She redialed Rob's number, expecting him to immediately pick up. Instead, she only heard a busy signal.

Rob must be trying to call me back.

Sighing, she put the phone down and waited for Rob's call to come in. After a few minutes she began wondering if Rob also got a busy signal, because he had tried to call her at the same time and was now waiting for her to call.

Sam was about to pick up her phone and call Rob again when the phone rang.

"Hello?" Sam answered the phone. It was her mother.

"Dear, do you have the television on?"

Sam could only wonder why her mother was calling at this time and couldn't believe she was worried about what was on the television.

"No, Mom. I don't have the TV on."

"Well, turn it on. You need to see this."

"Okay. What channel?"

"Any channel, Dear. I don't think it matters."

Sam turned on the television and was instantly greeted by a local news anchor reporting the news.

"...seems as if a volcano has erupted in New Mexico," the anchor announced. "We are not exactly sure what is going on, because we've lost contact with our Albuquerque and Santa Fe affiliates. Additionally, affiliates in the greater Denver area have also been unresponsive."

The news anchor paused as if she were getting additional information from her ear piece.

"This just in. Our Dallas affiliate is reporting that the Valles Caldera in New Mexico has erupted."

She seemed a bit confused by the news and looked past the camera to someone behind it.

"What does this mean?" the news anchor asked.

Even for a local news anchor, this was very strange behavior. Sam decided that she would switch over to Fox News for more information.

A familiar news anchor was reporting additional facts about the eruption. There was a map of the United States in the top left corner of the television screen. The title on the map said "Blast Radius", and there was a large circle that was centered on what looked like Santa Fe, New Mexico and it covered a large area in every direction. It looked like it went as far North as Denver, Colorado and as far East as Abilene, Texas. Then fear set in as she saw that the Blast Radius went as far as Las Cruces, New Mexico to the south and beyond Flagstaff, Arizona to the west.

She immediately began dialing Rob's number again, only to discover that she was still on the phone with her mother.

"Mom, I have to call you back," she said and hung up without waiting for a reply.

She redialed Rob again, only to be met with that annoying busy signal. She decided to call her oldest son, Jacob, next and also got the same. She burst into tears when her call to Isaac, her youngest son, produced the same result.

God, please tell me that they are okay!

But deep in her heart, she knew that her pleas would not be heard. With the realization that she had probably lost her entire family, she began to shake. The phone fell from her hand on to the floor and she curled up into the fetal position and held herself tight. Never in her life had she experienced so much pain. It was more than she could bear and soon the pain would consume her. A moan escaped her throat and soon turned into a scream of desperation.

"Noooooooo!" she heard herself scream. "Lord, I cannot go on without my family!"

Her body trembled and shook as she lie on the bed and then suddenly she went limp and lost consciousness.

At first, Sam wasn't sure where she was or what had happened. She was lying on a bed and soon it became clear that she was in a hotel room. She became aware of the sound of a television and sat up to see.

"What?" escaped her lips.

"...unfortunately folks, we haven't seen the end of this..." a news anchor announced.

For a moment, Sam couldn't remember what had happened, but then it all came rushing back to her in a flood.

"Oh, God, why?" she murmured, as she began to cry again.

Sam was about to lie back down on the bed when her phone rang. She looked toward the end table for her phone, but found that it wasn't there. The phone rang again and she discovered it lying on the floor, next to the bed. She bent to pick it up as it rang for the third time. The caller ID told her that it was her mother.

"Mom?" Sam answered and then began crying again, like she had heard the news of her family's death for the first time.

"Dear, Brian and Michele are on their way to pick you up," her mother said softly.

"Oh, Mom, why? Why did this happen?" Sam cried.

"Oh, Honey, I don't know. I'm so sorry, Dear."

The rest of the conversation was a blur to Sam, and after she hung up the phone, she simply stared at the television while she waited for her brother to come pick her up.

None of what the news anchor said that day made any sense to her. She wouldn't truly understand what happened for a few more days.

Chapter 67

Oklahoma City

Roger Steel sat in his office going over his budget for the next fiscal year. He had months to finalize it, but he felt that you could see the future in the numbers. He had become successful for two reasons: first, because he knew geology and second, but more importantly, because he was passionate about his business. Based on the data in front of him, it looked like the next year would be very profitable for his company. That was when the rumbling started.

At first, he wondered if it was another earthquake. Seismic activity had dramatically increased over the last twelve months. He turned in his chair to face the office window. His office looked west, out over the city. Suddenly, the entire window began to wobble. This shudder was different from any other earthquake he'd ever felt. Far over the horizon he could see a dark cloud growing. Never in his life had he seen such a cloud, ever growing upward and spreading out to cover the entire horizon. It had to be many miles away, but was expanding quickly. As he began to wonder about the cloud, his administrative assistant rushed into his office.

"Roger! There's been an event!" his assistant exclaimed.

"An event?" Roger questioned, as he turned toward his assistant.

"Yes, the Valles Caldera just erupted!"

"Oh my gosh!" he said, as he turned back to the window.

Now it made sense. The cloud of smoke and ash continued to expand and grow toward Oklahoma City. He hadn't spent much time studying volcanoes, let alone calderas, but he had a pretty good idea of some of the math associated with such eruptions. He turned to his computer and quickly brought up a map of the United States. He had no way of knowing the scale of the eruption, but based on the cloud that was growing, it had been big.

"Darcy, I don't think the blast will get as far as us, but I really don't know," he said. He paused a moment before continuing. "But that cloud that we see out the window will consume us and move well east of Oklahoma. The ash in the cloud will most likely cover the ground, upwards of 12 inches thick, once it all settles. Call your family and make sure that they get indoors as quickly as possible. We only have 10 to 15 minutes before it reaches us."

"Okay."

"Darcy, this ash is toxic and will kill most that inhale it. We need to shut down the HVAC system here and stay inside until the dust settles."

"Okay."

Roger could see that Darcy was terrified and did his best to settle her fears.

"We'll be okay, Darcy. As long as we stay indoors," Roger added.

Darcy nodded before leaving the room to make her calls. Roger wondered how long they would have to stay inside.

Days? Yes, it will be days. He thought to himself.

Roger lived alone, so he didn't have anyone to call. He turned back to the window to watch the ash cloud work its way toward him.

Chapter 68

Juarez, Mexico

Maria put the last tee-shirt out on the line to dry. She wiped the sweat from her brow and wondered when the heat was going to break. The temperature had been hotter than usual this summer. Miguel was close by, kicking around a soccer ball. Sweat dripped from him as well, but the heat didn't seem to have the same affect on him as it did his mother. Her son, Miguel, was ten years old and was full of spirit. If she let him, he would spend his day kicking around that old ball. Maria smiled at the joy that he seemed to find in kicking it.

As Maria watched her son play, a rumbling began to grow behind her and to the north. Her smile slowly changed to a frown as she turned away from her son and toward the north. There was a large cloud moving toward them and the rumbling sound grew as it came closer to them.

"Miguel, come inside!"

"Awe, Mom," Miguel complained.

"Now! Inside!" Maria almost screamed as she ran toward him.

Miguel's eyes opened wide when he saw the cloud that caused his mother to yell so loud. Maria grabbed his hand as she reached Miguel and they ran together toward their home. Maria closed the door behind them, but deep in her heart she knew that the door wouldn't stop the cloud. She didn't know what the cloud was, but she knew that it would overcome them. She pulled Miguel into her bedroom and shut the door. Immediately, she knelt next to her bed and beckoned Miguel to do the same.

"Pray with me, Miguel," Maria pled. Miguel nodded and they began.

"Our Father in heaven, hallowed be thy name, thy kingdom come, thy will be done..."

Maria and Miguel didn't get a chance to finish their prayer because the cloud of fire and ash finally reached them. It tore through their home with unparalleled force, and flattened most of the city.

Chapter 69

Camp David

Air Force Two landed at Ronald Reagan National Airport and the Vice President of the United States was being rushed to Marine Two that awaited his arrival. From there, they would be flown over to Camp David and would be met by whatever cabinet members were able to get there. Once the Vice President was in the bunker, the 25th Amendment would be invoked and he would become the sitting President of the United States.

Harold "Hal" Jones looked out over the city as the helicopter flew north. Becoming the President had been a lifelong dream, but this wasn't the way he wanted it.

"Is there any word on my family?" Hal asked the head of his secret service detail.

"Yes, Sir. Your wife and children are currently in route to Camp David. They should arrive shortly after we do."

"Thank you, Jack."

Agent Jack Miller had been in charge of the Vice President's security detail from the beginning of his term. He had a great resume, and he even had been on a presidential detail for two other past presidents. Hal always felt safe with him around.

"You are welcome, Sir."

When Marine Two arrived at Camp David, everyone was rushed inside and the Vice President, along with several cabinet members, was taken to the bunker where they met the Chief Justice of the Supreme Court.

"Hal, good to see you!" the Chief Justice said.

"Nathaniel, good to see you as well," the Vice President replied.

"I have received word from the President that we need to invoke the 25th Amendment," the Chief Justice stated.

"Yes, Nathaniel, we do."

"Okay, well, let's proceed."

After a brief ceremony, Harold Jones became the next President of the United States.

Chapter 70

Zack

After driving down I-90 for about 5 hours, Zack decided that he would stop for lunch in Chamberlain, SD. Chamberlain was a small town of about 2,300 people. Zack drove about a mile off the freeway before getting to the downtown district. It was a small downtown that covered a few blocks. There was a hardware store, a barbershop, several small retail shops, and a couple of bars. He pulled up to a small bar and grille and parked his truck.

The door to the bar squeaked a bit when he opened it and the bartender looked up. She was young, probably in her mid to late 20's. Zack walked up to the bar and sat down.

"What would you like to drink?" the bartender asked.

"Bud please, and a menu," Zack replied.

The young woman grabbed a menu from under the bar and handed it to Zack. Then she turned to pour Zack a beer.

The menu was typical of what you'd find in most small town bars throughout the country. Deep fried appetizers, a variety of burgers and sandwiches, and all you can eat fish on Friday's. When the bartender came back with his beer, she asked him what he'd like to eat.

"How's the Reuben?" Zack asked.

"It's pretty good. Would you like to add fries?"

"Sure, that sounds great!" Zack answered.

Zack turned his attention to the television that was behind the bar. It was tuned into some local news program. The news anchor was talking about the local football team and how they were expected to reach the playoffs this coming school year.

Zack smiled and looked about the room.

I guess all small towns are the same.

There were a few other guys at the bar and six of the ten tables had groups of people enjoying their food and drink. Zack had spent most of his trip thinking about Christin and wondering if he'd made the right decision. He wondered if he should have tried harder to convince her to come with him. He was beginning to get depressed when the bartender showed up with his food.

"Here ya go. How does everything look?"

"Looks good, thank you."

The bartender pulled catsup and mustard from beneath the bar and put it in front of him, along with silverware and a couple napkins.

"Enjoy and let me know if you'd like anything else."

Zack enjoyed a few bites of his Rueben before the patrons of the bar began to get visibly excited. At first, he didn't understand what was going on. They all seemed to be watching the television. Zack looked up and began listening to the local news anchor who was visibly shook.

"...it seems that there has been an explosion...no...uh...they are telling me that it is an eruption," the news anchor said. "A volcanic eruption near Santa Fe, New Mexico," she added.

Zack took another bite of his Reuben and continued to listen to the news broadcast. The news anchor didn't seem to have a lot of information and there were several pauses. She seemed to be completely confused.

"Would you like another beer?" the bartender asked from the other side of the bar.

Zack nodded in affirmation.

"...okay, we have more news. Wait! What? Is this right?" the news anchor asked. "How is this possible? Okay, okay...well it seems that this volcano...no this caldera in New Mexico has erupted. The blast radius is approximately 300 miles. There is no way this is right. Volcanoes aren't that big..."

Zack shook his head.

"...Seriously?..."

The news anchor was now visibly distraught.

"..Apparently, the blast was centered near Santa Fe, and has destroyed almost everything as far north as Denver, CO!" the anchor said. "It went as far south as Juarez, Mexico..."

The anchor began trembling and Zack could see tears rolling down her face.

"Did she say Denver?" the guy two seats down asked.

"Yeah, holy shit!" the guy he was next to replied.

The anchor had regained some of her composure and continued.

"To the east, it went as far as Dallas, and to the west, beyond Flagstaff. There is total destruction within this blast range. How many people is that?" the anchor asked.

She seemed to lose her composure again, and that is when reality hit Zack.

"Oh my God!" Zack said. "I have to go home!"

He threw down a $20 bill and ran out of the bar.

When he got to his truck, he pulled out his phone and dialed Christin. She picked up after the first ring.

"Zack, did you see what happened?"

"Yes! Yes I did. And I'm coming home right now!" Zack exclaimed. "But I won't be there for another 5 hours, assuming traffic is flowing."

"Oh, I'm so glad you're coming back," Christin said.

Zack could here relief in her voice.

"Okay, I have to hang up so I can get on the road."

"Okay, see you soon!" Christin said.

"See you!"

Zack started up his truck and got on the road. He looked down at his gas gauge and decided that he'd better get some gas before he left. He also decided that he needed to call Ford.

Chapter 71

Ford

Ford could hardly believe his eyes. The news was very clear about the Valles Caldera erupting. Abby sat next to him with a look of absolute terror on her face. John and Tom sat on the couch staring in utter disbelief in what they saw.

"What does this mean, Dad?" John asked.

"John, I don't know."

"Nothing like this has ever happened. At least during human history," Tom spoke up. "The closest eruption like this might be the eruption of Mt. Vesuvius near Pompeii, Italy in the first century."

"Right, but this is a magnitude of 1,000 times more," Ford guessed.

"Right, holy cow!" Tom exclaimed.

Soon the room became quiet again as everyone concentrated on what the news anchor was saying. He kept emphasizing that this event was larger than any event ever recorded in human history. He began talking about the long term affects of the eruption when Ford's phone rang.

At first, Ford wasn't going to answer it, but when he noticed that it was Zack, he immediately picked up.

"Zack, where are you?"

"I'm in South Dakota, but I'm heading back to Wyoming."

"What?" Ford asked.

"I have to go back to Christin, but I will convince her that she needs to come with me to Michigan."

"Zack, this eruption is immense. The ash cloud might get as far north as the southern portion of South Dakota, but it depends on the jet stream," Ford stated. "You'll definitely want to stay as far north as you can. I think we'll be fine here in Michigan. At least initially."

At that, his entire family turned and looked toward him. Each of them expressing some type of concern.

"How far are you from Hulett?"

"I'm about 5 hours away, assuming traffic is flowing."

"Okay, how long until you can get back on the road?"

"Well, that depends on how much begging I have to do. I told Christin that I was on my way back, but I still haven't told her that we need to get to Michigan. The fact that the ash cloud may get as far north as Hulett might be enough to convince her."

"Zack, it just might."

"Ford, I should get off the phone. I will let you know when I am back on the road toward Michigan."

"Drive safe, Brother!"

"I will. Talk to you soon!"

Ford hung up the phone and looked at his family.

"Dad, what did you mean by 'initially'?" John asked. Both Tom and Abby seemed to be waiting on pins and needles for the answer.

"Well, John, let's think about the consequences of this eruption. Obviously, there will be near complete destruction within the blast radius. Millions of people are dead. I can't even fathom how many have died already," Ford said. "But then, let's think about the ash cloud. On the news, they're talking about it stretching as far east as the Mississippi River and possibly more. Think about all that land between the Rocky Mountains and the Mississippi River."

"That's where they grow food and tend cattle," Tom said.

"Yes, that's right. Millions and millions of acres of farm land will be buried under feet of volcanic ash. That land will be unusable for decades. Millions of cattle and other livestock will die within days. What does that mean to our food supply?" Ford asked.

No one said a word. After a few minutes Ford broke the silence.

"Listen guys, I've been preparing for something like this for a long time. We have enough food to last us many, many years, even if we help other people along the way. Which we will. But we have to be careful. We can't go around telling everyone that we have food and water," Ford said. "I don't know if you are aware of this, but grocery stores only have about three to five days worth of food on their shelves."

"How is that possible?" John asked.

"John, it is possible because every day people are buying food and every day the stores replace what was bought with food that comes in that day. Most stores receive shipments every day, but at least five times a week," Ford answered. "So now think about the source of the food being cut off because of this disaster. Eventually, the food trucks quit delivering food to the stores. Within a week, our grocery store will be emptied."

Ford let those words sink in before he continued.

"What will happen when people start to realize that there is no more food?" Ford asked.

"It will be chaos," Tom answered.

"Yes. Which is why we need to keep our food stores to ourselves. It is the Christianly thing to share, and share we will, but we still need to be careful."

"So what do we do now?" John asked.

"Well, John, I'm glad you asked. Right now, you and I should go into town and grab a few things while Tom and your mother work on a few tasks that we need done. Like I said, I've been preparing for something like this," Ford replied. He looked knowingly to Abby, who nodded. Ford found no solace in being right, but he was happy that he had been preparing.

"But, Dad, how could you know that this was going to happen?" John asked.

"John, my son, it is all in the Bible."

"It is?"

"Yes, and we have more to learn, because this is only the beginning."

Chapter 72

Zack

Zack was speeding west down I-90 and traffic was pretty light. That was until he got close to Rapid City, South Dakota. That is when traffic came to a standstill. He was still about 2 hours from home. Traffic was lined up as far as he could see and not much traffic was traveling on the eastbound lanes. He could see the exit to Ellsworth Air Force Base about a mile ahead of him. He wondered if there was a back road that he could take to get around Rapid City. Since he literally had his truck in park, he decided to pull up a map on his phone and see if there was a better route. He had difficulty finding a road that would get him past the series of hills that made up the terrain around Rapid City. Finally, he was able to plot a course that would take him north and then west, skirting the city. Hopefully, this route was open and he would be able to get back on I-90 after he passed Rapid City.

Zack put the truck in gear and began driving on the shoulder of the road toward the next exit. He was greeted by multiple honking horns, and one idiot actually pulled off the road in front of him attempting to block his path. Zack veered further off the road barely avoiding a collision.

"Asshole!" Zack yelled out the window as he waved at the man with his middle finger in the air.

Once off the freeway, Zack had to turn south to avoid the Air Force base. Going south seemed counterintuitive, but he knew that was the route he had to take. Almost immediately, he took a right and started heading west again. He drove a mile and a half down the road and turned right again and headed north. Once off the freeway, he was better able to get a view of the traffic situation. A few miles down the road he saw a lot of flashing lights and assumed that there must have been a bad accident. Ahead of him he could see a check point station that allowed entry to the Air Force base. There were multiple flashing lights there as well. Fortunately, shortly after driving under the freeway overpass, he turned left and headed west.

The dirt road was aptly named Country Rd and it took him around the southern perimeter of the Air Force base. There seemed to be a lot of activity there. Zack wondered if that was because of the bombings at the United Nations or because of the eruption of the Valles Caldera.

Zack headed west for several miles before turning northward again. Before long, Zack was driving down a deserted road heading north. He took comfort in the fact that he was the only one out there, because frankly, he was still a loner. The thought of being alone made him think about Christin. He looked at his phone and had no signal. He hoped that was because he was out in the boons and not because of the destruction caused by the eruption. He drove north for a long time before he was finally able to turn west again. Ahead of him was a taller hill and the road he was on looked to go right into it.

After driving a half hour or so, he finally saw the freeway ahead of him. He glanced at his phone and was relieved to see a couple bars of service.

He pulled into the parking lot of a restaurant that was right off the freeway and dialed Christin's number.

"Hello?" Lizzy answered.

"Hey, Lizzy. Can I speak to your mom?" Zack asked.

"Yeah sure, Zack. Hang on a second."

Zack waited for a few minutes and started to wonder what was going on.

"Hi, Zack!" Christin exclaimed. She seemed to be out of breath. "Sorry it took so long. I was out in the garage putting some stuff together."

"No problem," Zack replied. "I just wanted to let you know that I was delayed in Rapid City. It looked like there was a big accident, but I'm really not sure. Anyway, I'm still about an hour and forty-five minutes away."

"Oh, okay."

"Listen, Christin. I was talking to Ford, and it looks like the ash cloud from the eruption may come as far north as us. He's not really sure, but I would really like to get you and Lizzy out of there."

"Zack, I'm with you. The news is saying that we might get a foot of ash here. They are telling people to head north."

"Okay. I would still like to head to Michigan," Zack replied. "My friend has a place there that can accommodate a lot of people. He has been preparing for this for years."

"Preparing for years?" Christin asked. "How is that possible?"

"Christin, I don't know. He says it's all in the Bible."

"In the Bible?" Christin wondered.

"Yeah, in the Bible. Once we are there, he can tell us everything about it."

"Okay. Well, I am almost done packing our things, but honestly, I don't know what else to bring other than clothes and a few food items."

"I have a lot of stuff packed into my truck. I'm wondering if we should grab my covered trailer and fill it with stuff too. That will delay our trip, but we'll be able to bring a lot more stuff with us. Also, I'm concerned that there will be enough gas along the way. I have several tanks that we can bring with us."

"Wow, I never even thought about gas!" Christin said.

"Okay, Christin, I should get off the phone. I'll see you soon."

"Okay, drive safe. I can't wait to see you!" Christin exclaimed. "I know it's been less than a day, but I really miss you."

"I miss you, too!" Zack said with a smile. "I will see you soon."

Zack hung up the phone and couldn't help but smile. He was heading back to get Christin and Lizzy and he couldn't be happier. He knew that the next days, months, and possibly years would be tough, but at least he would be with Christin.

Chapter 73

Sara

Sara was sitting next to Chris on the bed of his hotel room. The television was on, but neither of them seemed to be watching it.

"First, Turkey attacks Iran," Sara began. "Then the United Nations is destroyed. And now this? What in the world is going on?"

"Sara, our world will never be the same again," Chris said. "The eruption of the caldera will change the face of the United States. It will change the face of the rest of the world. Much of the world's food comes from the states that were virtually destroyed by the eruption. How long will it be before we run out of food?"

"I know. This is crazy," Sara was at a loss for words.

"Listen, I know this is probably the wrong time to even think about this, but..." Chris started. He stood up from the bed and pulled something out of his pocked. He knelt down in front of Sara and continued.

"Will you marry me?"

Sara went from shock to utter and complete shock. At first, she didn't know what to say. Of all the things going on, Chris' proposal was the most surprising of all. Suddenly, her heart began to race and she could feel warmth grow in her face.

"Oh my gosh, yes!" Sara blurted out. "Oh my gosh, yes!"

Chris stood and slid the ring onto Sara's ring finger and looked into her eyes.

"I love you more than life itself, Sara."

Sara was all smiles. It was as if everything on the news had never happened. She jumped up from the bed and threw herself into his arms. Her excitement turned into passion as she began to kiss Chris.

I can't believe this! I am going to marry him!

"I love you so much, Chris!"

They stared into one another's eyes for a long time until finally the reality of their situation started to come back. Chris and Sara sat back down on the bed, arm in arm, and just held each other.

"I think we need to go see Sam's friend, Ford. There is more coming and we need to understand what is going on," Sara said.

"Yes, I agree. But first, I need to call the Director and tell him what is going on."

"Okay, I'm going to call Michele and see if she wants to come with us."

Chris' head was spinning and he shook his head slightly. What a whirlwind it has been. He looked at Sara again and smiled.

How is it that I could be so lucky?

Sara smiled back and picked up her phone.

CHAPTER 74

Atlantic Ocean

After leaving the Mediterranean Sea, the Iranian submarine made its way toward the east coast of the United States. It successfully avoided detection for days. It had been more than a week since it received its last communication from General Hasim. Due to radio silence, the entire crew was unaware of the events that occurred in the Middle East and the United States. The submarine commander's orders had been to position itself a hundred miles off the coast of the United States within range of Washington, D.C. Only the commander and his first officer knew about the payload of the special missile that was locked in the armory.

"Commander, what are your orders?" the first officer asked.

Bahram Hosseini had been a submarine commander for more than two decades. Early in his career, he had trained with both the Russians and the Chinese. Over the last year or so, he had spent some additional training with the new Chinese submarine that Iran had purchased. The technology was on par with almost anything in the ocean. The stealth technology barely exceeded that of the United States. It was this technology that had allowed Bahram to get as close to the U.S. as he had. His first officer, Abbas Karim, had been with him for five years. Bahram couldn't be happier with his first officer.

"We are overdue to hear from the General, Abbas," the commander replied. "Prior to departure, the General shared with me his desire to bring the Great Satan down once and for all. It is my belief that he wanted us to launch our missile and detonate it at a high level, thus creating an EMP field that would take out the power grid on the east coast of the United States."

Abbas smiled a bit before speaking again.

"How much longer do we wait? How much longer can we evade the Americans?"

"Abbas, prior to the close call that we had yesterday, I would have been more likely to wait, but I think that the time to launch is almost here. Tell the men to prepare the weapon."

"Your will be done, Sir, Allahu Akbar!"

"Allahu Akbar!" the commander replied.

The USS Gerald R. Ford wasn't originally commissioned to leave port for another few years, but due to the state of war throughout the world, the President of the United States had ordered its deployment sooner. The Gerald Ford was the most sophisticated aircraft carrier in the world, and it was escorted by 1 cruiser, 3 destroyers, 4 submarines, and a variety of other support vessels. Having left port a day earlier, it made its way east out into the Atlantic Ocean.

Rear Admiral Jack Johnson was in command of the entire carrier strike group. He looked out over the bow of the carrier through the window of the command center. The skies were clear and the sea was calm. It couldn't have been a better day at sea.

"Sir, we have a ghost," the first officer announced. Victor Smith was an accomplished first officer who had worked with Admiral Johnson for several years.

Occasionally, a radar blip would appear and then immediately disappear. They had been working out the glitches in the system and the new radar system still needed calibration tweaks.

"At what vector, Victor?" the Admiral asked.

"Bearing 5 degrees starboard about 20 nautical miles out."

"Okay, let's re-calibrate the system and continue to monitor it."

"Sir, that will take about 3 minutes."

"Understood. Carry on," the Admiral replied.

The first officer commanded the radar man to calibrate the radar system. While they waited, the admiral continued to enjoy his view.

"Sir, we picked up a radar signature ahead," the Iranian radar technician announced. "I think it is a carrier group, but I'm not sure."

"Can we evade?" the submarine commander asked.

"Sir, I doubt it. It is only a matter of time before we are discovered," the technician answered.

The submarine commander turned to his first officer and spoke.

"It is time!"

The first officer turned and went into action.

"Bring us to launch depth and prepare the weapon," the first officer announced. Immediately, the submarine angled upward and began to move toward the surface of the ocean.

Within minutes, the submarine had reached launch depth and the first officer spoke.

"Sir, we await your command," the first officer stated.

"Launch the weapon!" the commander announced.

In the command center of the USS Gerald R. Ford, the first officer announced that the calibration was complete and the radar blip had been confirmed. The blip had become more pronounced, meaning only one thing.

"She's coming up to launch depth, Sir," the first officer announced.

"Prepare torpedoes!" the Admiral commanded.

"Bays 1 through 4 are ready, Sir."

"Fire!"

The submarine launched the ballistic missile and then all hell broke loose.

"Sir, we have multiple signatures headed our way."

"Evasive maneuvers," the commander yelled.

Immediately, the submarine dove and launched several anti-torpedo devices. These devices were created to confuse the guidance systems within a torpedo. The evasive maneuver worked. All of the torpedoes were neutralized.

"Sir, they've launched a missile. Its trajectory suggests it is a high altitude ballistic missile," the first officer said. "Our four torpedoes were neutralized."

"Launch four more torpedoes and fire the anti-missile guns," the Admiral commanded.

In a split second, four additional torpedoes were launched at the enemy submarine and the anti-missile guns went active. These new guns launched supersonic shells. These shells were meant for taking out all types of missiles. Unfortunately, they lacked the range to take out the ballistic missile launched by the submarine.

"Sir, the missile is out of range."

"Contact Washington!" the Admiral commanded.

The submarine dove more than 500 feet in a matter of minutes. The submarine designed by the Chinese was amazing. The submarine commander thought that they were in the clear for sure.

"Sir, four more inbound torpedoes."

"Evasive maneuvers!"

The submarine dove again, but at that depth, maneuvering so quickly was difficult. Three of the four torpedoes were neutralized, but the fourth found its target. The explosion rocked the command center and they were met with a mix of fire and water. None onboard would survive the attack on that day.

"Sir, the enemy submarine has been destroyed."

"Yes, but I fear we were too late."

Chapter 75

Andrews Air Force Base, Maryland

Sergeant William Tanner was sitting at his radar terminal at Andrews Air Force Base, when a warning alarm went off. He was able to immediately identify the incoming bogey.

"Captain, we have an incoming bogey!" the Sergeant announced.

"What is it?" the Captain asked.

"Sir, it has a missile signature!"

"Activate anti-missile defense systems," the Captain ordered.

Immediately, the room was ablaze with activity and the Captain focused his attention on the Sergeant's terminal.

"What is the heading, Sergeant?"

"It looks to be headed for the center of the city."

The Captain turned to the other men in the room.

"What's going on back there?"

The closest man to the Captain spoke.

"Sir, the missile is on a high level trajectory and it's already out of our range!"

"What?"

"Yes, Sir, our missile defense system can't take it out."

The Captain picked up the phone and spoke.

"Get me the Pentagon!" he commanded.

"Ten minutes until it reaches the center of the city, Captain."

"Shit! What is taking them so long to pick up!" the Captain yelled.

"This is the Pentagon. How may I direct your call?"

"Oh for Christ's sake, get me General Masterson!" the Captain screamed into the receiver. "This damn new phone system. I thought they got all the bugs worked out of it!"

The Captain's face was red with anger.

"Somebody's ass is gonna be put in a sling!" the Captain yelled, not necessarily talking to anyone in particular.

"Five minutes, Captain!"

"This is Masterson," a voice on the other end of the line answered.

"General Masterson, we have a high level bogey with a missile signature heading toward Washington. We only have minutes before impact."

"What? How?"

"It must have been launched from a submarine that was sitting on our doorstep."

The Captain could hear the General yelling at someone in the background, but he couldn't make out what he was saying.

"Damn it! How did you let this happen!" the General reprimanded the Captain.

"Sir, we had no time."

"That is unacc..."

Suddenly the lights went out and there was a rumbling overhead. After about 30 seconds, emergency lights turned on. The Captain and his team were three levels below the base.

"You two, head upstairs and assess the situation," the Captain said, pointing to two armed guards who turned in unison toward the elevator.

The first one pressed the elevator call button and it was clear that it wasn't working. They looked at each other and headed for the stairs.

"Idiots!" the Captain said, shaking his head.

"Captain, I'm sure you are aware of this, but I suspect that the missile detonated at a high level creating an EMP effect. My guess is the entire eastern seaboard is out of power. And it will be a long time before it comes back."

Chapter 76

Ocean City, Maryland

Steve Wilson was sitting in a chair on the beach watching the waves come in when he saw the missile fly overhead. He slowly stood and turned to watch as it flew high above the city. In an instant, there was a flash of light and a loud thunderous crash.

"Aaagh," Steve screamed, putting his hands over his eyes.

After a moment, he pulled his hands away and all he could see was white. Whatever that missile was, the flash of light had fried Steve's retinas.

Slowly the white in his eyes darkened, until all he could see was darkness.

"Help me, I can't see!" he yelled.

But no one would come and Steve would never see again.

Chapter 77

Samantha

Sam was sitting on her parents' couch being consoled by her sister, Sonia. Brian and Michele were in the other room helping Sam's mother clean up the kitchen. They had already taken down her father's bed after the funeral home came to pick him up. Sam was glad to see that go. It was only another reminder that she had lost everything.

On the television, there was continued coverage of the eruption in New Mexico. Scientists reported this and that, explaining what the country could expect next. Earlier, the Vice President did a brief newscast. He explained that the President was in Colorado when the eruption occurred and that his well being was yet unknown. He announced that the 25th Amendment had been evoked and that he was now the acting President of the United States.

There was a group of 'experts' on the television that were discussing the political ramifications of the 25th Amendment being evoked. Sam could hardly understand why they were concerned about politics when the world was on the verge of collapse. Then, all of a sudden, the picture went blank.

Both Sam and Sonia thought that was strange. Sonia grabbed the remote and changed the channel to CNN. Still blank. She switched it to ESPN and then MSNBC, both of which were blank. Finally, she switched it to the local station that was about 10 miles away.

The local television station was playing an old rerun of the Andy Griffith show, but a moment later a news anchor came on and interrupted the program telling the audience that there was breaking news. There was a flurry of activity in the news room. Anchors were getting seated and other people were running on and off screen.

"Sorry about that...we have breaking news. After everything that has already happened, it looks like the shit has really hit the fan," the male anchor announced.

His female co-anchor looked over at him with a shocked look.

"Did he just say, 'Shit'?" Sonia asked.

"Yes, I think he did," Sam replied.

The woman anchor went on to describe the situation in Washington and the rest of the east coast.

"We are unclear what exactly happened, but it seems that the entire east coast has lost power. New York, Washington, Philadelphia, Atlanta, Charlotte. You name it and they don't have power. It seems that most everything east of the Ohio River is down."

"Like I said, the shit has hit the fan!" the male anchor added.

"Wow, that guy has lost it," Sonia said.

There was a pause as more information seemed to come in.

"Speculation has it that a nuclear warhead was detonated at a high altitude above Washington, D.C. They are saying that this explosion created what is called an EMP. I guess EMP stands for Electromagnetic Pulse. The corresponding EMP took out the entire eastern power grid," the woman anchor said. "Wait, is that even possible?"

"You're damned right it's possible. You know what, I'm out of here!" The male anchor got up, tore off his microphone, and stormed off camera.

"Sorry about that folks," the woman anchor apologized. "We'll have more information as soon as possible."

Sam and Sonia looked at each other.

"EMP? What is that?" Sonia asked.

"I'm not entirely sure, but I'll bet Ford would know," Sam replied.

She picked up her phone and dialed Ford.

Chapter 78

Ford

"Hello, Sam," Ford answered the phone. "Listen, I don't know how much longer we'll have cell phone service. I also don't know how much longer before martial law is enacted. With the President out and the VP in, who knows? Even now the VP is probably out of communication because of the EMP. I think you and yours should get up here as soon as possible."

"I think you're right," Sam replied. "We've been preparing for my dad's funeral, but I am not sure that we are going to have one now. I am going to talk to my family and see if I can convince them to come with me to stay with you."

"Great. We have a lot of room, but please bring as much food, water, and supplies as you can manage. Sam, we are in it for the long haul. Things are going to go bad very soon."

"Okay, Ford. I'll text you when we are on our way. If you don't hear from me, assume that I'll be up there by the end of the day tomorrow."

"Okay, but sooner is better. Local authorities might start locking things down."

"Okay, Ford, but first, I have another question. Can you clarify what an EMP is?" Sam asked.

"Yeah, an EMP is an Electromagnetic Pulse. It can be created by detonating a nuclear bomb at a high altitude."

"Okay, but what does that mean?" Sam asked.

"Well, the EMP basically fries all electronic devices. Specifically, those that are actually functioning at the time of the EMP. For instance, if you had a battery powered radio that didn't have batteries in it and so it isn't running when the EMP is detonated, afterward when you put batteries in it, it would probably work. But I'm not exactly sure."

"Okay, interesting," Sam replied. "Thanks, Ford. We'll see you soon."

"We'll see you soon, Sam."

Chapter 79

Christopher

Chris tried multiple times to get Langley on the phone, but with no success.

"The EMP has knocked out their communications, too," Chris said.

"And we thought things were crazy before," Sara said.

"I think we should pack up and head over to Samantha's parents' house and see what they are doing," Chris said. "I think we need to talk to Samantha's friend as soon as possible."

"Yes, I agree. I'm basically ready to go. I can leave in five minutes. I will call Michele and have her meet us over at Samantha's parents' house, too."

Chapter 80

Zack

Zack arrived in Hulett and went directly to Christin's house. She and Lizzy were basically ready to go.

"I'm so glad to see you, Zack!" Christin said as she ran up to him and hugged him fiercely.

"I'm glad to see you, too!" Zack replied. "Are you guys ready to go?"

Christin had packed several suitcases and had several boxes of food and water ready. Zack had barely enough room in his truck for all their stuff, but he could manage until he picked up his trailer.

"Yes, I grabbed everything that I thought would be useful. Hopefully, I didn't grab stuff that we don't need."

"I'm sure this will be fine. I want to head back to my place and grab my trailer. We'll fill that up too and maybe pick up stuff on the way. Most importantly, I want to grab extra gasoline, because who knows how long gas will be available."

"Wow, right!" Christin said. "This is unreal. There is so much to consider. So much to worry about."

After loading up Christin and Lizzy and all of their stuff, Zack headed out to his ranch. When they arrived, he gave both Christin and Lizzy the job of collecting various things that he thought they might need on their trip and afterward.

"Most of the stuff you'll find in the garage, on and around the work bench. I'm heading into the house to grab my ham radio. It may come in handy later," Zack said.

After about an hour, they had packed up everything into the trailer and were ready to leave. Zack turned around and looked at his ranch, wondering if he'd ever be back. Christin, sensing his concern, came up behind him and hugged him.

"I don't know if I'll ever be back. I hope that I will. I've spent most of my life here. I love this place," Zack said, looking at Christin. "However, you'll love Michigan. It is beautiful! No mountains, but trees and water everywhere. Ford has a great spot, too."

"I'm sure we'll get along just fine," Christin replied.

"Okay, let's get out of here. Are you ready to leave, Lizzy?" Zack asked.

"Yup!" Lizzy exclaimed and smiled at both of them. She seemed to be taking the big move better then they both thought she would.

"Okay, hop in the truck and let's go...and no you can't drive," Zack joked.

Chapter 81

Ali

The Mahdi sat behind an ancient desk in the office of his home in Istanbul. He was an intimidating picture of a man. Ali couldn't think of another human being that intimidated him, but the Mahdi sure did.

"Mahdi, you called for me?" Ali asked.

"Yes, Ali. I have a new project for you. This project is of utmost importance. Care must be given, because any wrong move and your life could be in jeopardy. The President of Turkey has initiated the ground invasion of the Middle East. We need to bide our time until he has accomplished total victory. Once victory is accomplished, we will act."

"Sir?" Ali asked.

"Once victory is accomplished, the President will be removed from office and the Vice President will take over. At least for a short time."

"How will the President be removed, Sir?" Ali asked.

"He will be assassinated. There can be no connection to me or you. So care must be given."

"Yes, Sir. I will formulate a foolproof plan and let you know when I'm ready," Ali stated.

"No, from this point on, you are not to have contact with me, at least in public. The ground invasion won't last long. Six months at tops. Most of the Iranian leadership has already been removed and their troops have been severely beaten. The presence of Turkish ground troops throughout the Middle East will likely be enough to gain victory."

"How will I know when to act?" Ali asked.

"I will send word. Your plan must be foolproof before the end of the year."

"Yes, Sir. Yes, Mahdi," Ali said.

"Go now. May Allah be with you," the Mahdi encouraged.

"Allahu Akbar!"

"Allahu Akbar."

CHAPTER 82

Istanbul, Turkey

The Turkish President gave the command to begin the ground invasion. Troops had been stationed along the Turkish border, as well as at multiple airstrips. Tank brigades rolled into Syria, Iraq, and Iran. Air transports landed in Saudi Arabia, Yemen, Egypt, and other areas throughout the Arabian Peninsula.

The President sat at his desk and looked over his attack plan.

"I will control all of the Middle East within a matter of months. No one will rescue Iran from my power!" the President said greedily, as he looked up from his war plans and smiled.

CHAPTER 83

Camp David

The acting President of the United States, Harold "Hal" Jones sat in the President's office at Camp David. He never imagined his presidency being like this. New Mexico, Arizona, Colorado, much of Utah, and the western portion of Texas and Oklahoma were almost completely destroyed by the eruption of the Valles Caldera. His advisors estimated that over 20 million people lost their lives because of the eruption.

The caldera dumped several feet of ash as far west as Palm Springs, California, and most of the southern portion of California had anywhere from 6 inches to 12 inches of ash. The ash field ranged as far as the northern border of Nebraska to the north, as far as Memphis, Tennessee to the east, and as far as Chihuahua, Mexico to the south. Another estimated 10-20 million could lose their lives in the months to follow due to ailments associated with the inhalation of the volcanic ash.

An estimated 9 million cattle were killed by the blast, with an additional 20 million expected to die during the next month. Tens of millions of chickens were killed in the initial blast and millions more would die from the ash. The total estimated dead would exceed 50 million.

The amount of crops lost in the affected areas was incalculable, but food production in the United States was expected to drop by more than 60%. The consequences of this loss would affect the entire United States, as well as the rest of the world.

The Secretary of Transportation reported that travel in New Mexico, Arizona, Colorado, Utah, and the western portions of Kansas, Oklahoma, and Texas would be impossible for the foreseeable future. Travel difficulties would exist throughout all of Kansas, Missouri, Arkansas, Louisiana, Nebraska, Nevada, and Southern California, due to ash.

The Secretary of Defense reported that military installations in the affected areas were going to be nonfunctional for months, if not years. Not to mention 90% of all assets on the eastern seaboard had been knocked out by the EMP.

We are sitting ducks! the President thought.

The acting President tasked a team to reestablish communications at Camp David so that there was some semblance of governmental control.

"I need to get on TV as soon as possible, otherwise this country is going to implode," Hal said to himself.

His science advisors didn't know what impact the emissions from the volcano would have on the air quality locally. Some advisors said that the amount of material that was projected into the atmosphere could create a mini green house effect, and there could potentially be a decrease in global temperature. One scientist said that another ice age could result. Hal would not accept that outcome, not that he had any control over it.

There was a knock on the door.

"Enter," Hal said.

The leader of his communication team came in and gave him an update.

"Sir, we have established communications with a television network in Chicago. They are saying that their national affiliate in New York has been silent since the EMP. They don't expect them to be back on air in the foreseeable future, but they think they can get a message out to most of the states in the Great Lakes region, as well as the Ohio Valley. Many of the northern states, like North and South Dakota and Montana, will be accessible, but the west coast is out of the question."

"Okay, when can they be ready?" the acting President asked.

"They are ready now, Sir."

"Okay, tell them that I'll be ready in 15 minutes."

Hal was now alone in his office. He lowered his head and buried it into his hands. Shaking his head, he spoke aloud.

"What the heck am I going to tell the people? What can I say that will give them hope? How can I give them hope, when there is no hope?"

And then he started to sob.

Chapter 84

Ford

Ford was sitting at his desk, pouring over his notes.

"What the heck will happen next? Turkey will definitely complete their conquest of the Middle East, but what will happen after that?"

Ford stood up and looked out his window. It was getting late and the sun was working its way to the horizon. Sam and her friends and family were expected to be at the lodge by late the next day. Ford had spent the day preparing for them, but now he needed to prepare everyone for what was to come next.

"The next rider will be on a black horse. He will bring famine and pestilence, and there will be earthquakes. The eruption of the caldera has virtually ensured that there will be a shortage of food in the United States and probably throughout the world. Turkey's actions within the Middle

East will also have an impact on the supply of oil throughout the world. An oil shortage will have negative effects on almost every industry."

Ford paused to think about everything. Part of him was glad that he had studied Bible prophecy, but there was also a part of him that wanted blissful ignorance. He felt a lot of pressure to interpret prophecy correctly, so that he could lead his friends and family in the right direction.

"Okay, I have famine covered, but what about pestilence?" he asked himself. "Pestilence will rise because our water supply will be contaminated, or because healthcare options will have decreased, or maybe municipal garbage collection will stop. Imagine what will happen in urban areas when garbage collection stops."

A vision of rats taking over the streets came to Ford's mind. He started shaking his head.

"Is it possible that we've lost our federal government? Will local governments begin ruling themselves? What will happen to public services like police and fire departments? The power grid going down on the east coast will create chaos. They won't have power for months, or maybe years."

Ford sat down hard in his chair and began to feel a tremendous amount of fear and stress. It was all he could do to not start sobbing.

"Lord, please guide me and help me see the path that I am supposed to follow. Please give me the strength to follow your path and to hold on to my faith. In Jesus Christ's name, Amen," Ford prayed.

Prayer had always given Ford strength and he was thankful for the peace that began settling over his heart.

That was when he heard a commotion from the living room.

"Ford, come quick!" he heard Abby say.

Ford quickly got up and ran into the living room. On the television, the acting President of the United States was explaining the situation regarding the eruption, as well as the power outage on the east coast. He asked everyone for prayers.

"I ask you to pray for me, and for those in government. I ask that you pray for those who lost their lives. I ask that you pray for those affected by the power outage. And I ask that you pray for those in your own community. We have a tough road ahead, but we will prevail. Americans are strong. I have faith that you all will follow the golden rule and do on to others as you would have done on to you. God bless you all, and God bless this United States of America," the acting President said.

The screen went blank for a moment and then a news anchor began commenting on the acting President's speech.

"Ford, what do we do next?" Abby asked.

"That is a great question. We spent the day getting prepared for our guests, but I wonder if we need to get prepared for more people. I also wonder if we need to get ready to defend ourselves. I have no idea which way this whole thing will go, but my gut tells me that soon it will go bad. I think food supplies at grocery stores will run out very soon and that is when things will get really bad," Ford replied.

Chapter 85

Samantha

Sam was sitting on the couch at her parents' house when Chris and Sara arrived. She heard her mother greet them at the door. Sam wanted to get up and greet them as well, but just couldn't summon the energy. The loss of her family, combined with the loss of her father, was enough to pull her into a state of depression, but the added state of chaos around the world almost threw her into a state of hysteria. It was impossible for her to concentrate on anything. Her thinking seemed to be circular, always coming back to her family in New Mexico or to her father.

Sara and Chris were ushered into the room by her mother. Sam just realized that her mother seemed okay.

She is one tough cookie, Sam thought.

"Hi, Samantha," Sara said.

"Sam, you can call me Sam," Sam replied.

"Okay, Sam," Sara said.

There was a moment of awkward silence as Sam's mother left the room. She was keeping herself busy in the kitchen. It was Chris who finally broke the silence.

"Sam, we just wanted to express our deepest condolences for the loss of your father and your family," Chris said and began to fumble for more words.

"We can't imagine what you are going through. We also know that you hardly know us, but we want you to know that if you need anything, anything at all, we are here for you," Sara continued for Chris.

Sam feigned a smile. It was all she could summon.

"Thank you," Sam said. Not wanting more uncomfortable silence, Sam asked them a question. "What are you two planning to do now?"

"We need more answers about the Mahdi, so we are going to head north to see your friend," Sara replied. "We'd like to see if you'd like to come with us."

Sam sat in silence, considering the offer.

"I wasn't sure if I was going to go up there at first, but after the EMP, I think going north is the best option. I am trying to get my mother and siblings to head north as well. However, they are pretty anchored here and don't want to go," Sam said. "Ford thinks that with the federal government potentially out of the loop, local governments will start enacting curfews and potentially some version of martial law. He thinks that travel may soon be restricted."

"I believe your friend may be right," Chris responded.

"So because of that, I would like to leave in the next hour or so. The car that I rented is small and won't carry too much stuff. How big is your car?" Sam asked.

"Ours isn't much bigger. Maybe we could go turn them in and get a bigger vehicle. Maybe an SUV or something," Chris answered.

"Yeah, that sounds like a good idea."

"Okay, we'll head to the car rental place right now and come back with an SUV. Then we'll load up whatever stuff you want to bring and then follow you back to the rental place. That should give you time to get things situated here. Then we can drive together to Ford's place," Chris said.

"Okay, I will see you back here in an hour."

Chapter 86

Zack

Zack, Christin, and Lizzy had been traveling north on highway 85 for about 2 hours when they turned off the radio. There were a lot of conflicting stories on the radio. Some talked about the governor of North Dakota sealing off the state. Another news story said that I-94 was closed from Fargo to Bismarck.

"Switch on the CB and see if we can get firsthand news about this closure. If that is the case, then we need to find a new path," Zack said.

Christin turned on the CB and handed it to Zack.

"Hey, out there. Looking for any confirmation that I-94 is closed," Zack said into the transmitter.

They drove in silence for about 5 minutes and repeated the message. After three more attempts, they finally got a reply.

"Affirmative stranger. I-94 is closed between Fargo and Bismarck. I just got stuck on the western side of the Missouri River in Bismarck. The State Police have barricaded both sides of the bridge," the CB voice said.

"10-4. Are there any other routes east over the river?"

"That's a negative. All three bridges have been closed."

"10-4," Zack said and looked over at Christin. He wasn't sure what to do.

"I'm headed south on highway 6. I assume they'll let me into South Dakota, but I really don't know. There's another bridge on highway 12 in South Dakota," the stranger on the CB stated.

"10-4. Thanks for the information and good luck," Zack said.

Zack saw a sign ahead that said Buffalo, SD was 5 miles ahead.

"Let's stop there and figure out where to go next," Zack said. Christin just nodded.

As they neared Buffalo, there was a Conoco gas station. Zack pulled in and stopped next to a gas pump. Gas prices had already gone up by a dollar since the eruption. Zack wondered how much higher they would go.

"Christin, could you and Lizzy pick up a South Dakota map? I could use a Mt. Dew as well," Zack asked.

"Sure," Christin said with a smile.

Zack put his credit card into the automated pump. He suddenly wished that he had grabbed more cash.

"How much longer will credit cards work?" he said aloud.

He watched as Christin and Lizzy walked toward the gas station store. Zack couldn't help but smile. Even with all this craziness, he was still happy. Happy to be with Christin.

A few minutes later, the pump stopped and he put away the dispenser. Just as he got back into the truck, Christin and Lizzy came out of the store with a bag of supplies.

"Hey, did you find a map?" Zack asked as Christin got into the truck.

"Sure did. And here is a Mt. Dew," she said with a smile.

"What else did you find?" Zack asked.

"Oh, just a few essentials," her smile broadened.

"Essentials?"

"Yeah, we got beef jerky and Twinkies!" Lizzy exclaimed. She could hardly contain her excitement.

"Jerky and Twinkies! Perfect!" Zack laughed.

Zack opened his Mt. Dew and took a long swig. Then he opened the map and began to read it.

"Want a Twinkie?" Lizzy asked.

"Sure," Zack replied, taking the Twinkie that Lizzy had in her hand. He opened the wrapper and took a bite of the cream filled cake. "Wow, it's been a long time since I had one of these things," Zack said. "Not bad. Not bad at all."

Out of the corner of his eye he could see Lizzy's smile grow. Then he brought his attention back to the map. After a few minutes, he spoke.

"So it looks like the road back there about a half mile will take us east," Zack said, motioning behind them with his head.

"That road is state highway 20 and we'll take it about 70 miles and then head south on state highway 73 for about 40 miles. Then it looks like we take US 212 about 100 miles. At that point, we'll get to a bridge that goes over the Missouri River. Hopefully it's open."

"What if it's not open?" Christin asked.

"I'm not sure. I guess we'll figure it out at that point. We should know in 3 or 4 hours," Zack replied. "Are you ready to go on an adventure, Lizzy?"

"I sure am! Let's go!"

Zack and Christin both laughed. Zack started the truck and they were on their way.

Chapter 87

Ford

Ford and Abby were sitting on the porch swing enjoying a nice summer breeze. There was only so much bad news a person could handle. Sitting on the swing had always been their happy place. Ford took a deep breath and could smell pine needles, freshly cut grass, various flowers, and even the rich smell of freshly worked dirt. He couldn't help but smile.

"Where are you going to have everyone stay?" Abby asked.

"I have a couple rooms ready in the barn."

The pole barn had been converted into multiple living quarters where Ford imagined friends and family would stay when things started getting bad. He was very thankful that God had guided him to prepare for the end.

"Okay, that is good," Abby said. "When do they get here?"

"Well, I'm not exactly sure, but I expect them soon."

As if on cue, a large SUV pulled into their long driveway and slowly drove toward them. Ford and Abby got up to meet their guests.

Ford could see Sam in the back seat, and his heart was happy that she had been able to make the trip. His heart hurt because of the loss that she had endured the last few days. Ford assumed the man driving was the person that Sam had told him about. The SUV came to a stop and Sam was the first to get out. She walked toward Ford and Abby and she began to smile. Abby was the first to greet her with a strong hug.

"So good to see you, Sam," Abby said, "and I'm so sorry for your loss. Please let us know if you need anything."

"Thank you, Abby," Sam replied, as a tear rolled down her cheek. "Thank you for letting us come up."

"Alright, alright. My turn ladies," Ford said, as Abby and Sam released one another. Sam came up to Ford, smiled and gave him a big hug.

"How are you doing, Ford?" Sam asked.

"I am well," Ford replied. "So glad you came. I'm so sorry about your father. And Rob and the boys."

At those words, Sam broke down. Ford held on tight and the tears gushed from his eyes as well. Abby came in and hugged both of them. It was all hugs and tears for a few moments. When they finally separated, Ford noticed Sam's friends both had tears in their eyes as well.

"Hi, I'm Ford," Ford said, extending his hand to the man.

"Chris," Chris replied, "and this is Sara."

Ford released Chris' hand and accepted Sara's.

"It is very nice to meet you, Sara. Nice to meet both of you," Ford replied. "This is my wife, Abby."

After everyone exchanged pleasantries, Ford spoke again.

"How about we go inside and have a chat?"

"Sounds good," Chris replied and Sara nodded.

Ford sat at the head of the dining table with Abby across from him. Sam was to his right and Chris and Sara were to his left.

"So, Chris and Sara, Sam tells me that you are interested in Bible prophecy," Ford started.

"Yes, but specifically, we are interested in this Mahdi," Chris replied. "Honestly, we aren't sure what questions to ask." Sara nodded, but then spoke.

"We need to know what will happen next," Sara said. "We need to find the Mahdi and stop him."

"Stop him?" Ford questioned.

Chris and Sara looked at each other and then Chris spoke.

"Sam already knows this, but you should know that Sara and I work for the CIA. We believe that the Mahdi was behind the attacks in Paris, Nashville, New York, and Washington, D.C. last year," Chris said.

Ford didn't seem too surprised. He looked toward Abby and she smiled.

"Well, I guess that doesn't really surprise me. So you know about the connection between the Mahdi and the Antichrist, correct?" Both Chris and Sara nodded.

"I believe they are the same person, but I am no expert, by any means. It is easy to look at the things that have already happened and see the Antichrist's fingerprints. However, looking forward and anticipating his next move is more difficult," Ford said. "With that said, I think the prophet Daniel gives us some clues as to the events that will occur before Jesus comes back. So, let's talk about the Book of Daniel for a moment."

Ford got up and walked into the living room. A moment later, he came back holding a leather bound Bible. There were dozens of book marks throughout the book and it looked like it had been well read. Ford sat down and opened the Bible to the book of Daniel. He flipped a few pages until he finally settled on chapter 8.

"I'll summarize some of what you already know," Ford stated. "In Daniel 8:3, we are introduced to the two horned ram. We find out later that this ram represents the kingdom or empire of Persia. Some commentaries suggest that this prophecy was fulfilled in ancient times, but there are clear end-times fulfillments as well, as I'll show you shortly. So for now take my word for it."

"Okay," Chris replied and Sara nodded.

"So last year we saw Iran, modern day Persia, conquer the entire Middle East, with the exception of Israel," Ford began. "This is the end-times fulfillment of the prophecy. In Daniel 8:5, we are introduced to a goat with a prominent horn. With some analysis, we discover that the goat represents Turkey. This scripture talks about the goat crossing the entire earth without touching the ground and striking the ram furiously. The goat then knocks the ram to the ground and tramples him. Just in the last few weeks, we saw Turkey launch an unprecedented airstrike on Iranian military assets throughout the Middle East. Just yesterday, before the EMP, I heard that it was confirmed that the Ayatollah was killed in the nuke that hit Tehran, Iran. My guess is that the military leader in charge of the Iranian Revolutionary Guard Corps (IRGC) was killed in the other large nuke attack. The Turkish military flew across the Middle East without touching the ground and has virtually destroyed most of the Iranian military. There are also news reports that a full ground invasion has commenced. Without any leadership, it will be a matter of weeks or months before Turkey controls all of the Middle East."

Ford paused to let all that information sink in before continuing.

"But that is all information that you might already have. What does this have to do with the Antichrist? Well, we are almost there. One more important event must occur first. Let's look at Daniel 8:8," Ford said, and then read the scripture from the Bible.

"The goat became very great, but at the height of his power his large horn was broken off and, in its place four prominent horns grew up toward the four winds of heaven," Ford read.

"Okay, so if I remember correctly, horns represent leaders, correct?" Sara asked.

"Exactly," Ford said, putting his index finger on his nose.

"Is the first prominent horn the current president of Turkey?" Chris asked.

"Yes, I think he is," Ford replied.

"So at some point in the future, when the conquest of the Middle East is complete, he'll be taken out. Probably assassinated, right?" Chris asked.

"That seems very plausible. Maybe he'll get sick and die, but the scripture says 'his large horn was broken.' To me, that says that he'll be taken out," Ford replied.

"So who takes him out?" Sara asked.

"The scripture doesn't necessarily say, but I'm sure you two might have some insight to all of that."

Chris and Sara looked at one another.

"Prior to coming here to Michigan, we were on our way to Turkey to investigate a potential coup d'état, but we never made it. The Turks launched their attack on Iran the night before our plane was supposed to take us to Istanbul," Chris said. "This is all classified, so I would appreciate your discretion."

Ford smiled and said, "Well, we are all friends here. No worries there. Things have changed anyway."

"Yeah, I suppose you're right," Chris said.

"So do you have any idea who might commit this coup d'état?" Ford asked.

"Honestly, we didn't have a clue, but Sara and I were beginning to believe that the Mahdi was behind it," Chris replied.

"My gut tells me that you are probably right," Ford said. "But let's talk about the ramifications of the four prominent horns that replace the large prominent horn. With the presumed assassination of the current leader of Turkey and the entire Middle East, there will be a power vacuum. I see the Vice President of Turkey taking control over Turkey itself. I see a leader in Egypt, Iran and Saudi Arabia also stepping up. So I speculate that these four regional leaders will carve up the Middle East. Maybe there will be some treaty, maybe not. I think there will still be a lot of unrest and that opens the door for the Antichrist."

"How so?" Sara asked.

"Let's read a little more from Daniel, specifically Daniel 8:9. The scripture reads, *'Out of one of them came another horn, which started small but grew in power to the south, and to the east and toward the Beautiful Land.'* This scripture talks about another leader rising up and growing in power. If you look at the four regions where the four horns reside, only one of them can grow to the south and to the east, and that is Turkey."

Ford looked at everyone, waiting for any possible questions. When no one said a word, he continued.

"The next verse ties this new horn to the Antichrist. Let's read. Daniel 8:10-12 says, *'It grew until it reached the host of the heavens, and it threw some of the starry host down to earth and trampled on them. It set itself up to be as great as the Prince of the host; it took away the daily sacrifice from him, and the place of his sanctuary was brought down. Because of rebellion, the host of the saints, and the daily sacrifice were given over to it. It prospered in everything it did, and truth was thrown to the ground.'*"

"Sorry, you lost me," Chris said.

"Yeah, it's a tough one. Let's break it down. This new horn, or leader, grows in strength to the point where he declares himself greater than Jesus, who is the Prince of the host. This leader will eventually put an end to the daily sacrifices. The daily sacrifices refer to the sacrifices that are performed by the Jewish high priest. By the way, these sacrifices can only be performed in a temple, which most of you may know doesn't exist yet. There is an effort underway right now to get this temple built. I believe plans for the new temple have already been drawn up and many of the sacred priest robes have already been recreated. Construction of the third Jewish temple could begin almost any day. Anyway, this also ties the new horn to the Antichrist. In Revelation 13, we find out that it is the Antichrist that puts an end to sacrifices and offerings."

"Okay, so this new horn is the Antichrist. I have to admit that I'm a bit confused, but I'll take your word for it," Chris said. "How does this help us?"

"To be honest, earlier you asked how you could stop the Mahdi. I think the answer is that you can't. If the Mahdi is indeed the Antichrist, as I believe he is, there is no stopping him. At least, no human will stop him. Only Jesus will stop him, when He returns," Ford said.

Chris seemed a bit dejected. As a new Christian, his old belief system was still on the fringe of his mind. Part of him still thought that he could do something to stop the Mahdi.

"What am I supposed to do then?" Chris asked.

"Many of us, me included, assign worth to ourselves based on the work we do and how successful we are at our job. But our worth is not based on the job that we have, but on the work that we do for God, for Jesus. Our faith, and how we share it with others, is how God will judge us," Ford started. "So I would suggest that you take a step back from your job with the CIA and ask God what path he wants you to follow now."

Everyone nodded and seemed to accept this new reality.

"The world is no longer what it was yesterday. It is clear that we are living in the end-times. We need to evangelize more now, than ever. Jesus told us that we are supposed to share the word of God. However, know that we will be persecuted for our beliefs. Many of us will die as martyrs," Ford said. He paused, as if thinking about what to say next, and then said, "How about we all go outside and enjoy the rest of this beautiful day. Spend some time outside before dinner and then afterward we'll talk more."

Everyone seemed to agree that Ford's idea was a good one. Chris and Sara went hand in hand outside and sat on the porch swing. Abby called down to John and Tom to help her with preparing dinner.

"Let's go for a walk," Ford said to Sam.

Chapter 88

Samantha

Ford kissed Abby and told her that he was going to go for a walk with Sam. Sam followed Ford out the back door.

"This view is amazing. There is so much green!" Sam said. "I really miss the green. I don't look forward to going..."

For a moment, Sam had forgotten that her home had also been destroyed when the caldera erupted. A tear escaped her eye. Ford put an arm around her and whispered.

"It's going to be okay. The only thing that I can say to encourage you is, know that your family is now with God and they won't have to go through the persecution that will come very soon."

"Yeah..." Sam sniffled. "I know, but it's so hard."

Ford and Sam reached the top of a small hill where Ford had put a small bench. It provided spectacular views of the valley and the forest that was part of his property. They sat on the bench in silence for several minutes.

"How long do we have before we will suffer persecution?" Sam asked. "I am not prepared for that."

"I don't know. When the Antichrist declares himself God and sets up the abomination that causes desolation, it will begin in earnest. But I suspect those who are followers of Satan will begin to persecute everyone very soon," Ford replied. "I'm not talking about people who practice Satanism. I'm talking about your every day bad guy. You know, the bad guy who will take what he can get and possibly kill anyone to get it."

Sam nodded in agreement.

"I wish Zack was here," Ford said. "We need more people like Zack to help defend our group."

"Chris seems like a good one for that. I have a suspicion that Sara might be a badass, too," Sam said with a smile. "Maybe you should try to convince them to stay."

"Do you know if they are Christians?" Ford asked.

"Yes, I think they are."

"Okay."

"What about Zack?" Sam asked. "Is he a Christian?"

"I don't know. I don't think so, but I think he will be on our side," Ford said. "But we need to work on him when he gets here."

"When he gets here?" Sam asked.

"Oh, yeah. I forgot to tell you. He's on his way from Wyoming. I expect him in a couple of days," Ford said. "He's bringing his new girlfriend and her daughter."

"Oh, it will be so great to see Zack," Sam said, and then her mind went back to something that Ford had said.

"So what did you mean earlier when you said that we need to evangelize?" Sam asked.

"Sam, I believe we need to fight for souls. We need to leave the confines of our homes and find people who aren't saved and share the gospel with them," Ford said. "I wanted to pick up a ton of Bibles to share with people, but I haven't gotten them yet. I guess ordering them from Amazon is out of the question now." Ford smiled despite himself.

"I wonder if there are any local book dealers that would have a bunch of Bibles in stock. Maybe local churches would have them too," Sam said. "I'd like to look into that. It will give me something to do. I need something to do."

"That sounds good. We all probably need to start working on special tasks like that. I'll bring that up later after dinner," Ford said. "Speaking of dinner, let's head back. I'm sure dinner is close to ready. Maybe we can help with it."

"Sounds good. Thanks, Ford!" Sam said. "I couldn't do this without you and your family. Thank you!"

"You are part of my family, Sam!" Ford exclaimed, and then hugged her tightly.

Chapter 89

Christopher

Chris sat next to Sara and held her hand while they swung back and forth on the porch swing. It was still fairly early in the afternoon, but the sun was making its way toward the west. Chris imagined that the sunset was amazing from that swing.

"So, what are you thinking?" Chris asked Sara.

"I was just wondering what is going on back home."

"Me too. I was thinking about calling Langley again," Chris said. "If we can't get a hold of the Director, I think we should continue our investigation from here. I feel like there is a lot more that we can learn from Ford."

"I agree," Sara started. "I would like to get back to my house and get a few things, but I'm thinking that getting there might not be possible soon."

"I would think that air travel is very limited. You can't fly in the south and southwest because of the ash cloud. You can't fly in the east because of the power outage," Chris noted. "I imagine that local governments will have enacted curfews and potentially some form of martial law. Without some form of federal government to guide them, who knows what might be happening."

"So, we try to call the Director again, and if we can't get through, then we ask Ford if we can stay. Is that what you're thinking?" Sara asked.

"Yes, I think that is the plan."

The front door to the house squeaked a little as it swung open. Ford came out onto the porch and let them know that dinner was ready.

"It's a great swing, isn't it?" Ford asked.

"Yes, very relaxing. Thank you," replied Sara.

"Well, dinner is ready. So please come in and join us."

"Will do," Chris replied.

Chris and Sara followed Ford into the house and sat down at the dining table. Abby and the boys were placing all sorts of food dishes on the table.

"It smells amazing!" Sara exclaimed.

Abby smiled and said thank you.

"How about we all say grace?" Ford asked, extending his right hand to Sam and his left to Chris. Everyone else followed suite and took hands.

Ford prayed, "Lord, please bless this food to our bodies. We thank you for the nourishment that it will bring. Lord, I thank you for bringing our new friends to our home today and pray that they stay safe. Lord, I ask you to encourage all of your followers to reach out to those who have not yet accepted Jesus as their personal savior. Lord, please give us all the strength to follow your word and to share it with others. In Jesus Christ's name, we pray. Amen."

"Amen," everyone replied.

Abby began passing food around the table and everyone felt blessed to share a meal together.

Chapter 90

Ford

Throughout dinner, there was a little bit of conversation, but not a lot. Everyone seemed pretty preoccupied with the food and Abby received multiple compliments from everyone. When dinner was done, Abby asked John and Tom to help her clean up.

"Tom and John, could you boys please help me clean up so that your father can go in the living room with our guests and talk?" Abby asked. They both nodded.

Ford and everyone else went into the living room and sat.

"So, I've been thinking," Ford began. "Chris and Sara, I don't know what you have back at home and I don't know if you have families or pets, but I would like to invite the three of you to stay with us," Ford continued, as he shifted his eye contact to Sam.

"That is very gracious of you, Ford," Chris said. "Sara and I were talking about that earlier while we sat on the porch. We will continue attempting to contact our boss and see what they would like us to do, but in the meantime, we would love to stay. We are more than willing to do whatever it is we need to do to help around here."

"Great," Ford replied, and then looked at Sam questioningly.

"Ford, you know that I would love to stay here, but I have to head back and be with my family," Sam said. "My mom is still grieving, as are the rest of us. We need to be together."

"Yes, I understand, but I also want you to know that your family is welcome here as well," Ford replied. "As you'll find out shortly, we have more than enough room for everyone."

Sam smiled and nodded, but didn't reply. Ford waited a little longer before talking again.

"Okay, let's get back to the Mahdi," he began. "I believe the Mahdi is on the scene in Turkey. I don't believe he is the current president and unlikely the Vice President, but he most certainly has already found a place for himself in the government somewhere. I would guess that he is either directly behind the Vice President, in the chain of command, or darn close."

Chris and Sara nodded, but didn't reply.

"Chris, as you and Sara said, he is most likely already planning his take over."

"Right, we had some chatter, but now all our resources are scattered and we are blind to what is going on over in Turkey," Chris replied.

"Honestly, like I said before, I really don't think it matters if we know who he is or not. He will do what he is prophesied to do, regardless if we know who he is," Ford said.

"So what can we do then, Ford?" Sara asked.

"Let's talk about where things go from here, and then we'll circle back to answer that question," Ford answered.

"Okay."

"So once the leader of Turkey is taken out, there will be a leadership vacuum in the Middle East and four new leaders will pop up, most likely in the regions of Turkey, Iran, Egypt, and the Arabian Peninsula," Ford said. "I believe their reign will be short lived, because the small horn will grow in power to the south and to the east. Somehow the new leader of Turkey will be removed and this new small horn, the Antichrist, will grow in power and re-conquer the Middle East. At some point after doing this, he'll set himself up in the Jewish temple and declare to the world that he himself is god. The world will be amazed at the power that this man possesses. I believe this will occur at the mid-point of Daniel's seventieth week."

"Seventieth week?" Chris asked.

"Yes, in Daniel 9, the prophet talks about seven weeks that will precede the coming of Jesus. A week, in this case, refers to a year. So there are seven years. Halfway through the seven year period, which is forty-two months, the Antichrist will set up in the temple an abomination that causes desolation. At this point, the persecution of Christians, and possibly Jews, will be ramped up like no time in human history."

Ford paused again to see if anyone had any questions.

"It is this persecution that I believe we need to prepare for."

"How do we prepare for that?" Sara asked.

"First, each of us needs to accept Jesus as their personal savior, if we haven't already," Ford said.

"We're all good there," Chris said.

"Great. Next, we have to start helping others who are not saved," Ford said.

"Okay, so how do we go about doing that?" Chris asked.

"I believe we need to venture out and talk to people. This may sound weird, but I think we need to start at churches," Ford said.

"Won't people in churches already be saved?" Sam asked.

"Well, you'd hope so," Ford began, "but that isn't always the case. Many of these people will have had their faith shaken by all the events that have occurred recently."

Everyone nodded in agreement.

"So we need to reach out to them, and make sure they have all been saved. After that, we need to seek out other people. You guys, things are really going to get crazy soon. I think if we were to go to the grocery store right now, it might be in chaos. It also might be completely empty."

That statement shocked everyone.

"What kind of defenses do you have set up here?" Chris asked. The wheels were obviously turning now.

"Great question, Chris," Ford answered. "I can walk you through the details of everything later, but let me tell you that we are doing pretty well on guns and ammo, but I could use some advice in regards to setting up a defense perimeter. Another reason that I'm glad you two are staying."

Chris and Sara nodded.

"Regarding food, we have enough food to last us several years. We'll need to find new food sources. We'll have to hunt and gather. I believe we'll find ourselves taking in new people too, so our food reserves will have to be increased."

No one said anything, but everyone seemed to nod with understanding. Sam simply smiled and was secretly thankful for everything that Ford had done to prepare for this day.

"In addition to food stores, we have seeds for growing crops and there is an abundance of wildlife in the surrounding land. We have two real good sources of well water, as well as the river that runs through the property, if necessary. As you may have already seen, we have a fair number of solar panels on the barn and a wind turbine for the generation of electricity."

"You have quite a place here, Ford," Chris said.

Abby, John, and Tom walked in and sat down.

"Thank you. We have worked hard to get everything ready," Ford said, as he acknowledged his family.

"Tomorrow, I would like to give everyone a small list of tasks to do, so that we can finalize preparations," Ford said.

"Sounds good!" Chris exclaimed. He seemed a bit excited to have purpose.

"We are more than happy to help," Sara replied.

"Ford, I would like to head home tomorrow and see if I can gather up my family and get them to come up here," Sam said. "Chris and Sara, I'm hoping that I can use the SUV. Would that be okay?" Sam asked.

"Yes, Sam, anything you need," Chris said, as he looked at Sara for confirmation. Sara nodded in agreement.

"Sam, I wish that I could come with you and help, but we have a lot of work to do here," Ford said. "How long do you think you'll be?"

"I don't know. Maybe a week. Hopefully not longer than that."

"Okay, we have a spare CB radio. Let's put that in the SUV and hopefully we'll be able to communicate with it," Ford suggested. "Midland is just out of range, but it's close. We should be able to stay in communication most of the time."

"Sounds good!" Sam said. "I really appreciate everything that you and your family have done here." Sam and Abby made eye contact and they both smiled lovingly.

"Well, let me show you where you'll be sleeping tonight," Ford said.

After he got back from the barn where the others would be sleeping, he found Abby in the living room.

"Hey, Babe," Ford said.

"Hi," Abby said with a smile. That smile always made Ford melt. "Is everyone all set for the night?"

"Yes, I got them all tucked in for the night," Ford laughed.

Abby smiled, but then her smile faded.

"Have you heard from Zack at all today?"

"No, I haven't. I was going to call him one more time before I go to bed," Ford replied. "I sort of expected to see him by now. I'll call him right now."

Ford pulled out his phone and dialed Zack's number. It rang six times before going to voicemail.

"Hey, Zack, this is Ford. Wondering where you are, Bud. I hope you're well. I sort of expected to see you tonight. Maybe tomorrow. If you get this message, give me a call or text me. I just want to make sure that you're good, Bro. See ya, Man."

Chapter 91

Samantha

After breakfast the next morning, everyone gathered outside to send off Sam. Sam hugged Abby.

"Take care of these guys," Sam said, as she motioned to Ford, John, and Tom.

"I'll do my best. It's like herding cats sometimes," Abby replied. Everyone laughed. It was good to laugh. There wasn't a lot to laugh about anymore.

Sam shook Chris' hand and hugged Sara.

"Try to behave while I'm gone," Sam said to Ford.

"I will, but no guarantees," Ford replied. "Be safe, Sam. Call me on the CB a few times, maybe every 15 minutes or so. That way we can get an idea how much range they have."

"Will do. Be safe, Ford," Sam said, as she gave Ford a big hug.

Sam got in and started up the SUV. She grabbed the CB radio and said, "Hey, this is Sammy, over."

Everyone laughed.

Sam backed out of the driveway and waved to everyone.

"I sure hope that she'll be okay," Abby said.

"Me, too," Ford said, as he put his arm around her and waved to Sam.

CHAPTER 92

Ali - six months later

For the last several years, Ali spent most of his time planning attacks on infidels. The attack he was currently planning was on a fellow Muslim. That really didn't matter much to him. It was what the Mahdi wanted. However, the president of Turkey would be a difficult target to hit. He had a full complement of security, 24/7. Only someone close would be able to pull off the assassination.

Ali was sitting at his desk in his home office when Abutab came in. She was a striking young woman in her mid-twenties. She wore tight jeans and a white tank top. This type of attire was typical in a predominantly secular Turkey, even though traditional Muslim dress was making a comeback as the country moved back toward Islam.

Recently, Ali had discovered the President's weakness for beautiful young women. He believed that that weakness could be exploited to achieve success in his mission. Abutab worked in the Presidential Palace as a maid and often had access to the President's sleeping quarters. She had caught the President stealing glances at her on several occasions and felt that she could get close.

"Why would you do this?" Ali asked Abutab.

"The man is detestable. Several of the girls that I work with have been harassed by him. More than one has been raped by him, but fear reporting the crime. He promised them death if they ever said anything."

"You do realize that there is a good chance that his security team will figure out what happened?" Ali asked. "The consequences of getting caught will most certainly be death."

"I am aware."

"So why do it?" he asked. "You are young and beautiful. You could marry a rich man and want for nothing."

"Yes, but I'd only be slave to that man's desires. I wish to choose my own destiny. Allah, be praised."

"I see," Ali began. "How can I be certain that you will not indict me?"

"I have nothing to gain by indicting you."

"Okay," Ali said, seemingly convinced. "There are a couple of options. One, you could slip him some poison. Two, you could slip him a knife to the throat or other vital organ. In either case, you'll need to be sure you are successful and cause no alarm. His security detail will be close, and we can't guarantee that his sleeping quarters aren't under video surveillance. So you might have to get close, possibly intimate."

"I am prepared to do what I must."

CHAPTER 93

Istanbul, Turkey – The Presidential Palace

It was late and the President was sitting at his desk inside his sleeping quarters. He was reading reports from the battle field. He planned to announce his complete conquest of the Middle East the next day. Most of his advisors knew about this announcement, but they didn't know about his second announcement. He planned to declare a new caliphate and name himself the new Caliph. A smile grew on his face.

"Total conquest in less than six months. Who else could have done such a thing?" he asked the walls.

Then, there was a knock on the door. He looked at the clock and noted that it was well past midnight, and closing in on 1:00 a.m.

"Enter," he said, without turning to face the door.

"Good evening, Sir," said a young sweet voice. The President smiled and turned toward his guest.

There, before him, was a dazzling young woman with long dark hair and dark eyes. He recognized her as one of the maids on his staff. Instead of the normal uniform, she wore a sexy version. It was something that you might find at a Halloween party on the campus of an American university. The skirt was high up her thigh, with a white ruffle around the bottom, and the top was low cut and tied off just below her bosom.

"Well, good evening, young lady," he said playfully.

"Sir, I was wondering if there was any cleaning that you needed done." she said, and smiled in a devilish way that really got the President's blood flowing.

"Well, I am certain there is something I can have you do."

"Hey, check this out," the one guard said to the other. He was flipping through the security camera feeds when he came to the feed coming from the President's sleeping quarters.

"That feed is supposed to be turned off after 10:00 p.m.," the second guard said. "Looks like that last team forgot to turn it off. We should probably switch it off."

"But look at that," the first guard said, pointing to the screen.

On the screen, the President was lying down on the bed. They couldn't see his lower body, but he seemed to be without clothes. A young woman was standing between the President and the camera.

"Is that a sexy maid costume?" the second guard asked.

"Yes, I think it is. Whoa!"

Just then, the woman removed her top, revealing her back to the camera. The President seemed to be pleased with what he saw. A moment later, the young woman straddled the President. It was clear what they were about to do. The second guard clearly began feeling uncomfortable.

"We have to turn this off," he said, as he reached to turn off the feed. "If we get caught watching this, we'll lose our jobs or worse."

The screen went blank to the dissatisfaction of the first guard.

"Yeah, I suppose you're right," the first guard said, still staring at the blank screen. "Wow, that girl was something else."

"Yes, she was."

Chapter 94

Mahdi

News of the President's death spread quickly throughout Turkey, and the Vice President was quick to claim the role of President. He quoted the constitution as the basis of his claim. Most members of the Turkish parliament were agreeable with his claim, but some weren't and there was a bit of chaos over the next couple weeks.

Ali knocked on the door and waited.

"Come in," said a voice on the other side.

Ali opened the door and walked in. The Mahdi sat in a chair reading the Quran.

"Such a great work, the Quran," the Mahdi said.

"Praise Allah," Ali replied.

"You've done well."

"Thank you, Mahdi."

"The young woman, where is she?" the Mahdi asked.

Ali couldn't hide his shock. He had told no one his plan, not even the Mahdi. The woman ensured him that she had told no one. The Mahdi's somber face transformed into a smile.

"I see all, Ali," he said plainly.

"I'm sorry that I doubted you," Ali said, fearing the Mahdi would be angry with him.

"Have no fear, Ali," the Mahdi began. "Your secret is safe. No one knows."

"But..." Ali began, but decided that finishing might be a bad idea.

"How?" the Mahdi completed his question. "I am the Mahdi. I see and know everything."

Ali dropped to his knees and laid his chest and arms down on the floor. It was a position that he assumed countless times while praying to Allah.

The Mahdi enjoyed the worship that he received from Ali, but after a moment, he spoke.

"Rise, Ali. You are my trusted servant and your deeds will be rewarded, in this life and in the next."

Ali slowly rose and finally stood in front of the Mahdi, still reluctant to make eye contact.

"So, tell me, Ali, where is the girl?"

"Sir, I have her in a secure location. Originally, I intended to let her go, but she could incriminate me if she chose," Ali replied.

"Bring her to me and I will take care of her," the Mahdi commanded. "I will bring her into my service. I have more work for her. Did you see the security tape from the President's sleeping quarters?"

"No, Mahdi, I did not."

"She does wonderful work," the Mahdi stated and then smiled broadly.

"I will go and retrieve her for you now," Ali said.

"Bring her by tomorrow afternoon."

"Yes, Mahdi, praise Allah."

"Be well, Ali," the Mahdi said. With that, Ali took his leave of the Mahdi.

Chapter 95

The Middle East

After the prominent horn of the goat was broken off, four prominent horns grew up toward the four winds. The Middle East was now divided into four new regions, ruled by leaders in Egypt, Iran, Saudi Arabia, and Turkey.

The economic environment in the Middle East turned sour because of the chaos that resulted from the war being waged throughout the region.

Cairo, Egypt

The attacks on Cairo by the Turkish military many months ago had killed the Egyptian President and many members of parliament. The Vice President was out of the country at the time of the attacks, but didn't have the political clout to claim the vacated office of the President. It was the leader of the

Al-Nour party, which held the belief that the government should follow Islamic law, also known as Sharia law, whose claim ended up being accepted. Egypt quickly would go from a vastly secular government to one that followed radical Islamic law. Egypt would claim all of Egypt and the western portion of Jordan under its control.

Baghdad, Iraq

With much of the city of Tehran destroyed by the Turkish attacks, it was easy for a mid-level military leader to claim leadership of Iran. He controlled much of what was left of the Iranian Revolutionary Guard Corps. He claimed eastern Iraq and all of Iran for the new Iranian government that would form soon. It would make Baghdad the new capital of Iran.

Riyadh, Saudi Arabia

The palace of the king of Saudi Arabia had been destroyed by the Turkish military and much of the city would be uninhabitable for years to come because of the nuclear attack. The top echelon of the royal family was also killed. It was a minor prince who was able to claim the throne and be accepted. Peace would be difficult to maintain because many other minor princes would continually challenge the new king's leadership. All of the Arabian Peninsula was claimed by the new kingdom of Arabia.

Istanbul, Turkey

The Vice President was sworn into office, as the new President, and began assembling advisors around him. He quickly asked the Mahdi to be his Vice President. The Mahdi gladly accepted the new role. However, the new President didn't know the true identity of his new Vice President. With the rest of the Middle East being controlled by lesser leaders, the Mahdi convinced the President that it was time to establish a diplomatic relationship with Israel.

The United States

The eruption of the Valles Caldera created a huge reduction in food production and distribution worldwide. For decades, much of the world had become dependent on food coming from the United States. The price of even the most basic food items became almost out of reach for the majority of the world's population.

Scarcity became the norm and famine was on the rise. The people of the world looked for a savior, but found none. The United States was no longer considered a superpower. Almost overnight, it had become a third world country. The United Nations also no longer held any power over the world after the majority of its body had been destroyed in the terrorist attack. Europe had its own problems and was on the verge of a civil war between its people and the Muslims who had slowly invaded for decades. Russia had been weakened by its war with Turkey and others, and China was weak from the war that ravaged in the east. There was a leadership vacuum and it would soon be filled. This new leader would rise up and people worldwide would praise him for saving them. It was only a matter of time.

"When the Lamb opened the third seal, I heard the third living creature say, "Come!" I looked, and there before me was a black horse! Its rider was holding a pair of scales in his hand. Then I heard what sounded like a voice among the four living creatures, saying, "Two pounds of wheat for a day's wages, and six pounds of barley for a day's wages, and do not damage the oil and the wine!"

— Revelation 6:5-6

Epilogue

Jerusalem, Israel

The Prime Minister was standing by the large window in his office that looked out over the city. He never got tired of the view he had of Jerusalem. So much had occurred during the last several months. Turkey had conquered the entire Middle East, after it all but destroyed the Iranian military. Equally shocking, was seeing the reports on the death of the Turkish President. The news about the rise of the four regional leaders added to the Prime Minister's stress. There would be chaos if someone didn't step up and take control soon. As the Prime Minister stood there, a knock sounded on his office door.

"Come," the Prime Minister commanded.

The door opened and in came the man that he was waiting for.

"Shalom, Adam," the Prime Minister said.

"Shalom, Prime Minister."

Adam Ehrlich was Israel's Ambassador to Turkey.

"What do you have to report?" the Prime Minister asked.

"Sir, he just arrived," Adam replied.

"Send him in."

"Yes, Sir," Adam said, and in a moment he returned with the Vice President of Turkey.

"Sir, let me introduce you to Muhammad al-Malik, the Vice President of Turkey, and previously the Turkish Ambassador to the United Nations."

The Prime Minister stood and walked around his desk to greet the Vice President.

"Very nice to meet you Muhammad," the Prime Minister said with an outstretched hand.

The Vice President shook his hand and said, "It is very nice to meet you too, Prime Minister. We have a lot to talk about."

"Yes. That we do."

"If you are ready, we can go over the document," the Vice President said.

"Yes, let's. Please sit," the Prime Minister replied, motioning to the chair in front of his desk.

Unbeknownst to the Prime Minister of Israel, before him sat the Mahdi, the prophesied savior of the Islamic world. The Mahdi, the Vice President of Turkey, handed the Prime Minister a simple ten page document that outlined the proposed treaty between Israel and Turkey. The Prime Minister surveyed the document for a moment and finally spoke.

"It looks good, but I have one question," the Prime Minister said.

"What might that be, Sir," the Mahdi replied.

"Why only seven years?"

Recommended Reading

The Holy Bible (New International Version)

The Septuagint (1851 Translation by Sir Lancelot C. L. Brenton)

The Islamic Antichrist by Joel Richardson

The Mideast Beast by Joel Richardson

Mystery Babylon by Joel Richardson

Daniel Revisited by Mark Davidson

The Harbinger by Jonathan Cahn

The Mystery of the Shemitah by Jonathan Cahn

Revelation Deciphered by Nelson Walters

Thank You

I would like to thank you for reading my book. I really hope that you enjoyed it. I did quite a bit of Bible research while writing this book and I continue to do so. It is my goal to create a story that God would be proud of. If you don't have a personal relationship with Jesus Christ, I would like you to consider starting one as soon as possible. I do believe that Jesus Christ will return soon. In my heart, I believe that it will happen during my lifetime. Obviously, I could be wrong, but it doesn't hurt to prepare yourself now.

Matthew 24:30 *"Then will appear the sign of the Son of Man in heaven. And then all the peoples of the earth will mourn when they see the Son of Man coming on the clouds of heaven, with power and great glory."*

If you want to bring Jesus into your life, but you are not sure how, please contact me at cliffwellman@hotmail.com and I will try to guide you.

Reviews

If you liked this book, please find it in your heart to give me a 5-star review on Amazon and Goodreads.com. As an independently published author, reviews are very important to me.

Social Media

Please like and follow me on Social Media and check out my website.

Facebook: https://www.facebook.com/TheRoadToRev
https://www.facebook.com/CliffWellmanAuthor

Twitter: https://twitter.com/RoadRevelation

Websites: http://www.TheRoadToRevelation.com
http://www.CliffWellman.com

Charity

When I began this journey, I decided that I would share my good fortune with others. The first book in The Road to Revelation was dedicated to my father who lost his battle with cancer in the summer of 2016. It still pains me that he was never able to read the entire book. During the last days and weeks of his life, Hospice of Michigan was there for my father, mother, and rest of our family. It would have been far more difficult to get through that trying time without them. Because of their service, I have decided to give 50% of the profits from The Road to Revelation series to charity.

Current charities include:
- Hospice of Michigan
- St. Jude Children's Research Hospital
- St. Vincent DePaul
- and other local charities.

In addition to these charities, my family has setup a scholarship in my father's name at the high school where he spent the majority of his career teaching.

I have been blessed to have an exceptional family and believe that we should those in need. I encourage you to do the same. If you can't spare the money, maybe you can spare your time. Give locally and give often.

Thank you again for reading my book.

A sneak peak at book 3

THE ROAD *to* REVELATION

Darkness Falls

Clifford T. Wellman Jr.

Chapter 1

Ford – present day (one week into treaty)

Snow was falling as Ford walked up the driveway to the main house from the pole barn. The winter had been as cold and snowy as he'd ever seen, and it was still only January. Scientists were blaming the terrible winter on the eruption of the Valles Caldera in New Mexico. So much ash had been pumped into the atmosphere that global temperatures decreased slightly and there were some scientists that said the world was headed for the next ice age, but most people didn't believe it. Ford didn't believe it, but he was beginning to wonder.

He opened the backdoor and walked into the mudroom. Stomping his feet, he was greeted by a wave of warm air and the smell of something delicious coming from the kitchen. After taking off his winter gear and putting it away, he yelled into the house.

"Hey, where is everyone?"

"I'm in the kitchen," Abby replied.

Tom and John must have been out of range, because he didn't get an answer from them. Tom, his oldest son had come home from Oklahoma City just prior to the eruption. Ford and Abby were forever grateful that he made it home before getting caught up in the ensuing chaos. John would have been a freshman in college had the eruption and EMP not changed the landscape of the United States. Instead, he was home with his parents until life in the United States returned to normal. Although Ford doubted things would ever be the same.

Ford walked into the kitchen and found Abby at the stove stirring the contents of a pot. He walked up and kissed her neck while hugging her from behind. The light scent of her perfume caressed his nose.

"Mmmm, smells delicious," Ford exclaimed.

"Bean and ham soup," Abby said. "I also have bread baking in the oven. Dinner should be ready in about fifteen minutes."

"Do you need any help?"

"No, thank you. I think I have it covered," Abby replied, with a smile.

"Okay, I'm gonna go into the living room and sit by the fire."

In the living room, a fire was burning in the fireplace. Ford tended to the fire and then added another log.

Crack!

Ford stood in front of the fireplace for a moment warming his hands. He loved the sights, sounds, and smells that a fire provided. For him, a fire was the best thing about wintertime. He sat down in his chair and picked up the Bible. Over the last year, it had become perfectly clear to Ford that they were living in the last days. First, Iran had conquered the Middle

East. Then, Turkey used tactical nuclear weapons to decimate the Iranian army before completely invading the Middle East. It was only a matter of time before Turkey was in total control. The recent death of the Turkish president concerned Ford and when he saw the Middle East being divided into four regions, he knew that these were the events prophesied in chapter 8 of the Book of Daniel.

"Hmmm," Ford said to himself. "How much longer do we have before the Antichrist rises?"

Before he could answer his own question, he heard an automobile honking its horn. He got up from his chair and went to the front window. Standing in the driveway was a truck that Ford didn't recognize and when the driver got out, he didn't recognize him either. For a moment, Ford thought about grabbing his 45 just in case, but then at the last moment, he had a feeling that everything was okay. That was when something unexpected happened. The front passenger side door opened and out came his lifelong friend, Zack.

"Abby! It's Zack!" Ford exclaimed.

Zack's beard was long and he walked with a slight limp. Ford had not heard from Zack in almost six months. The last he heard was that Zack was leaving Wyoming and heading to Michigan. At the time, Zack had told Ford that he would probably be at his house in 3-5 days, but he never arrived. Ford put on his boots and jacket and opened the front door.

"Hey, Man," Zack said, as Ford came up to him and gave him a big hug.

"Oh man, I am so glad to see you! Where have you been, Brother?" Ford asked.

"Dude, that is a long friggin' story," Zack replied, and then he turned around at the sound of the rear passenger door opening. Out came a pretty woman who was probably ten years younger than Ford and Zack.

"Ford, this is Christin," Zack said, as he put his arm around her. She extended her hand and Ford accepted it. "Christin, this is Ford."

"It is very nice to meet you, Ford," Christin said.

Ford looked past Christin, looking for her daughter. Sensing the question to come, Christin broke down crying. Zack turned fully toward her and held her in his arms. Ford's heart sank into his stomach, knowing that something tragic happened on their trip from Wyoming to Michigan. Ford looked away and toward the stranger who had come out of the driver's side door.

"Hi, I'm Ford."

"Michael Justice," the stranger said, accepting Ford's outstretched hand.

"You've had a long journey. Let's go inside and we can talk in there," Ford said.

Inside, everyone was greeted by Abby, Tom, and John.

"Christin and Michael, this is my wife, Abby, and my two sons, Tom and John."

"Very nice to meet you," Michael Justice said, extending his hand first to Abby, and then next to Tom and John.

"Nice to meet you," Christin said. She had somewhat recovered from her breakdown, but Ford wondered what happened to them on their way to Michigan. He decided that he would talk to Zack separately later.

"Hi there, Zack. It is so good to see you safe," Abby said before giving Zack a big hug.

"It's good to see you too, Abby," Zack replied. After a moment Abby released him and spoke.

"Would anyone like coffee?" Abby offered.

Zack and Christin accepted graciously. Michael declined, but asked for water.

While Abby went to fetch drinks, the rest of them went into the living room. Ford realized that soon they were going to need another couch to accommodate more guests.

"Hey, John, could you call Chris and see if he and Sara can join us."

"Sure, Dad," John replied and then he went into the kitchen to call Chris over the intercom. Ford and Chris recently installed the intercom system between the house and the barn where Chris and Sara had their sleeping quarters.

Zack and Christin sat on the couch to the left of Ford. Christin leaned toward the fireplace and warmed her hands by its heat. Michael sat on the couch across from them. He didn't seem entirely comfortable in the house of a stranger.

Zack leaned in toward Ford and began talking.

"Ford, things have gotten really bad out there," he began. "As far as I can tell, society has all but broken down."

"That might be somewhat of an exaggeration," Michael interjected, "but it's close. There are some good people still out there, but there are also gangs of truly evil people roaming around." Michael seemed to become more comfortable now that they were talking.

"Well, you're right, Michael, but things are only going to get worse," Zack replied, turning his attention back to Ford.

"Listen, Ford, I don't think the federal government has any control anymore. As far as we can tell, several states have sealed off their borders between their neighboring states." He looked over toward Christin for a moment as if he was wondering if he should go on. Just then Abby came in with beverages.

"Thank you, Abby," Zack said. "It's so good to see you guys." He looked back toward Ford and continued talking.

"We had a very difficult time getting east of the Mississippi River. It cost us a pretty penny and I don't even want to talk about what happened in Mankato, Minnesota. The Mackinaw Bridge is closed as well."

"Closed?" Ford questioned. "So how did you get here? Did you go south through Chicago?"

"No, Chicago is a mess too. Well, the city is fine, but security is insane. The President moved the government there until power is restored in the east. Needless to say, it's a mess in Chicago," Zack replied.

"Okay, so if you didn't go over the bridge and you didn't go through Chicago, how did you get here?"

Zack looked over at Michael and nodded.

"Ford, I have some connections within various departments of the military," Michael began. "In this case, I was able to contact a friend in the Coast Guard who happened to be stationed in Cheboygan. He got us across Lake Michigan, but that cost us too.

"Ford, we started our journey with a truck and trailer full of stuff. You know, survival stuff, but none of that stuff made it here. We arrived here with basically the clothes on our backs and a few other odds and ends. The truck out there we had to steal after we got across the lake."

Ford's eyebrows rose, showing his surprise. Zack was a law abiding citizen, so things had to have been bad for him to steal a truck.

"Listen, Ford, we're sort of tired. How about we get some rest and then we'll talk more later. We have been on a long, dark road," Zack said.

"Yeah, good idea. We'll talk more tomorrow. Let me show you your place."

Just then Chris and Sara came in and Ford introduced everyone.

"Chris and Sara, I'll be back right after I show these guys their place."

"Sounds good, we'll be in the living room," Chris replied.

Everyone got dressed for the cold weather and started out the door. Zack and Christin went first, but before Ford could leave, Michael pulled gently on his arm.

"Hey, I'd like to talk to you once we get them settled," Michael requested.

"Okay, sounds good," Ford replied. "I'm interested to learn more about you," Ford smiled.

"Ditto," Michael replied. He didn't smile, but Ford had a feeling that his face might break if he did. He looked like a hard man and smiling might be a facial expression that is very foreign to him.

Chapter 2

Michael (one week into treaty)

Michael followed Ford back to the house from the barn after getting Zack and Christin settled.

"So what happened to Christin's daughter?" Ford asked.

"That is a personal and tragic story," Michael replied. "I think that is something that you and Zack should talk about."

"Okay." Ford opened the door for Michael and they went into the mudroom. After removing their winter gear, they joined Chris and Sara, who were visiting with Abby in the living room. The boys must have gone back down to the basement. They seemed to spend more and more time there.

"You look military," Chris said to Michael as he entered the room. Sara looked at Chris, sort of surprised by his direct questioning of a person they just met.

"Ex-Military," Michael replied, assessing Chris. "You too, eh?"

"Yeah, something like that," Chris replied. His vague answer didn't seem to bug Michael at all.

"I spent twenty years in the Army," Michael said. "I retired after doing four tours in Iraq and Afghanistan."

"Special Forces?" Chris questioned.

"You're an agency man, aren't you?" Michael said.

"Yes. Well, I was. Not really sure there is an agency anymore."

"Yeah, you're probably right. There might not be much of an agency anymore, but, yeah, I'm an ex-Army Ranger."

Chris smiled and nodded. *A ranger could come in handy*, he thought to himself.

Ford took advantage of the moment of silence to speak.

"Are you planning to stay?" Ford asked Michael. Michael was a bit surprised by the offer, after only knowing Ford for a few minutes. He was sure that Ford saw the surprise in his face, but he didn't say anything. "Listen, if you're a friend of Zack's, then you're a friend of mine," Ford said.

Chris, Sara, and Abby all nodded. Michael looked around the room with a sense of disbelief, but also with a sense of relief. The last six months had been tiresome and wore on his soul. It was nice to be among like minded people that he could hopefully call friends soon.

"Yeah, I'm planning to stay," Michael started. "For as long as you'll have me."

"Dinner is probably ready," Abby spoke up. "Would you like to join us, Michael?"

"Yes, Ma'am, that sounds great!"

Chapter 3

Ford (one week into treaty)

After dinner, Sara helped Abby clean up. Ford, Chris, and Michael went back into the living room to talk.

"Michael, so what can you tell me about the state of things out there?" Ford asked.

Michael nodded his head and seemed to be thinking about where to start. He cleared his throat and began.

"Well, after the eruption in the west and EMP in the east, it seems that much of the federal government has broken down. There are rumors that the President was buried under a mountain base in Colorado, and it is suspected that he is dead."

"What?" Ford exclaimed.

"Yes, news is vague, but we also heard that the Vice President was sworn in and is now the acting President. It is said that he moved what was left of the government to Chicago," he began. "My military contacts told me that the EMP totally fried the primary electrical grid all along the east coast. Their best guess was that it wouldn't be back up and running for another twelve to eighteen months."

"Whoa," Ford expressed his disbelief. Chris said nothing and simply shook his head.

"Yeah, I know. Crazy, right?" Michael asked. "So it has been just over six months since power went down. Most urban areas ran out of food in a matter of days. I have a buddy who lived in Brooklyn, New York at the time of the EMP. He was fortunate enough to be in upstate New York when the EMP went off. He was working on his hunting cabin in the Finger Lakes region. Prior to me joining up with Zack and Christin, I had been communicating with him via ham radio. He told me that he heard reports out of New York City that within a week there were riots. Grocery stores were emptied and the power was out. They didn't have running water and the city stopped picking up garbage. Can you image what that place would smell like in a couple weeks?"

"I imagine it was horrible," Ford replied solemnly.

"My buddy said that he heard reports that state officials in New Jersey had closed all bridges and tunnels into their state. Apparently, they didn't think they could handle an additional eight million or more people migrating into their state, so most residents of New York City had no way to get out. Those on the north end may have been able to get out, but I have no idea. Last I heard, a very large portion of the city was on fire. That was four months ago, so I can't imagine there is much left. No food, no water, no police. The garbage piling up and I have to assume rats were everywhere. That is the virtual definition of pestilence isn't it?" Michael asked.

"The Bible spoke of such things happening in the time of the end," Ford said. Chris nodded in agreement.

"The Bible?" Michael laughed. "I don't mean to laugh, but what are you talking about?"

Ford smiled and said, "I totally understand your skepticism. Most people who haven't studied the Bible don't realize that we are living in the days leading up to the end."

Michael raised his eyebrows and smiled a bit.

"Here, let me show you," Ford said, as he grabbed the Bible off the end table. He opened the Bible to the Book of Revelation, flipped to chapter 6, and read verses 5 and 6.

"When the Lamb opened the third seal, I heard the third living creature say, 'Come!' I looked, and there before me was a black horse! Its rider was holding a pair of scales in his hand. Then I heard what sounded like a voice among the four living creatures, saying, "Two pounds of wheat for a day's wages, and six pounds of barley for a day's wages, and do not damage the oil and the wine!" Ford read.

"What?" Michael asked, shaking his head. "That doesn't make much sense."

"Michael, let me break it down for you," Ford started. "But first, I need to explain some stuff. You've heard of the four horsemen of the apocalypse, right?"

Michael nodded.

"Most people have, because they have been depicted in several movies. For the most part, the movies get it wrong," Ford began. "So let's talk about the four horsemen for a moment. The first rider was on a white horse. I'm not going to get into a lot of detail right now, but we can talk in the future if you have questions. Anyway, most scholars believe that the rider on the white horse is the Antichrist," Ford paused in case Michael had any questions. He simply nodded, so Ford continued. "The second rider was on a red horse. It is said that this rider will take peace away from the earth. The third rider was on a black horse. This is the one from the verses that I just read to you. The fourth rider is on a pale horse, sometimes called a green or dapple horse. He brings death."

"Okay," Michael said, still not convinced.

"So if we look at the scripture that I just read, it says that this rider on a black horse carries a set of scales. If you recall from history, scales used to be two plates suspended by a cable and balanced over a hinge. To weigh something, you took objects that had known weight and put them on one plate, and the object being weighed on the other plate. You kept adding known weights to the one side until the two plates balanced perfectly. This told you how much the item weighed. Anyway, the verse goes on to say *Two pounds of wheat for a day's wages and six pounds of barley for a day's wages.*"

Michael simply stared at Ford and squinted his eyes.

Ford smiled and continued. "To understand what this means, you have to understand how much wheat cost back in those days under normal circumstances. It certainly didn't cost a man a day's wages to feed himself for a day. He could work a day and most likely feed his family for a day or more. This verse says that a person will have to work an entire day just for enough food to last him the day. Well, what about his family? This verse implies that there will be scarcity of food, or famine."

Michael nodded as if he was beginning to understand.

"I don't want to get into too much detail right now, but there are other verses in the Bible that support the idea that, along with famine, there would also be pestilence and earthquakes," Ford said.

"Earthquakes?" Michael said. "We've had some of those."

"Right, all these signs are occurring. Look back at the second rider on the red horse who took peace away from the earth. You could argue that the world is more at war today than at any other time in history," Ford said.

"True. Hmmm. You've got some good points," Michael acknowledged. "Okay, maybe there's some merit to all this Bible stuff."

Ford smiled and said, "I am more than happy to talk more about this stuff any time."

"Okay, so what do we do now?" Chris said. Both Ford and Michael turned toward him, as if they had forgotten he was there.

"As Michael said, most urban areas on the east coast are probably a disaster. I have been wondering how big cities, like Detroit and Chicago, have fared with the food shortage. I expect that they have had some problems too, but probably not as extreme as what has happened in New York City," Ford said. "Our small town has had its share of problems. I heard from the Sheriff that a few gangs have been put down, but he is concerned that more people from bigger cities will make their way into rural areas like ours soon."

"Am I to assume that you have some stores of food and ammo here?" Michael asked.

Ford had a touch of concern about giving Michael all the details of their stores, until he knew him better, but said, "We are doing okay." He looked over at Chris and saw that he was a bit relieved by the answer that Ford gave Michael.

"One thing we could use is help setting up a secure perimeter around the property," Chris said. Michael nodded and was just about to say something when Abby and Sara came in.

Chapter 4

Abby (one week into treaty)

When Abby and Sara walked into the living room, Ford, Chris, and Michael were engaged in a serious conversation. Upon their arrival, the men immediately stopped talking and turned in unison toward the ladies. Ford's face was serious at first, but his demeanor changed as he began smiling at her. Abby couldn't help but smile back.

"So what's up?" Abby asked.

"We were just discussing the defense of our property," Ford began. "Prior to that, Michael was telling us some things about New York City. It isn't good out there, Babe."

Abby nodded. She could feel a lot of tension in the room and decided that maybe it was time to break up the meeting.

"Ford, it's getting a little late. How about we call it a night?" she asked.

"That sounds like a good idea," Chris said, as he looked toward Sara who seemed to be staring at him.

Ford agreed, "Sounds, good. Michael, tomorrow after breakfast, how about I give you the complete tour and we can begin planning."

Michael nodded and said, "Thank you for your hospitality. It has been a long few months and I am very thankful to be in a place where I feel somewhat safe."

Abby watched as Chris and Sara walked hand in hand to the barn with Michael in tow. The three of them all seemed to be talking together. Abby turned toward Ford and said, "I'm glad Zack is here. I don't know much about Michael though."

Ford nodded as if thinking, "He's not a Christian and so we'll have to work on that. Zack isn't either, and who knows about Christin, so we may have to work on all three of them. But I think Michael is a good man. Besides, Zack likes him."

"Yes, I suppose you're right. Ford, let's go to bed," Abby said, grasping his hand and leading him into their bedroom.

....

The Road to Revelation 1 – The Beginning now available at Amazon on Kindle and paperback.

The Road to Revelation 2 – World at War now available at Amazon on Kindle and paperback.

The Road to Revelation 3 – Darkness Fall now available at Amazon on Kindle and paperback.

The Road to Revelation 4 – Life & Death available in late 2020.

Made in the USA
Columbia, SC
06 April 2021